ANYTHING FOR HER

ANYTHING FOR HER

A FRIENDS TO LOVERS BILLIONAIRE ROMANTIC COMEDY

JULIA GABRIEL

SERIF BOOKS

Anything for Her

Copyright © 2020 by Julia Gabriel

ISBN 13: 978-1-7343832-7-0

ACKNOWLEDGMENTS

As always, much love and appreciation to Ann Clement, J.B. Curry, Victoria Hanlen, and Anna James—fellow authors and friends extraordinaire.

PROLOGUE

Danny

(not the hero of this story)

I'm sitting in my spacious office at Get Fit with Danny!—the premier chain of functional fitness gyms in North America (as I'm sure you've heard)—going over revenue numbers with my CFO. Sales of new memberships are up! Renewals are up! We've been featured in the media fifty-six times in the past six months! We now have franchisees in all fifty states, plus Canada! I've just inked a deal to produce a line of workout videos!

Well, okay, so I'm not. But that's the point! I'm thirty-one years old and I'm sitting in my cramped office at the original location of Get Fit with Danny!—the premier chain of functional fitness gyms in the Avondale metro area (okay, Avondale is a town of twenty thousand so "metro" is stretching it)—with my parents, begging

1

them to invest more money in my business. And if they just would, the sky's the limit! Functional fitness is hot!

"The return on investment will be major. Just think of the retirement you'll have. Golfing every day, dad. That boat you've always wanted." (My mother rolls her eyes at the mention of the boat.) "And mom, you'll have the kitchen of your dreams. Plus unlimited privileges with the masseuse." (Take that, dad.)

"You know what I want in my retirement?" My mother pins me with a hard look. "Grandchildren."

"And you will, mom. I promise. All in due time."

"Danny, will you excuse us for a moment? I'd like to speak with your mother in private." My father cocks his head toward the door.

I go out into the hall and stroll down to the smoothie bar.

"Hey, Alicia. Give me a Power Kale Chia. Large." Alicia is wearing a pink Get Fit with Danny! cropped fitness top. Alicia has six-pack abs beneath that top. Don't ask me how I know. "And a small Strawberry-Banana." My mother loves those. My father, on the other hand, despises smoothies with a passion normally reserved for a certain professional football team based in Washington, DC.

I carry the smoothies back to my office and my mother's face lights up.

"Son, we'll give you the money." My father's face is still dark.

I fist pump in victory. In my mind, of course. I'm not an idiot.

"On one condition."

What? I hope they don't want a controlling share. My father's idea of fitness is eighteen holes of golf.

"You find yourself a nice girl to settle down with and get married. It's high time."

"And by nice girl, we don't mean one of those cheap floozies you're always running around with," my mother clarifies.

"Cheap floozies are the only kind of women in this town. Except you, of course."

"There are plenty of nice girls in Avondale if you open your eyes, Daniel." Dad stands. Apparently this meeting is over.

"And how long do I have to find one of these mythical nice girls?" How long does it take to procure a mail-order bride? Anyone know?

"We'll give you the money in installments," my father says.

Damn, they've really thought this through. In the time it took me to walk to the smoothie bar and back.

"One third when you bring us an acceptable woman to meet. One third upon your engagement. The final third on your wedding day."

"Are you kidding me?"

"That's our final offer, Danny."

I escort my parents off the premises—I mean, to the front door. I watch them get into their car and drive off.

Well.

That didn't go as planned. Understatement of the year.

Get married? I've never been a one woman kind of man. What's the point of having a body like mine—honed and chiseled through thousands of hours of sweat and reps—if you're going to limit yourself to one woman? I'm a sky's the limit guy—in business, in coaching, in life.

I pass the smoothie bar. Just ask Alicia here. How many orgasms did I give her last night? More than her husband has given her in the past month, no doubt. To calm myself, I stroll around the building and survey all I've built. It's a lot. But it could be so much more. My goal is to be a star in the fitness industry.

No, scratch that.

My goal is to be *the* star in the fitness industry. I want Get Fit with Danny! to be a household name. Like yoga. Or Richard Simmons. I just need more capital.

I stop at the long glass window outside one of the fitness classrooms. There's a barre class happening right now. All those gorgeous women in skintight leggings and sports bras, bending and twisting, their faces flushed like they've just had a lovely orgasm. I count the number of "cheap floozies" in the class. And by "cheap floozies," I mean "women who have slept with me." I stop counting when I get to half the class.

Is it my fault that I am god's gift to women? I'm practically god's only gift in Avondale! Women throw themselves at my feet!

The class turns en masse toward me and the women begin pulsing their thighs, their pretty heads bobbing, their faces the very picture of exercise concentration. My gaze stops on a woman near the back. Amy is her name? She works at the high school, I think. Teacher, maybe? Social studies? Home ec? I coach the state championship football team at the school, but I can't be expected to keep track of who teaches what there. She catches my eye and I give her a little smile.

No, she is not one of the cheap floozies I've slept with. Amy puts the mouse in mousy. The nerd in nerdy. But her body's not bad these days. She was definitely a little chubby when she started coming here. That's the power of Get Fit with Danny!

She's probably a virgin still. That would send my mother over the moon. Grandchildren born of a virgin womb? But I shudder at the thought of sleeping with her. My taste does not run to the good girls. It just doesn't. What can I say?

I watch her for a few minutes more. The class moves from pulsing to flushing it out and then down to the floor for planks. She's pretty good at barre. I'll give her that. Maybe she's interested in becoming an instructor. I could use another one, especially with my plans for growth. Sky's the limit, baby!

CHAPTER 1

Amy

18 months later

"All right, ladies and gentlemen. What's a class reunion without a few embarrassing party games?"

A bouquet of cheers and groans blooms inside the banquet room of the Avondale Country Club.

"Come on, guys, your parents love this first game at their reunions," the deejay adds.

The cheers wilt.

I look around the room. It's all decked out with gaudy streamers and twinkling disco balls. Has it really been fifteen years since we all graduated from high school? The signs emblazoned "Welcome Class of 2006!!!" seem to think so. On the one hand—surrounded as I am by friends, not-quite-friends, and not-friends-anymore—it does all feel like yesterday.

There's Angela Alessi, still skirting the bounds of propriety—and the dress code—in an outfit that will surely flash her underwear when she sits down. If she's wearing any, that is. The day Angela Alessi came to school with no underwear on has long since been incorporated into Avondale High School's collective mythology.

And there's George Noonan, who spent his teen driving years in a used hearse—and apparently rented one for tonight, as well. When I got to college, I discovered George wasn't half as unique as he fancied himself to be. Practically every high school in America has that one kid who drives a used hearse.

On the other hand, of course, high school feels like eons ago. Sometimes the books I teach at the high school feel newer and fresher to me. Jane Eyre? Didn't she graduate last year? Danny and I debated not even coming. Danny Walker is my fiancé, the former quarterback of the Avondale state championship football team, current coach of the Avondale state championship football team, and owner of the Get Fit with Danny chain of functional fitness gyms.

"Here's the first game, folks!" The deejay's voice brings me back to the present. Apparently the Class of 2006 has been downgraded from "ladies and gentlemen" to "folks."

No argument there.

"So think back to fifteen years ago," the deejay continues. "Who was that guy or gal you always wanted to kiss but never had the opportunity to? Who were you dreaming of while you were supposed to be paying attention to Mr. Mannheim in biology? Who was the pillow you practiced on?"

God, the deejay is milking the buildup for all it's worth. My eye roll mirrors everyone else's.

"Well, tonight's your big chance. Look around this room, find

8

the person you never got to kiss in high school, and lay one on 'em. Spouses and partners? Step aside. This is all just in good fun."

Good grief. I know who came up with this game. The reunion steering committee was composed solely of members of The Sass Pack, those girls who knew from kindergarten on that they were innately better than everyone else.

A breeze of nervous laughter floats up to the party streamers hanging from the ceiling like Spanish moss. Couples split apart and begin the hunt. I watch in horror as Angela Alessi leads The Sass Pack straight toward me and Danny.

Oh, come on. You can't tell me none of you ever kissed Danny in high school. In fact, I'm pretty certain that the only girl Danny didn't kiss in high school was me.

"Spouses ..." the deejay warns.

I take a deep breath and then three giant steps backward, secure in the knowledge that Danny loves me. The wedding date is even finally set—July 16th. I take another giant step, just for good measure, and back into someone standing behind me.

"Oh! Sorry! I wasn't watching where I was going ... oh, Ethan. Hi."

Ethan McNamara pulls me closer, so close I can smell the laundry detergent he washed his blue dress shirt in. Tide. Same brand Danny insists on. Only the best for me, babe, he always says.

"What are you doing?" I try to insert an inch or two of daylight between his Tide-scented chest and my blouse.

"Kissing the girl I never got to in high school."

I roll my eyes. "Like you ever wanted to—"

Ethan's lips are warm and soft, and taste faintly of the cheap beer the cash bar is serving. (Danny has a twelve-pack of better stuff in the car.) Ethan never wanted to kiss me in high school. I spent plenty of time at his house, so if he had wanted to kiss me, he had ample opportunity. Hell, I used to sleep in Ethan's bed at least two or three times a month. Ethan had been so not into me, his parents didn't even mind.

My friendship with Ethan was platonic with a capital P.

"So was that everything you imagined it would be?" I say sassily when he lets the kiss gently end.

I'm about to take a step away when Ethan pulls me back into his chest and cups my head in his palm. "Sweetheart, that wasn't even close to everything I imagined."

Then his lips are on mine again, and not in a tentative I-wish-we'd-kissed-when-we-were-sixteen sort of way. No, this kiss is bold and ballsy, his mouth taking what he wants, our tongues tangling together ... and it's glorious. Choir of angels singing in the heavens glorious, and for an instant I never want it to stop. Why didn't Ethan and I kiss when we were teenagers? If I'd known he knew how to kiss like this ...

Slowly, I become aware of the dead silence around us.

"Ethan," I mumble into his lips.

I can feel Danny's presence in the split second before it all happens. When Danny is angry, it's like his body sucks in all the energy in a room, the way the ocean retreats before a tsunami, then releases it all in one devastating blast.

Ethan McNamara, the boy whose family had been my refuge during the darkest days of my father's losing battle with heart disease, is about to get blasted.

Danny claps a heavy hand on Ethan's shoulder and yanks him away from me.

"What. The. Fuck. Are you doing." Danny's voice trembles with rage, the way it does when one of his players fumbles a ball at the five-yard line.

If Ethan knows what's good for him, he'll back away, respect his position in the Avondale Class of 2006 ecosystem. But he doesn't. Because he's Ethan. Instead, he opens his mouth and says, "Kissing your girlfriend. What does it look like?"

Danny's fist hits Ethan's face with such force, I'm certain his cheekbone just shattered. I throw my arms around Danny and do what I can to hold him back. Not that I can hold him back for long, but if I'm lucky—and that's a very big if—I can buy Ethan enough time to get the hell out of here.

Danny tries to shake me off, but I hang on like a puppy to a chew toy. "Baby, baby," I coo. "Calm down. It was just a kiss. Just a stupid game."

Leave, Ethan. Please just leave. I try to communicate telepathically with him, not that this style of communication has ever been in my wheelhouse.

Ethan stands his ground though, even as his cheek and eye are bruising into a lovely shade of demonic pea green.

"Okay, fellas." The deejay jumps in. "This is what I meant when I said spouses need to step back."

Danny flips off the deejay without even turning around. He's gearing up for round two on Ethan's face when Angela Alessi sidles up to him.

"Danny," she coos.

She's better at cooing than I am. Of course she is.

She strokes her manicured hand down his tensed forearm, managing to "accidentally" scratch my wrist in the process. "He is so not worth it. He's just a bug on the ass-crack of life."

Danny relaxes in my arms and I let go, even as I'm one part

puzzling over the "bug on the ass-crack of life" metaphor and two parts irritated that Angela's simpering is working. I hurry to the bar to get Danny a beer, remembering when I get there that all they have is cheap swill. I ask for water, instead. Out of the corner of my eye, I see Adam Boyer shepherding Ethan into the hallway. I hope he's leaving for good. Ethan and I go way back as friends but I am, for the first time in my life, well and truly angry with him.

When I return to Danny with the water, he's seated on a banquet chair with Angela and her friends hovering around him like hummingbirds. He tosses back the water in one shot, then stands up.

"We're leaving, Amy." He grabs my hand tightly and pulls me toward the exit. "I told you we shouldn't have come."

He punches open the door to the parking lot. Behind us, the reunion starts to settle back into itself. The tidal wave has receded and people are cautiously returning to the beach.

"Okay then, kiddos. I think we'll skip over Spin the Bottle and go straight to Telephone." I hear the deejay's forced laugh. "Though I guess today it should be called Text, huh? Doesn't quite have the same ring, does it?"

Well, there's one thing I can agree with Danny on. We shouldn't have come to this stupid reunion.

On the drive home, Danny seethes. Which is better than Danny going ballistic. But worse than Danny merely fuming.

"I want my money back," he says eventually. "That was the worst reunion I've ever been to. If I ever see that punk again, I'm gonna snap him right in two. Damn nerd. Probably didn't kiss any girls in high school. Or any since. He's probably gay."

I sit there silently, staring straight ahead as Danny rolls through one stop sign after another. Ethan hadn't kissed like he was gay. Not that I've ever kissed a gay guy. That I know of.

"I don't even remember him being in our class." Danny is not letting this go.

Ethan had kissed quite well, actually. Like a man who's had some practice. I sneak a quick glance sideways toward the driver's seat. Better than Danny, if I were going to tell the truth, which of course I'm not. Not in present company, anyway. But I'm perfectly happy to spend the rest of the drive home silently turning that inconvenient truth around and around in my mind, examining it from every possible angle, and enjoying the way it makes my spine positively tingle from neck to coccyx.

I've never had a kiss that made my tailbone tingle.

CHAPTER 2

Ethan

"Danny Walker?" I let Adam Boyer shove me into his pickup truck. "Ouch! Watch it." I rub my elbow where I've just banged it on the sharp edge of the truck's door.

"Shut up and get in before he decides to come after you." Adam runs around to the driver's side and gets in. "Honestly, Ethan? There was no one else in there you could have picked? You had to choose Danny Walker's fiancée?" Adam turns the key in the ignition. "It's not like you never kissed Amy Casales in high school, anyway. You were just taunting the man. Why?"

"I wasn't trying to taunt him. And Amy and I never kissed back then. It wasn't like that."

"Ethan, you are the worst fucking liar I've ever known. Remind me again how you were able to create a game app and make a shit-load of money?"

"Because I'm not a liar?"

I glare out the window of Adam's truck as it bounces and bumps over the back roads of central Pennsylvania. It's the second weekend in June and the trees are bright with summer leaves, but I ignore the lovely scenery. I can't wrap my head around Amy being engaged to Danny Walker. What the hell had happened? Sure, Amy and I lost touch after high school—something that was as much my fault as hers—but Danny freaking Walker? I just can't make heads or tails out of that. Amy isn't exactly Danny's type.

In high school, Danny dated big tits and big hair. Well, "dated" was probably overstating things a little. In any case, Amy is short, brunette, and, while not exactly flat as a board, not terribly well endowed either. Amy is cute. And plenty of guys like "cute." But Danny Walker has never been one of them.

Adam slaps my thigh. "Your mother used to brag to my mother about how Amy Casales was teaching you the ways of women. You're telling me that wasn't code for 'shagging you blind?'"

I roll my eyes and punch him in the upper arm, causing the truck to swerve toward the center line.

"That's exactly what I'm telling you." I am well aware that my mother was under the impression that Amy and I were having sex all those nights Amy spent at our house. She had both adored Amy and desperately wanted me to have a girlfriend, so I never did much to correct her erroneous impression of what was going on beneath the covers in my room.

"Well, shit. If I'd known that, I would have done her. Ouch!"

I punch him in the arm again. "It's not like I didn't want to."

"Well then, why didn't you? You were wearing a chastity belt or something?" Adam pulls his arm away just in time.

"No. She spent the night at our house when her dad was in the hospital. She was generally upset and worried sick those nights. I didn't want to take advantage of her."

"Ooh. Saint Ethan." Adam sticks out his arm. "If you hit me again, I will pull this car over."

I laugh quietly. "I do deserve a fucking medal or something."

"After tonight, I'd say so. Kissing Danny Walker's fiancée. Man. You purchased a set of balls with all that money you made. You buy hair for your chest, too?"

I pretend to rip open my shirt. "As a matter of fact, I did."

We ride in silence through town until I finally ask the question that's been gnawing at my gut all evening. "How long have they been engaged?"

"Oh, I don't know, man. A year or so, maybe? I heard the wedding's sometime this summer. I work out at one of his gyms, but I don't talk to him much."

"Why the two of them, though? They just don't make sense together."

Adam shrugs. "Danny's kind of a catch in town. He owns a good, solid business. Coaches the football team. Who would have thought the old lunk would turn out to be such a savvy business-man? And he's not bad looking. She could do worse, I suppose."

"But what does he see in her?" Not big hair and big tits.

Adam was quiet for a long minute, long enough that I knew I wasn't going to like whatever I heard next.

"I just know the gossip."

Another long moment of silence.

"So don't shoot the messenger, okay? Word on the street is that his parents were pressuring him to settle down and start a family. They looked around town at the available prospects and decided on

Amy. She's not divorced or thrice-married. Not already saddled with four kids. Respectable job."

"In other words, she was good wife material."

"I don't see Amy much around town, but I haven't heard that she's unhappy or anything. Well, she's probably unhappy now after that little stunt you pulled tonight. Danny will probably spend all night lifting weights to work out his aggression over you instead of boinking her."

I hope that is true. An image of tiny Amy Casales in bed beneath the bulked-up body of Danny Walker fills my mind, and it's an image I don't like.

I know it shouldn't bother me. We're thirty-three years old. Plenty old enough to be married and settling down, as my mother never tires of reminding me. I pull out my phone and shoot off a quick text to her. Why hadn't she ever mentioned Amy and Danny being engaged? Even though she and Dad live in a nice active adult community in New Athens near me, she's still plugged into the Avondale grapevine. She's probably still in touch with Amy's mom, for that matter.

I stare at my phone, waiting for a response. When none comes, I shove it back into my pocket. She and Dad are likely out golfing or playing competitive bocce.

Amy has every right to get married.

But why Danny Walker? Why not Adam here? I'd be okay with Amy and Adam getting married.

Oh, screw it. I would so not be okay with that.

CHAPTER 3

Amy

I glance up at the round-faced clock on the wall. I hope this faculty meeting starts on time. It's the last day of school and we're all sitting in the high school media center, waiting for Principal Gardner to arrive. In the student parking lot just beyond the windows, car engines are revving and the celebratory whoops and whistles sound louder than I remember from years past.

Or maybe I'm just getting old. I'm definitely getting impatient in my dotage. I need to swing by the bakery after this meeting to pick up wedding cake samples and take them to Danny. The wedding is so close, I can hardly believe it. Next month! It's time to start finalizing decisions like cake flavors and flowers and salmon versus chicken. I was never one of those little girls who started planning her eventual wedding in kindergarten. Or even in high school.

But here I am anyway! I'm set to marry the town's most eligible bachelor. And owner of the premier chain of functional fitness gyms in North America, I might add. With franchisees in all fifty states, plus Canada! And a newly inked deal to produce a line of workout videos! (I'm not just the soon-to-be wife of the owner, I'm also a client and instructor—as the newest ad campaign says.)

When Charlie Gardner walks in, I snap back to the present. These final staff meetings consist of an end-of-year speech from Charlie—basically saying, "whew, we survived another year of these hellions"—and the announcement of promotions for next year. I'm ninety-nine percent sure that I am going to be named the new chair of the English department. The former chair, Genevieve Ludwig, had a surprise stroke over spring break and abruptly resigned. The position has been vacant for the past month and a half. I was the only internal staffer asked to interview for the job.

I sit up a little straighter. I picked a seat near the front instead of way in the back, which is where I normally sit for staff meetings. Easier to check my phone for texts from Danny that way. But today, my phone lies quietly with the ringer turned off in the bottom of my purse. I dressed carefully today. I'm wearing a new shirtdress—jersey so it wouldn't wrinkle—and new pumps with chunky low heels. It's a look that I hope conveys authority and gravitas.

Even Danny said I looked nice when we kissed and got into our cars in the garage this morning. I'll be honest—I wanted to drag Danny back into the house and shag him silly. I am so damn horny these days. But Danny is so romantic, he wants to wait until our wedding night before we have sex. I know, I know. Danny Walker saving himself for marriage? Danny didn't even save himself for the ninth grade prom.

But that just goes to show that a person can change. We're thirty-three years old. We're not high schoolers anymore. Danny is no longer a manwhore and I'm no longer the yearbook's "most likely to die a virgin." Unless I die before the wedding next month, that is. But that is so not happening!

Charlie launches into his intro. *What a year ... more high points than low, but we're all ready for summer ... staff turnover yada yada yada ...*

I try to focus on what he's saying, but it's the same thing he says every year. At last, he gets to the part I'm waiting for.

"As you know, we have a few department chair positions to fill and I'm happy to make those announcements now. First up, the mathematics department ..."

Great. He can't do them alphabetically?

"World languages ..."

I discreetly check the clock again. The bakery closes at three today and it's already one. That gives me two hours but still, I need to factor in time to mingle here, say goodbye to everyone—not that I won't see them around town over the summer—accept congratulations, and then drive to the other side of town where Tiers of Joy is located.

I clap enthusiastically for Lorelei Sanders as she shakes Charlie's hand and accepts her promotion to chair of Family & Consumer Sciences. I like Lorelei. She's my best friend in town, despite the fact that she slept with Danny in high school. It's hard for me to hold that against her, though. Pretty much every girl slept with Danny back then. Except me, of course.

Not that I'm some prude. I'm dying to finally lose my V-card. It's been even worse since Danny's mother helped me move into his house last month—into the guest room. His parents are old-fashioned about things like that. But I'd be lying if I said I don't lie there in bed thinking about sneaking into the master bedroom and surprising Danny. He's adamant that we abstain until our wedding night, however. Plus, there's the minor fact of me being a teacher. The last thing I want is for students to be Snapchatting about Ms. Casales banging the football coach before we're married.

Even though that's exactly what's going to happen next month.

"And now, last but not least ..."

I drag my mind out of the gutter and sit up even straighter.

"Genevieve left—" Charlie pauses for effect. "—big shoes to fill in the English department."

Everyone titters because Genevieve famously has size eleven feet.

"But I'm confident they will be filled effectively."

I scoot forward onto the edge of my chair, ready to stand.

"Please welcome our new English chair, Malcolm Jones!"

My butt is in the air before my ears process that "Malcolm Jones" is not "Amy Casales." I sit back down, my face burning with embarrassment, but fortunately no one is paying attention to me. I look just like everyone else, craning their necks to see who the hell "Malcolm Jones" is.

Charlie wastes no time in explaining. "Malcom comes to us from Cheswick Township, outside Philly, and is bringing some exciting new ideas to Avondale High."

What the ever loving fuck? They hired someone from out of town? I have exciting new ideas too! If Charlie would ever listen to them.

I watch as "Malcolm Jones" picks his way from the back of the library to where Charlie stands. Malcolm is tall and thin, balding, and of some indeterminate age between thirty and fifty. He looks like a Malcolm.

He shakes Charlie's hand and turns to the assembled faculty to "say a few words." I totally tune this out. I'm not angry.

Not even enraged.

Nor am I seething, fuming, or about to go ballistic. Adjectives that would make me write on a student paper, "Do you really need these? Show, don't tell."

No, I am just good old-fashioned pissed.

I deserve that job. I've been teaching here since I graduated from college. I graduated from this high school! Did my student teaching here! I've done every thankless service task anyone has ever asked me to do here.

Chaperone the homecoming dance? Check.

Sell tickets to basketball games? Check.

Direct traffic in the parking lot during morning drop-off? Check.

Cheerfully serve on five thousand committees?

Okay, so not five thousand and not cheerfully. But I did it! I've never said "no" even once to anything Charlie or Genevieve asked of me. Not once!

Why even ask me to interview if they were taking the search outside?

I can feel my pulse pounding behind my eyes. I glance up at the clock on the wall behind Malcolm's head, squinting through my blurred vision at the time. I need to get those cake samples and get to Danny's office during the gym's mid-afternoon slowdown. But I need a word with Charlie first.

The minute Malcolm stops talking, half the room stands up en masse and heads for the exit out to the parking lot. I linger, waiting until Charlie has finished saying goodbye to the ass-kissers. Then I approach him.

"Charlie."

"Amy. Ready for summer?"

So that's how he's going to play it? Feign ignorance?

"Can I speak to you in your office before I leave?"

"Uhh ... sure?"

We walk to his office and he shuts the door behind us.

"What's up, Amy?"

"I interviewed for that job."

"Yes, you did."

"And, correct me if I'm wrong, but I was under the impression that I was the leading candidate."

He nods.

"So why didn't I get it? You hired someone from across the state?"

"You're getting married this summer."

"And?"

"Well, I was shooting the breeze with Danny at the end-of-year sports banquet and he said, uhh ... umm ... he said that you two are planning to start a family soon. And that you're planning to be a stay-at-home mom." Charlie looks at me warily. "Which is great! My mom was a stay-at-home mom. And my sister! Even my wife! Our kids love having her at home ..." His voice trails off as his tiny reptilian brain registers the expression on my face, the one that's telegraphing the message, "You have got to be kidding me."

It's true that Danny and I have discussed starting our family sooner rather than later. We both want kids! And we're not exactly spring chickens anymore. But never have we discussed the idea of me staying home afterward. Nor would I ever entertain it. I love teaching. Even on the days when the moon is full and the kids are behaving like werewolves, I still love it.

"I am returning in the fall, Charlie. Why would I have bothered interviewing for the position, if I weren't? Not to mention submitting a proposal for a girls' mentoring program."

"Ah, yeah. About that."

"What about that? The Board of Education didn't approve it?"

"No, no. They approved it. But, ah, Ms. Monroe will be sponsoring it."

"Kylie Monroe? She's twenty-three years old! She still needs a mentor herself!" One that would advise her not to steal someone else's pet project out from under them.

"I know, but …"

"But you told the board that I wasn't returning in the fall."

"Something like that," he mumbles.

As I storm out of Charlie's office, I mentally add another item to the afternoon's to-do list: stop at Danny's favorite deli, Knuckle Sandwich, to pick up two Italian cold cut hoagies. Or, as he calls them, "slop on a roll." Danny and I need to discuss this, and food will put him in a better frame of mind. One of us, at least, needs to be in a good mood.

Right now, that is not me.

The Broad Street location of Get Fit with Danny is nearly deserted when I arrive, all hurried breathlessness as I pass the smoothie bar and skirt the edge of the giant workout room on my way to Danny's office. A white paper bag with two wrapped slop-on-a-rolls is tucked under one arm as I try to balance a flat white bakery box filled with cake samples in the other.

I'm glad the gym is empty at the moment—fewer people to interrupt the cake tasting. Danny is always happy to jump into the middle of a group class and "show 'em how it's done" or urge people on to "higher, faster, stronger." It's this attention to his members that makes his chain of fitness clubs so successful. But I need Danny to myself for a bit.

At the end of the gym, I take a left into the long hallway that leads back to Danny's office. I shift the bakery box so it rests partly on my hip and then knock on his door. I can hear his voice inside, which is good. That means he's on the phone and not out running with a private client. I wait a minute to give him a chance to end the call, and then knock lightly again.

Still no "come in!"

Hmm. I told him I'd be stopping by this afternoon with cake samples. He knows that the last day of school is always early dismissal. Mid-afternoon is the best time to do this—the lunchtime workout crowd is gone, yet it's too early for the after work folks. This window of time gives me Danny's undivided attention for wedding decisions.

I try the doorknob and find it unlocked. I push the door open with my hip and back into the room to keep the door from jostling the bakery box.

"Danny? I'm here with the cake—" The words die in my throat as I spin around to face Danny's desk—and the naked back of the person sitting on it.

The naked back of the *woman* sitting on it.

Danny's head pops up from between the woman's legs.

"Fuck! Amy! What are you doing here? Get out!"

The woman coolly turns her head to glare at me. Angela Alessi? She didn't leave town after the reunion? And why is she glaring at me? Like I'm the one who's not supposed to be here. In my fiancé's office. With the cake samples for our wedding.

"Amy. Leave. Now."

There's so much going on in my brain right now, I can barely see. I must be dreaming. I must be asleep. There's no way I'm standing in the doorway of my beloved's office and seeing him with another woman. A cheap floozy from high school, no less! And with our wedding only one month away! One month from the day we were finally going to have sex!

And then a tiny spot of clarity begins to form in the fog of my brain. Lorelei had gently tried to warn me. Leopards don't change their spots. But I ignored her gentle warnings. I so wanted to believe that Danny Walker had changed—for me. Turned over a new leaf. Been transformed by the love of a good woman.

Changed his spots.

I tighten my grip on the bakery box, then pull the white sandwich bag from where it's wedged between my arm and ribs.

"I brought you lunch. But I see you've already eaten."

I hurl the bag—with its oil and hot pepper laden hoagies inside—with as much force as I can muster (I'm not just the owner's ex-fiancée, I'm also a client!). The bag nails Angela Alessi right between the shoulder blades.

Her naked shoulder blades.

I slam the door on the way out.

Smithy's Rock is an outcropping in the mountains outside Avondale, a spot popular with hang gliders, underaged drinkers, and the occasional person who wants to end it all. I'm none of those. I fall into the fourth category of Smithy's Rock visitors—people who just need to sit and think in the glory of nature. *Really* think.

How did I get myself in this predicament?

You fell in love with the town's resident playboy.

Oh right.

I feel like the scales have fallen from my eyes. I'm normally Miss Responsibility. I don't do wild and crazy. What was I thinking, falling in love with Danny? I was as shocked as anyone when we started dating.

That should have been my first clue.

I gaze out over the valley floor hundreds of feet below and shove another piece of cake into my mouth. Praline with chocolate mousse and almond buttercream icing. I've already eaten the red velvet with cream cheese icing, the white chocolate with raspberry cream filling, and the coconut-lime. That leaves just the pink champagne with strawberries and chocolate espresso with dark chocolate frosting.

I don't want the cake to go to waste. And it's not like I need to worry about fitting into a wedding gown next month.

My stomach isn't feeling so great at the moment, but ask me if I give a flying rat's ass. If I have to, I can always just lean over the rock and barf into the valley. I doubt I'll be the first—or the last—person to do so.

It all makes sense now, Danny wanting to save himself for our wedding night. I've been wearing out my vibrator, biding my time until the magic day. Danny's been biding nothing, apparently. He's still the same old man whore he always was.

I am so furious I want to scream. Instead, I grab the slice of pink champagne cake and hurl it out over the rock ledge, imagining the splat when it hits the ground. It was so satisfying to hit Angela with the hoagies. I know, I know. It's terrible and childish.

But there it is.

How long has this been going on? If Angela Alessi has moved back to town, I haven't heard of it. She left Avondale right after graduation, striking out for Los Angeles and the hopes of an acting career. It strikes me as incredibly unrealistic (not to mention incredibly naïve) to believe that she's a one-off. Danny proposed to me over a year ago after a whirlwind courtship. We fell for each other hard and fast after Danny hired me to be one of the new weekend barre instructors. Or so I thought. Did the cheating go that far back?

I hold out my left hand and stare hard at the two-carat diamond sparkling in the late afternoon sun. I pull it off and, for a split second, contemplate hurling it off of Smithy's Rock. I think better of the idea, though, and shove it into the side pocket of my purse.

Romantic! What an idiot I am.

I knew Danny's reputation as a skirt chaser was well earned. But it never occurred to me that he wasn't being exclusive with me now. Because otherwise what was the point of marrying me? Danny could literally marry any cheap floozy in Avondale.

I eat the last of the wedding cake samples, fold up the box, and with a heavy heart trudge back to my car. How on earth did I manage to lose a promotion, my fiancé, and anything even remotely resembling self respect all in one day?

CHAPTER 4

Ethan

My flight back home isn't until tomorrow and I have a few hours to kill before I'm supposed to meet Jack for dinner. I point the rental Porsche in the direction of the old neighborhood. My parents sold their house five years back, when I finally convinced them to retire near me in New Athens. I bought them a brand new home in an "active adult" community there. I'm an only child and it was either move them to me or endure years of my mother nagging me about moving back to Avondale so she can spend time with her grandkids.

Grandkids I haven't produced yet, I might add.

Plus, no way in hell would I move back here. Why did Amy stay? I mean, I get why she stayed during college. Her dad had died, her mom was alone, and the nearby state school offered her a full scholarship. So she commuted from home. But why take a job here after graduation? It makes no sense to me. There's nothing going on in Avondale.

The old neighborhood looks pretty much the same as it did when I was a kid. Smallish houses set close together, with uniformly square front yards. Three doors down from my childhood home is the Casales house, freshly painted and with flowers planted in newly dug beds. I pull the Porsche up to the curb and get out. I've got time to say "hi" to Amy's mother. And ask for Amy's cell number.

There's no answer when I ring the bell. I rap loudly on the wooden door. Still nada.

I get back in the car and drive around town for a bit. Growing up, Amy and I were like brother and sister. From the time we were born, our mothers hung out together. They traded child rearing tips (I slept through the night before Amy did) and celebrated milestones (okay, so Amy was walking a good three months before I managed that feat). We played together as toddlers, walked to elementary school together, rode the bus to middle school.

We would never have called each other "best friends," but looking back, that's what we were. It's so obvious now, I wonder why we didn't see it then.

And now? We're not even friends on social media. She still sends a Christmas card to my parents every year—*Say hi to Ethan for me. Love, Amy Casales.*

Why didn't I stay in touch? Yeah, sure, I was busy. School, work, relationships—the same old stuff everyone is busy with.

I drive to the town's lone coffee shop and order a coffee from the drive-through. Then I park in the lot and pull up Facebook. At first, I'm surprised to find that Amy doesn't seem to have an account. Then I remember that she's a teacher. I work with a lot of teachers in New Athens, and all of them are careful about their social media presence. High school kids can be miserable little fuckers.

Danny, of course, has a robust presence—and with security settings not restricted to just friends and friends-of-friends. I scroll through his pictures.

Danny and Amy in Paris!

Danny and Amy in London!

Danny and Amy on a white sand beach with turquoise water behind them, so perfect looking it could have been Photoshopped. I stare at the beach photo for a good while, ignoring Danny's perfectly sculpted physique in his tiny Speedo swimsuit. In the picture, Amy is wearing big dark sunglasses and a hot pink bikini. Her dark hair is pulled up into a ponytail on top of her head.

She is so effing adorable.

And sexy.

Deliciously sexy, with her hip cocked to one side. I think about chasing her through the surf. Lying beneath a cabana and drinking fruity rum drinks with her. Holding her sandy hand as we walk back to our hotel room and shower together. Then, our skin cleansed of sand and sunscreen, we tumble onto the bed and ... I need to stop this line of thought. I'm getting hard, for one thing. And for another, in the picture Amy is wearing a great big smile in addition to great big sunglasses. She's evidently happy with Danny Walker.

I mean, I don't get it. But who am I to wish otherwise for her?

I close out of the app as a text comes through from Adam. *Meet you in 30?*

Sure, I text back. *Where does Danny Walker live?*

Not a good idea, dude.

I'm just curious.

Yeah right.

But he texts the name of the neighborhood anyway.

If you aren't at Buns of Beef in 30 minutes, I'll call 911.

The neighborhood where Danny and Amy live didn't exist when we were growing up. It's a newer suburban-style development. McMansions and three-car garages. Every house is a slight variation of the same model. I drive slowly through the winding streets, wondering which one is theirs.

I spot a white baby beemer parked in an open garage. There's a "CO-EXIST" sticker on the bumper and the license plate reads, "Amy 1." I take in the house for a second, allowing myself to bask in triumphant superiority over Danny-effing-Walker. My house in New Athens is three times the size of his. Hell, my assistant has her own wing. Mostly so I don't get on her every last nerve, as she puts it.

After a few minutes, I drive away before someone sees me. I don't want to make more trouble for her.

At Buns of Beef with Adam, I can't stop wondering what Amy and Danny are doing right now. Having dinner? Watching TV? Arguing? Banging each other silly? I don't want to think of that last one.

Honestly! Adam here would be a better fit for Amy. He commutes to Baltimore every day for a terrific job at an insurance company, lives with his mother and younger sister in Avondale. He's safe, sane, steady as they go.

I know. I know. Who am I to swoop in all these years later and offer an opinion on her life?

Except I was the one who held her in my arms on the nights when her father was at Hershey Medical Center. I was the one who listened to all her fears of losing her dad, fears which came true. I was the one who dried her tears, went down to the kitchen, and made her hot chocolate the way she liked it, half chocolate and half marshmallows. Sure, the idea of hooking up with her crossed my mind once or twice. Okay okay, so it crossed my mind every damn night she spent in my room, sleeping in the pajamas my mother bought and kept at the house for her. But she needed my friendship more than I needed to hook up with her.

Yes, for a teenaged boy, I was bizarrely chivalrous.

After dinner, I stop at the package store, then drive back to the hotel and call my mother.

"Are you still in touch with Mrs. Casales?"

"Yes. Why? Did you see Amy at the reunion?"

"She's engaged to Danny Walker."

"I know. He's a nice boy."

"No, he's *not* a nice boy." I struggle—and fail—to keep my voice level.

"Ethan, why are you so upset?"

"He was a total dick in high school." Still a total dick.

"Language, please."

I roll my eyes. "So you knew that they were engaged?"

"Of course I do, Ethan. Your father and I lived in Avondale for over fifty years. We're still in touch with people there."

My parents were born and raised in Avondale. Actually, I'm still surprised that I got them to leave.

"You should stop by and say 'hello' to her mother."

"I did, but she wasn't home. Do you have Amy's number, by any chance?"

"No. Just Sylvia's."

"Any chance you could get her number?"

33

"I'll call Sylvia now and then text you. When are you coming home?"

"Tomorrow. Late."

"Your dad wants to play golf this weekend."

"I can't." I sigh. "I still need to go shopping for the wedding."

"Send Erin-Joi." Erin-Joi is my trusty assistant. "She does everything else for you."

That's true. My life would totally collapse in on itself like a dying star if it weren't for Erin-Joi. But I draw the line at having her buy gifts for friends and family. It's always so obvious when someone's assistant has done the shopping. I may be a billionaire, but I don't want to become so out of touch that I can't shop for my college roommate's wedding.

"Give dad a raincheck, please. And don't forget about Amy's number."

CHAPTER 5

Amy

The Avondale Hotel is really more of a motel, but it's on the very outskirts of town and, thanks to the new shopping center built last year, hidden from the main road. The location makes it less likely that anyone will spot my car and recognize it.

I stride up to the front desk, pulling my wheeled suitcase behind me, and ring the tiny gold bell.

"Ms. Casales! Hi! Are you looking for someone …?"

No one recognizing my car. Yeah. Clearly that was not the only thing to be worried about.

"Hi, Shelly." Shelly Brown is a former student of mine. She graduated last year. To make matters worse, her brother is a junior right now and a fullback on the football team. It won't take long for word of my whereabouts to reach Danny. If he cares about my whereabouts, which he might not.

"Is everything okay, Ms. Casales?" Shelly is the very picture of concerned in her stiff hotel uniform of white shirt and navy pants.

"Yes, everything's fine. Danny is, uh, having a guy's night at the house. So I need a room for the night."

"Oh. Okay. Sure."

My explanation doesn't sound convincing even to me, but whatever. I could crash at my mom's place, but I need a night alone to regroup before people start fussing over me.

Pitying me.

Before the gossip begins about how they all knew there was no way I'd be able to hang onto Danny Walker.

Turns out they were right.

"Just a room, Shelly. On the second floor, if you have one available up there."

"Yes, sure, Ms. Casales. I—I got several up there."

"Non-smoking, too."

It takes Shelly another fifteen fumbling minutes to input a room reservation into the computer system and successfully program a magnetic room key. It makes me begin to question my worth as a teacher, if my former students can't operate a computer and small pieces of plastic.

At last, Shelly manages to put me in room 203, at the far end of the left wing hallway. I grab a bottle of sparkling water from the vending machine on the way. I've never stayed at the Avondale Hotel. Why would I? I'm a hometown girl.

Inside, I see that the room decor is rather plain, but it's clean and that's all I need for the night. A quiet, clean place to think and get a decent night's sleep before confronting reality tomorrow.

By reality, I mean Danny.

I pile all the pillows against the headboard, kick off my shoes, and pop open the water. I should have stopped by the liquor store on the way and picked up a bottle of wine. Or vodka. This feels like a vodka kind of evening.

Isn't that what one is supposed to do in this situation? Drink and weep? Oddly, I don't feel like weeping. In fact, I haven't cried at all today. Not even at Smithy's Rock. I take a sip of water and relax back into the mountain of pillows. I wait for the tears to flow.

I take another sip.

Still no tears.

Damn it! I want to weep and rend my garments. It's been that kind of day. I'm entitled to an evening of weeping and rending.

I force myself to think of sad things. Natural disasters. Tear-jerker songs. Onions.

Still the weeping muse refuses to even knock on the door.

I sigh and drink more water. Maybe I'm in shock. I try to recall the symptoms of shock from my annual first aid training. Rapid, weak, or absent pulse. That's one sign. I press my finger to my wrist, then my neck. No, my pulse seems fine. Clammy skin is another. I lay my palm on my forehead. Nope. If anything, I feel a little too warm.

I get up to adjust the air conditioning, then flop back onto the bed and pick up the remote. I begin flipping through the television channels and end up spending the next twenty minutes watching a little of this and a little of that. The news, a reality talent show, a cooking competition, a standup comedian, part of a movie that Danny and I went to see last year. When I reach the high end of the channels, where the pay-per-view and porn are, I stop. I've never watched porn before. I assume Danny has. All men do, right? I was always okay with that. It's just pictures. No harm, no foul.

But hey—since there is now no long-awaited wedding sex in my near future, I might as well.

I click through the menu and purchase the first porn movie I see. "Angel Does Albuquerque." I take a long sip of water and settle in. Apparently the story involves Angel doing two men and … water spews from my nose and leaves a spray of dark spots on the hotel's white comforter.

Angel of Albuquerque is none other than Angela Alessi, formerly of Avondale.

I sit up, coughing, my eyes watering from the sting of carbonated water in my nasal passages.

Angela Alessi is a porn star?

Does Danny know that? I have the sneaking suspicion that he does. I wipe my eyes on a pillow and set down my bottle of water. I need to pay attention to this. I watch in rapt disbelief for several minutes, at one point even attempting to pull my legs back over my head the way Angela is doing on screen.

Turns out I don't bend that way.

Does anyone else in town know about Angela's, uh, stardom? Probably I'm the only one who *doesn't* know.

My cell rings. The caller ID says "New Athens." Ethan. I pick up, skip the pleasantries, and get right to the point.

"Did you know that Angela Alessi is a porn star?"

"The Angela Alessi we went to high school with?"

"That would be the one."

"No, I did not know that.

I let out a long exhale. Good. I'm not the only one who doesn't know.

"But how do *you* know?"

"I'm watching one of her movies right now."

Long pause.

"Umm … are you and Danny watching, um, porn right now?"

"No." As the word leaves my mouth, I realize the potential pickle I've just put myself in.

"Ames? What's going on? Where are you?"

"I'm at a hotel. I moved out of the house. Well, not officially, but …"

"And why is that?"

"I walked in on Danny and Angela having sex in his office today."

I hold the phone away from my ear, waiting for Ethan's outburst. Instead, all I hear is a long sigh.

"Ahh. So Angela isn't really a porn star. You just mean she looked like one when you walked in—"

"No, she really is one. I'm watching a porn movie at the hotel and she's in it. Angel Does Albuquerque."

"Which hotel?"

"What? The Avondale Hotel. It's new."

On the television, a third man walks into the scene with Angela. My eyes widen. "Damn, she's practically upside down. How do they do that?" I cock my head way to the side, trying to figure out where everybody's limbs are.

"Wait right there." He hangs up.

Two minutes later, a knock sounds on the door. It's the weeping muse, at last! I get up and peer through the peephole. No, it's Ethan, his bruised cheek still a lovely verdant green. I open the door.

"What are you doing here?"

"I'm here to watch Angela Alessi fuck upside down."

"No, I mean how did you know which room I'm in?"

"Shelly was easy to bribe. I'm staying here, too." He holds up two bags of cheese-flavored popcorn, a bag of licorice, and a bottle of tequila. "I raided the vending machine."

"They have tequila in the vending machine?" I must have missed that.

He rolls his eyes and barges right on in. We settle onto the bed to watch Angela Alessi fuck upside down, polishing off both bags of popcorn and half the licorice in the process. I'll be paying for today's diet tomorrow, for sure. Every time she makes a fake porno moan, we each take a slug of tequila. Before long, I'm listing on the bed like a dinghy that's slowing sinking.

As the credits roll, Ethan says, "Well. That was interesting."

I let out a long, low moan and Ethan theatrically takes a drink. He holds out the bottle to me. Just the thought of another hit of tequila sends me rushing for the bathroom, where my stomach does a triple-twisting Simone Biles and I promptly hurl the contents of my entire day into the porcelain god. Wedding cake, popcorn, licorice, tequila.

I feel my hair being lifted off my neck. I push up off the toilet, not meeting Ethan's eyes. Just when I thought the day couldn't get any worse ... suddenly I am tired. So very, very tired.

"What's going on, Ames?"

Ames. That was always Ethan's pet name for me, dating back to the days when our vocabulary could be measured in the dozens of words. According to our parents, Ethan couldn't quite manage the second syllable when he was learning to talk, and the name stuck.

"It's a long story."

"I got all night."

"Let me wash up." I brush my teeth and rinse my face, not caring about Ethan seeing me without makeup. It's just Ethan, for pete's sake! He's seen me in worse states, sadly.

Back in the room, he's lying on the bed, pointing the remote at the television.

"Just like old times." I flop onto the mattress next to him. It's not just like old times, though. We're in a hotel, not his bedroom. His parents aren't downstairs. And Ethan has, uh, filled out a bit since high school. I wonder if my mother knows that. If so, it's a fact she has thus far failed to mention.

Well, he's not pumped and buffed like Danny but he's not the skinny nerd he used to be. And he still has that thick wavy hair I used to yank on when we were still in diapers. Ditto for the pretty blue eyes that were always kind and smart.

He's also totally rich these days, according to my mother. He created some app she can never remember the name of. He probably has a beautiful girlfriend who's too sophisticated to come to a dumb class reunion in dumb Avondale.

In other words, he has a great life. Yesterday, my life was fantastic! Today, not so much.

He reaches over and wraps his hand around mine. "Tell me what happened."

"I don't even know where to start."

"Start at the beginning. Isn't that what they say?"

"Well, okay. First, today was the last day of the school year and I thought I was going to be promoted to chair of the English department for next year but damn Charlie Gardner—he's the principal now—hired someone from out of town. A guy named Malcom."

I look to see whether I have lost Ethan's attention yet, but he's still watching me intently so I continue. "I interviewed for that job. I was the top—hell, the *only* internal candidate. And you know why I didn't get the job? Danny told him that we were planning to start a family right away, and that I wanted to be a stay-at-

41

home mom. We never had that conversation! And I *wanted* that job."

I can tell my voice has slipped into the hysteria register. If I don't cool it, I will break into tears, guaranteed.

"I'm sorry, Ames."

Ethan reaches out to brush my hair back off my face and in a heartbeat, I'm transported back to adolescence. How many nights had we spent just like this? The two of us platonically in bed, Ethan listening to me pour my heart out.

We're both too old for this now.

"You don't have to listen to this. You should just go. Please."

"I'm not going anywhere until you tell me everything that happened today. So Danny cost you your promotion. What happened after that?"

"I picked up wedding cake samples and two Italian hoagies and went to Danny's office. We were supposed to finalize the cake decisions. But when I got there, Angela Alessi was in his office. Naked. Danny yelled at me to get out and then I threw the bag of hoagies at Angela."

Ethan's eyebrows lift. "Bullseye?"

I nod and he holds up his hand for a high five.

"Good girl."

And then we are both laughing, the bed bouncing beneath us and I'm glad the hotel is practically empty. We're making enough noise to wake the dead.

Eventually we calm down and I swipe the tears from my cheeks with the back of my hand.

"What are you going to do now?" Ethan asks.

I shake my head. "I don't know."

"Not take him back, I hope."

I shake my head again. "No. I'm sure the entire town knows about my utter humiliation by now." I sigh and let my head do a Fosbury flop onto the pillow. "I can't think about this right now." I'm crashing from the tequila. "I need to sleep."

I close my eyes, vaguely aware of Ethan getting off the bed and then the sound of running water in the bathroom. And then silence.

CHAPTER 6

Ethan

In the morning, I awake before Amy does. I stare at the bright morning light streaming in through the drapes we didn't think to close the night before. I stare at it for a good five minutes until spots are dancing around in my vision. I turn to look at her.

Even in this stark early light, she's beautiful. Even after all these years, she is beautiful. Even after getting banged by Danny-effing-Walker, she is still beautiful to me.

That's not always the case, you know. Sometimes you spend the night with a woman and in the morning, she's got drool slobbering out of her mouth, her hair managed to braid itself into knots overnight, and she's cartoon-snoring at an ungodly decibel level.

But Amy's hair looks as glossy and bouncy as ever against the pillow, and her breath sounds soft and sweet in the even cadence of sleep. And those lips? The memory of kissing those soft, warm lips at the class reunion has me hard as a rock. Harder than watching Angel of Albuquerque last night, that's for sure.

And yet once again, there is absolutely nothing I can do about this. Just like when we were teenagers, I can't act on it. Amy had a shit day yesterday. Not getting the promotion she wanted. Walking in on her fiancé with another woman the month before their wedding. Somehow, even after all these years, I am still relegated to the role of Ethan the Comforter.

I consider the idea, though. I could lean over and kiss her, just a quick brush of the lips—I could say I was going for a friendly good morning kiss on the cheek and missed. I dismiss the idea just as quickly. We're friends. That's it. And who's to say that my sudden renewed interest in Amy Casales isn't a byproduct of Brad and Marissa's upcoming wedding. In the Caribbean. On the beach. Beneath a perfect azure blue sky. (I'm assuming.) With Everly in attendance. That would be Everly, former love of my life and woman who accepted my proposal of marriage (from bended knee, even!) only to rescind it in the car afterward. (She didn't want to humiliate me in the restaurant.)

And did I mention that she's bringing her new husband? According to Marissa, he's minor British royalty and has a "fabulous" accent.

Of course he does.

Next to me, Amy stirs and my opportunity for misbehavior is gone. I roll out of bed so as not to embarrass her. I slept in my jeans, though apparently I stripped off my tee shirt at some point in the wee hours of the night. It's lying on the floor in a wrinkled ball. I leave it there for now and make for the room's cheap plastic coffee maker. I rip open the plastic bags with their pre-packaged coffee pods, powdered creamer, and sugar. I drop in a pod, then uncap a complimentary bottle of water and pour it in.

I turn to look at Amy. She has one eye open, squinting skeptically at me, as though she's not sure whether she's awake or still dreaming.

"Oh god." She closes the eye. "We didn't do anything, did we?"

I see the hotel comforter ripple as she quickly pats down her body, checking for underwear.

"You mean like sex?" I ask.

"Yes, I mean like sex. Things are a little fuzzy due to the tequila, but I have a faint impression of sex."

"We watched a porno together."

"And that was it?"

"Yes, ma'am." The coffee maker is done sputtering. I carry the paper cup over to her. "Cream and sugar?"

She takes the cup gratefully, shaking her head. "I think this is a black coffee kind of morning." She takes a sip. "You're sure we didn't—"

"Yup, totally sure. You know I would never ..." Even though I'd lain awake half the night imagining doing the exact thing "I would never." Even though she is most definitely staring at my chest right now and it's making me hard again. I turn and pop another pod into the coffee maker.

"Don't turn around, okay?"

I hear the swish of the comforter, then the tiny click of a suitcase being unlatched.

"I got up in the middle of the night to change. My clothes smelled like puke."

"So that's what happened to my shirt," I joke. I sense a certain stillness in the air, and turn around.

46

Amy is standing there, clutching a bundle of clothes to her chest. I'm torn—between the utterly stricken expression on her face and the tanned, shapely legs that are not covered by the tiny little nightie she is wearing. If I had known that was lying next to me all night ... I take a deep breath.

"Oh god," she says again. "I'm sorry, Ethan. I was drunk. I didn't know what I was doing—"

And ... I'm losing the plot here.

"What?"

"I mauled you in the middle of the night, didn't I? I'm so sorry."

"No. Ames, what are you talking about? You didn't maul me. Why on earth would you think you did that?" Not that I would have minded being mauled. Right now, my nether regions are wailing "maul me, maul me baby" like backup singers on a farewell world tour.

A look I can't identify washes over her eyes, and then it's gone. She turns and heads into the bathroom. I dump two packages of powdered creamer into the coffee while I listen to the sound of the shower running. It's going to be a fake creamer kind of day.

CHAPTER 7

Amy

"Oh god." I let the hot water pour over my head. "I mauled Ethan McNamara last night. Or early in the morning. Or sometime between the tequila and the black coffee." He's just too sweet and nice to tell me. I cover my face with my hands and moan. My humiliation is complete. I can tell from the way my body feels that we didn't go all the way, which means he shut me down.

Of course.

Ethan wasn't interested in me back when we were both hormone-addled teenagers. He was always the perfect gentleman, which for a teenage boy, is simply code for "not interested." And it takes a lot for a teenage boy to not be interested in sex. I'm a teacher. I spend seven hours a day around the cretins.

And why would he be? I'm the only idiot saving myself for marriage.

I'm sure Ethan's no longer a virgin. I mean, no one is still a virgin at our age. Other than me. He probably has women lined up around the block. Rich, handsome ... gorgeous chest with just a smattering of curly dark hair, just the right amount to play with as you lie in bed.

Not that I have any personal experience of playing with a man's chest hair, but I do have a rich fantasy life. And a high-end vibrator (a Christmas gift from Danny last year).

I shampoo my hair and rinse, then turn off the water. The bathroom is filled with a fog of steam and for the first time in my life I don't wipe off the mirror with a towel. I'm too embarrassed to look at myself.

I propositioned Ethan. If only the Avondale Hotel had a proper bar, I at least could have propositioned a complete stranger.

It occurs to me that if I stay in the bathroom long enough, he might get bored and leave. I turn off the fan to listen for sounds of life on the other side of the door. It sounds pretty quiet. I comb out my hair and shimmy my damp skin into my underwear, shorts, and tank top. Then I open the bathroom door and find ... Ethan lounging on the bed, a cup of coffee in one hand and his phone in the other. Still shirtless. My fingers tingle at the sight of his chest hair.

"I thought you'd be gone." I stuff my dirty laundry into the suitcase and snap it shut.

"Why? My room is exactly like this one. I asked for the Presidential Suite and Shelly looked at me like I was speaking in tongues."

I'm sure he's used to staying in the Presidential Suite. To hear my mother talk, Ethan has more money than Bill Gates. He bought his parents a brand new house and new cars—a Range Rover for his dad and a zippy little Mini Cooper for his mom. Oddly enough, I can totally see Mrs. McNamara in that kind of car.

"I'm just kidding, Ames."

I muster a smile in acknowledgement.

"So what are your plans for the day?" he asks.

"Going to the house to get my stuff, I guess."

"Need me to come along?"

"No. I'll be fine. Then I guess I'll go to my mom's place and chant some spell and hope I can just magically disappear for the next three months."

"Come to the Bahamas with me."

"What?"

"Come with me to the Bahamas."

He has to be joking. Yet the expression on his face is completely serious. Not even a mischievous twinkle in his eye, which is a look Ethan has had in his repertoire since he was three years old.

"I can't do that."

"Why not?"

"Uh hello, teacher's salary? I can't afford to go to the Bahamas. Or anywhere, really."

"I'll pay."

"Why would you want me to come? Won't your girlfriend be upset?"

He laughs. "Ames, I don't have a girlfriend. If I did, I would have brought her to the reunion."

"Oh."

"But I need a girlfriend. Actually, I need a fiancée. My college roommate is getting married in the Bahamas and my ex-girlfriend will be there."

"So?"

"So when she dumped me five minutes after accepting my proposal of marriage, she said that she didn't believe I was capable of sustaining a long-term relationship. And maybe she's right, because here I am. But just for one week, I don't want her to think she's right. It'll make the whole trip miserable."

"You want me to pretend to be your fiancée for a week?"

He nods.

The thought of a week in the Bahamas ... I take a deep breath. Danny and I were planning to go to Hawaii for our honeymoon. Obviously, that's off now, so the prospect of some mindless sunbathing and fruity cocktails on a white sand beach is appealing. But I can't. I need to stay here and sort out the aftermath of my broken engagement. Things need to be cancelled. The church, the reception hall, the florist, the pianist, the deejay, the wedding planner .... yup, I'm going to be busy for awhile. It's too late to get our deposits back, of course. Danny's parents will be pissed about that, but it's their son's fault.

"I can't, Ethan. I'm sorry." I pull up the handle on my suitcase. "And I have to go." I glance at the alarm clock on the nightstand. "Danny should be out of the house by now. I need to get my things."

Downstairs, I stop at the front desk to check in on my checkout. I don't have one hundred percent confidence that Shelly processed things properly last night. Fortunately, she's not behind the desk this morning. An older woman smiles at me as I approach.

"Checking out, sweetie?"

"Yes." I wheel my suitcase to a stop, thinking about what lies ahead. Packing up my meager belongings from Danny's house. Clothes, books ... well, that's about it.

"Last name?"

"Casales. Amy Casales."

The woman's fingers fly over the computer keyboard. She seems to be more familiar with the system than Shelly was last night.

"Oh, there you are. You're all set. Your husband already paid." She looks up at me and smiles.

Husband? My first reaction is panic—Danny was here?

The woman squints at the screen. "McNamara is the name on the card." She looks up at me. "You modern girls these days."

Ethan paid for my room? I nod at the woman and turn toward the lobby door. I pull out my phone as I stride across the nearly empty parking lot toward my BMW (birthday present from Danny). I'm not sure whether I should thank Ethan or yell at him. Both, maybe. I drop the phone into my purse. I need to get my stuff out of the house in case Danny comes home for lunch. I'll deal with Ethan later.

CHAPTER 8

Ethan

Well, that went well.

Not.

I really wasn't expecting Amy to turn down an all-expenses-paid trip to the Bahamas. Who would do that? Maybe I didn't "sell" it enough. Now I'm stuck with the original problem—no plus-one for Brad and Marissa's wedding. And the wedding is next week.

Yes, I should be mature enough to not care what Everly thinks of me. I should be man enough to go to a wedding by myself. It's cold comfort that I could probably buy and sell her husband a thousand times over. Even if he is minor British royalty with a fab accent.

But apparently, I'm not.

I thought Everly was the love of my life. I planned that proposal for weeks. Got a reservation for two at a restaurant that is notoriously hard to get a table at. I had the restaurant's sommelier order in a special bottle of champagne just for the occasion. I remember every little detail from that evening! What we ordered—grilled Mediterranean octopus and wood-fired peppers to start, washed down with a lovely Amarone wine. We shared a salad of wild Italian grass (which is exactly what it sounds like—blades of grass in a nice vinaigrette). Then she had the filet mignon with garlic mashed potatoes, and I had seared Maine scallops with a side of angel hair pasta.

Everything was going according to plan. After we ordered dessert, the waiter knew to give us a few moments. I got down on one knee, smoothly produced the engagement ring from my pocket (thanks to hours of practice with Erin-Joi), and uttered those fateful words.

"Everly, will you marry me?"

She said "yes" and teared up as I slipped the two-carat heart-shaped diamond onto her perfectly manicured finger. Then we split cannoli and gelati (pistachio) with the specially ordered champagne.

And the whole time, she knew she wasn't really going to marry me. The. Whole. Damn. Time.

I was on top of the world for thirty minutes, my fingers itching to get on social media to tell the entire world that Everly had said "yes!" Then I got drop-kicked off the top of the world in the parking lot.

In the car, I leaned over to kiss her, but she turned her face away and took off the ring, handing it back to me. "I don't want to marry you, Ethan."

"What? Why not? You just said—" I looked back at the lights of the restaurant. I was confused. Hadn't she just said "yes" with tears sparkling in her eyes? Hadn't she just drunk my special, crazy-expensive champagne? Or had I imagined all that?

"I don't think you can go the long haul, Ethan. I don't think you're capable of sustaining a long-term relationship."

"What? We've been together for three years!"

She pressed the ring into my palm and folded my fingers closed around it. "I feel sorry for you, Ethan, I really do. You're going to be single your entire life."

"Not if you marry me I won't! Why did you say 'yes' then?"

"I didn't want to embarrass you."

"Thanks," I muttered, shoving the two-carat diamond back in my pocket.

"Take me home, please."

After I dropped her off at her apartment, I texted Erin-Joi. *She said no.*

"I'm so sorry, sir" came her immediate reply.

By the time I stumbled, dazed and heartbroken, into the house, Erin-Joi had already turned off the romantic harp music, swept up the trail of rose petals, and extinguished the scented candles in my bedroom suite. I mentally tacked on another ten grand to her annual bonus. In the bathroom, I flung open cabinet doors, ready to throw Everly's toothbrush and tampons into the trash, but Erin-Joi had already taken care of that, too.

Make that twenty grand.

I shake myself back into the present and haul my sorry, self-pitying ass back to my own hotel room where I shower and pack up my suitcase.

"I never liked that girl." Erin-Joi had said.

"Oh sweetie, these things are often for the best. There's someone better out there, waiting for you." (Mom.)

"Don't forget to return that ring and get your money back." (Dad.)

I still haven't done that. The ring remains, to this day, stashed in the back of my closet beneath a towering stack of sweaters my mother has bought me over the years and that I never wear. (I'm not really a sweater kind of guy. More tee shirts and soccer pants.) It's no secret in the city, obviously, that Everly and I broke up, but still—I hate the thought of walking into the jewelry store to return it. I'm not enough of a reprobate to ask Erin-Joi to do that, as well.

And if there's someone better out there waiting for me, she hasn't made her presence known yet.

CHAPTER 9

Amy

When I get to the house, Danny's banana yellow Corvette is parked in the garage. The garage door is open, which is odd. Danny is very protective of his car and practically paranoid that someone might steal it. I open my side of the garage and park next to the Corvette.

Inside, the house is quiet. Too quiet. It's unlike Danny to still be asleep at ten in the morning. He's not the type to oversleep the alarm. Actually, he's one of those super annoying people who wake up instantly and bound out of bed, full of energy and raring to go—like he spent the entire night dreaming of endless refills of coffee.

Speaking of coffee, the coffeemaker in the kitchen is silent and cool to the touch. I sniff. Nope, no lingering aroma of coffee in the air. So he hasn't been downstairs at all today.

I look at the kitchen and sigh. I'll never have this nice of a kitchen again. Not on a teacher's salary. Danny spared no expense when he bought the house. The kitchen's custom cabinets are painted a rich, ebony color—a lovely contrast with the white marble counters. The appliances are all high-end and stainless steel. There's even a standalone ice-maker for Super Bowl parties.

Ah well. It was fun while it lasted.

I walk into the great room with its soaring two-story ceiling to retrieve the novel I was reading from the coffee table. It's a psychological thriller about two women whose husbands keep turning up dead. It doesn't seem quite so farfetched at the moment.

I'm in the process of turning around when my eye catches on a jolt of red lying on the floor between the coffee table and the leather sofa. I lean down to take a closer look. It's a pair of shoes with bright red soles. Women's shoes. A pair of black platform fuck-me pumps, to be exact.

I don't own a pair of black platform fuck-me pumps.

Well. Apparently Angel of Albuquerque is here. Spent the night, evidently. That would explain why Danny's not awake.

"Honey, I'm home!" I shout as loud as I can, which is pretty darn loud—I'm a teacher, after all.

I'm greeted with silence.

Okay, so that's how they're going to play it. I picture the two of them lying in bed, holding their breath, trying not to make a sound.

Fine. I'll just pack up my stuff and go. It's not like I have a lot here, anyway. The furniture belongs to Danny. The dishes, the cookware, the towels. It occurs to me that living here has been a lot like living in an Airbnb.

I was scheduled to upgrade from the guest room to the master bedroom next month after the wedding. All along I assumed that was because Danny's parents are old-fashioned and didn't want us having hot, non-babymaking premarital sex. After all, Mrs. Walker helped me move into the guest room one Saturday, and unpacked and organized my clothes and toiletries. Now I wonder if the real reason for the guest room arrangement was because Danny didn't want me sleeping in the master bedroom a minute before he had to.

I take the stairs two at a time to the second floor. At the top, I shout, "Honey! I'm still home!" My embarrassment is turning to anger at a rapid clip. In the guest room, I pull two suitcases from the closet and cram in as much clothing as will fit. I run downstairs for a few garbage bags to fit the rest. I load up my car and go back to the room for the final suitcase.

I stop and look at the framed photograph of me and Danny on vacation that I kept on the nightstand. We were skiing in Vermont over a three-day weekend. In the photo, we're all smiles, our cheeks pink from the cold and wind, our eyes bright with what I thought at the time was love and happiness.

But I guess not. Who knew Danny Walker was an Oscar-worthy actor?

I grab the photograph from the nightstand and carry it out to the landing, where I stop about six feet from the closed master bedroom door. I set down the suitcase. Then I draw my arm back and throw the photograph with all my might. The glass from the frame shatters beautifully.

"Be careful when you come out," I yell as I pick up my suitcase. "There's glass in the carpet."

Downstairs, I get one more brilliant idea. A brilliant, petty idea, but I'll worry about regretting this later. I grab Angela's black fuck-me pumps from the great room and deposit them in the powder room toilet on my way out. In the movies, this is where the aggrieved, cheated-upon woman would set fire to Danny's yellow Corvette. I don't particularly want that on the memories page of next year's Avondale High School yearbook—*Remember when Ms. Casales lit up Coach Walker's 'vette???!!!*—so Danny and Angel of Albuquerque are getting off easy, really.

CHAPTER 10

Ethan

I press the doorbell of the Casales house and listen to the familiar melodious chime. For a split second, I feel about six years old again, ringing the doorbell to ask if Amy can come out to play. Then the weight of the ginormous bouquet of flowers I'm holding registers again in my brain. I may be an "emotional nitwit" (I'm paraphrasing Everly here), but one doesn't make the annual list of richest New Athenians (as decided by New Athens Style magazine) without a few fully functioning brain cells.

Mrs. Casales' face lights up the instant she opens the door and sees me.

"Why, Ethan McNamara! What a pleasant surprise."

I hold out the flowers. "These are for you, Mrs. Casales."

Her cheeks turn half a dozen shades of pink, and I wonder

whether Amy blushes that way—because Mrs. Casales is the spitting image of her daughter, only older and a bit heavier.

"Aren't you sweet, Ethan? Come on in. Amy's on her way."

I'm not sure how much she knows about what transpired between Amy and Danny. Or between Danny and Angela Alessi. I decide to tread carefully. There's already the risk of Amy being majorly pissed when she finds me here. But driving through Avondale this morning was just so depressing, I can't let her spend the summer here. Not after what Danny Dickhead did to her.

I also can't discount the possibility that Angela might decide to stay in town for awhile. I did a little research on the hotel's free wifi before checking out. Angela is really more of a porn actress than a porn *star*. She's made exactly two films—Angel Does Albuquerque and Angel Gets Her Wings. It doesn't look as though she has a busy filming schedule to return to immediately.

"Can I get you something to drink? Some tea? Or a soda? I don't keep that orange soda you used to drink by the gallon around anymore."

"Water would be nice, Mrs. Casales." I follow her into the kitchen at the back of the house. "I stopped drinking that soda a few years back. The dentist told me if I didn't stop, my teeth might be permanently stained orange."

Mrs. Casales also has her daughter's lilting laugh. She pours me a glass of water, then sets about unwrapping the bouquet.

"These are just lovely, Ethan. I'll have to send your mother a picture later." She fills a vase with water and plops the flowers in. "Did your mom ever get you Amy's phone number?"

"Yes, she did. Thank you."

"How was the reunion?"

"Good. It was very nice—"

She shoots me a look.

"Okay, so it was pretty lame."

"Those things always are."

I sip at my water, hoping she hasn't heard about me planting a kiss on Amy at the reunion. I try to keep the bruised side of my face turned away.

"Did you get in touch with Amy?"

"I did. Thanks." I'm guessing Amy hasn't told her mother that we spent the night together in a hotel room.

"I'm sure she told you what happened yesterday." Mrs. Casales shakes her head. "Just between you and me, Ethan—" She lowers her voice. "I always thought Amy was too good for the likes of Danny Walker. Don't know what she saw in him. And that Alessi girl? I knew she was destined to be a tramp when you kids were in preschool. Remember that birthday party?"

She looks at me expectantly, but I'm drawing a blank.

"The one with the moon bounce?"

I shake my head, still clueless. "I don't have a lot of memories that far back."

"Well."

I can hear the righteous indignation in her voice.

"It was Isabel Friedman's fourth birthday party and her parents rented one of those moon bounce things for you kids. And after the cake and ice cream, you all piled into it. Which was a bad idea, to begin with. All that sugar in your bellies. But after about five minutes, Angela pulled her sundress over her head, did this with it —" Mrs. Casales mimics someone waving a lasso over her head— "and then tossed it aside. Pretty soon, all of you kids had stripped down to your Captain Underpants."

"I'm glad I don't remember that," I say quietly.

"I knew right then that she was not going to be a *nice* girl." She glances up at the clock on the kitchen wall, the one that's been there as long as I can remember.

I need to lay out my idea quickly, before Amy shows up.

"Well, I need a favor from Amy and just wanted to run it by you first. I mean, I know Amy has the summer off, but the two of you might have plans ..."

Mrs. Casales waves away that notion. "Pfff. Now that the wedding's off, I'm sure Amy has no plans."

"I was hoping to hear that. Because I have a wedding in the Bahamas to go to. Next week, actually. And I could really use a date for it ..." I lay out the whole sorry story for Mrs. Casales. Everly, the two-carat heart-shaped diamond, the hours and hours I spent practicing, the specially ordered bottle of champagne, how delicious the entire meal was ("best gelati I've ever tasted").

I lay it on thick, to the point where her eyes are wet with sympathy.

"And gelati, you say? Oh, I love gelati. And she said 'yes' in the restaurant and then took it back in the car?"

I nod solemnly.

Mrs. Casales utters an oath I won't repeat here. "Girls these days. They just don't recognize a quality man when he's down on one knee in front of them, do they? They all fall for the ones like Danny Walker, a big lunk still living off of his parents' generosity."

I lift an eyebrow.

"Oh, the Walkers have poured so much money into those gyms of his. Excuse me, fitness studios. And I looked up the real estate records for that giant house of his. No way he came up with a twenty percent down payment for that on his own." She shudders. "Don't tell Amy I said this, but I am just so relieved that this is over.

I wanted to be supportive of her. She was head over heels in love with him. The Walkers are lovely people. And at least Danny is employed, which is more than you can say about a lot of the so-called men around here. But I always did just have a bad feeling about it."

Huh. This might be easier than I thought.

"Well, I would love for Amy to come to the wedding with me. Sounds like a trip to the Bahamas is just what she needs right now. All expenses paid, of course."

"Oh, Ethan, that is just the nicest offer. And I agree. Let Danny and that tramp go to his parents' timeshare in Hawaii. You and Amy will be in the *Bahamas*. And you know what? You should tell that Everly witch and prince whatever that Amy is your *wife.* Make her jealous."

"Hmm, I'm not sure Amy would agree to pretend to be my wife," I demur.

"Well, fiancée then. You and Amy go way back, Ethan. I'm sure she'll agree to do this for you."

Yup. A hundred bucks worth of flowers and … easy peasey.

Outside a car door slams and then a moment later, the screen door wheezes open.

"Amy, love? You'll never guess who's—"

"Some asshole parked a Porsche with Idaho plates in the driveway. You didn't see that, mom?"

Amy bursts into the kitchen. "Oh."

"How did it go?" Mrs. Casales pours another glass of water for Amy.

Amy bursts into tears.

"She was there!"

"What?"

65

"Angela was at the house!"

I see Mrs. Casales take a deep breath. "Did you get your things?"

Amy nods, tears streaking her cheeks, and I am torn between two impulses. Pull Amy into my arms and comfort her. Or storm out of the house and go rip Danny's face off for hurting her like this. As appealing as option number two is (and I'm not ruling it out for the future), I stick with the first impulse. I cross the kitchen in two long steps and pull her into my arms.

After all, I am Ethan the Comforter.

CHAPTER 11

Amy

Ethan smells like the Avondale Hotel soap and shampoo, and for some reason this makes me feel safe enough to blurt out, "I threw her shoes in the toilet!"

"Oh, Amy." I feel my mom pat me on the shoulder.

"I think they were those Christian Louba-whatevers. The ones with the red soles."

"Ouch." Ethan releases me. "Those are, like, thousand dollar shoes, Ames. Not that she didn't deserve it."

Angela can afford thousand dollar shoes? Her movie wasn't *that* good.

"Did you get all your things?" Mom asks again.

"Yeah. I got everything. They didn't even come out of the bedroom." I step away from him and frown. "What are you doing here? Is that your Porsche in the driveway?"

"I stopped by to say hello to your mom. And it's a rental car."

"He brought me flowers. Aren't they gorgeous?"

"You can rent a Porsche?"

"And he's taking you to the Bahamas!" I turn and look at my mom, giving a cursory glance to acknowledge the flowers. That's no mere "saying hello" bouquet. There are several bouquets stuffed into that vase.

I step away from Ethan. "Oh no. He's not, mom. I'm not going anywhere." Which reminds me. I rummage in my handbag and pull out the hundred dollars I withdrew from the ATM. I thrust the bills at Ethan. "This is for my room."

He holds up his hands. "I'm not taking your money, Ames."

"I can't let you pay for my hotel room."

"Why didn't you just come here?" Mom asks.

I back turn to Mom. "I told you, I needed some time to think."

I try to stuff the bills into the pockets of Ethan's jeans, but he covers my hand with his ... and holds it there just a beat too long. Suddenly it doesn't feel like Ethan's hand. Or rather, it doesn't feel like the hand of my *friend*, Ethan. It feels better than that.

He gently folds the money back into my palm and lifts my hand back to my chest. Which, you know, puts his hand right at my chest. Which also feels better than it should. A lot better. Clearly, I'm reacting to the sudden withdrawal of promised wedding night sex. Still, my body should not be glomming onto Ethan McNamara as a fix. This is Ethan we're talking about.

"He needs your help, sweetie. After what that Everly witch did to him?"

You know how books always describe brown eyes as being like "pools of dark chocolate?" Well, Ethan's eyes are like the vats of chocolate on the Hershey factory tour, and I'm falling headfirst into them. My tailbone is tingling with the memory of what I've been trying not to remember: that kiss from the class reunion. Meanwhile, behind me, Mom is prattling on.

"Go hang out on the beach for a week. Come back tanned and relaxed and with those nice streaks you get in your hair after you've been out in the sun too long. Things always look better after a vacation."

Hmm. Maybe she has a point. I was so looking forward to just lying on the beach in Hawaii, letting the warmth of the sun soak into my skin, listening to the sound of the ocean gently crashing into the sand, enjoying the peacefulness of it all. In reality, Danny would have been talking non-stop on the beach, if not to me then to one of his buds on the phone. Sometimes I think he lives to hear himself talk.

Ethan's not that way, though. If I told Ethan that I wanted to just lie there and chill in the music of nature, he'd silence his phone and zip his lips for as long as I wanted.

"You two could go to that Nautilus place." My mom is not giving up. "Isn't that in the Bahamas?"

"It is," Ethan concedes.

"See? When you were twelve, you asked Santa for a trip to Nautilus."

"I don't recall him making good on that."

"Yeah, well, sometimes Santa ..."

"Let me be your Santa," Ethan whispers, too quietly for my mother to hear, which is a good thing because the way he says it makes the words sound vaguely filthy.

"It's summertime," I mouth back.

"Christmas in July."

"Sweetheart." My mother's voice sounds more urgent now. "You and Ethan are old friends. The two of you will have a blast."

"We will." Ethan's face is serious now. "We'll do anything you want."

"Anything?" I waggle my eyebrows playfully, trying to get rid of his somber expression.

"Anything."

The way his lips move around that word—*anything*—like they're caressing each syllable is amplifying the tingling in my tailbone. Actually, the tingling is beginning to spread to other nearby locations.

"It's just for a week, Amy," Mom adds. "Don't overthink this."

A week of pretending to be Ethan's fiancée. How hard could it be? After the disaster that was yesterday, I deserve a week away from reality. While it might not be as wonderful as spending a week in Hawaii as a newlywed, a week with Ethan won't be horrible.

I dig my car keys out of my purse and toss them to my mother. "Well, I guess I'm already packed." I pretend to not notice the look of triumph that passes between her and Ethan.

I mean, my fiancé. LOL.

By the front door, Ethan picks up my two suitcases. I give my mother a hug because, well, she's my mom. Plus, she never did like Danny—I could always tell—and right now, that makes her a whole hell of a lot smarter than me.

I follow Ethan and the suitcases down the porch steps to the Porsche in the driveway.

"They're not going to fit," I say.

He looks at the car like he's seeing it for the first time. "Yeah, I guess you're right. That's okay. You can go shopping in New Athens before we leave." He picks up the suitcases and heads back to the house.

"I can't afford to—"

He cuts me off. "I'll pay for it. Don't worry about it."

I want to protest some more, but he's schlepping the bags up the porch steps. "These aren't going to fit after all, Mrs. Casales. My mom will take Amy shopping."

"You hear that, Amy? Mrs. McNamara will take you shopping. How fun!"

I give her a wan little wave. I'm starting to feel like a charity case. Cheer up Amy! Buy Amy all new clothes because she's poor!

Just as Ethan is opening the car door for me, my mom calls out a question.

"Oh Ethan? What is the name of that app you developed? I can never remember."

Ethan looks back at her and smiles a big happy smile. "Oh, it's a game, Mrs. Casales. It's called Pissy Puppy."

My jaw damn near hits the sidewalk.

In the car, I turn and say, "You invented Pissy Puppy?"

"Yup." He smiles proudly.

"That game is the bane of every teacher's existence."

"Sorry," he says, backing the car out of the driveway. But he says it in a tone of voice that doesn't sound sorry at all. "Wave to your mom," he adds.

I dutifully wave to my mom, who's frantically waving back and beaming from the porch. As soon as we're out of sight, she's going to call all her friends and tell her that I'm going to the Bahamas with Ethan McNamara, who invented Pissy Puppy by the way, and screw that Danny Walker.

In the security line at the airport, I turn to him again. "Pissy Puppy? Really?"

He shrugs.

An hour later and we are seated in first class. The flight attendant hands us heated towelettes. I say again, "Pissy Puppy?" Because I can hardly believe that Ethan is the mastermind behind that diabolical game. "Do you know how many faculty meetings I've had to sit through that were about that game specifically?"

Ethan waves a heated towelette at the airplane cabin around us. "First class, love, courtesy of one Pissy Puppy."

I look at the stream of people inching their way back to coach, dragging their larger-than-allowed carry-on suitcases. First class is already full. "How did you manage to get another seat so quickly?" I don't recall him even making a phone call after we left my mom's house. Unless he did it before I arrived.

"I always buy the seat next to me when I fly."

"You do? Just to have it empty?"

He nods. "It's more comfortable that way. More privacy for working, which is usually what I do on a flight."

I look around at our fellow first class travelers. We all look way more comfortable than the folks back in coach, even with every seat filled. Then again, this is my first time in first class.

"So this is how the other half lives," I murmur. He gives me a weird little smile.

"What?" I say.

"Nothing." But the weird little smile stays on his lips for a moment longer before disappearing.

The flight attendant returns with a tray of champagne. Ethan shakes his head, but I grab one of those flutes straightaway. Ethan's eyes are laughing at me.

"What?" I say. "This is my one time flying first class. I want the full experience."

"And you should have it." He holds my chin between his thumb and forefinger—just for a second, but it's long enough to buzz my tailbone. "Though we'll be flying first class to the Bahamas, too. So this is your *first* time, not your only time."

I take a small, exploratory sip of champagne. On the one hand, I'm expecting airline bubbly to be like airline food. Not that good. On the other hand, this is first class. I take another sip. Of course, on the other *other* hand, I'm a high school English teacher—I wouldn't know good champagne if it bit me on the ass.

Speaking of champagne, I hope the Walkers can return the cases they purchased.

"Earth to Amy."

"Sorry. I just remembered all the wedding contracts I need to cancel."

"I can have my assistant do it for you."

I really want to roll my eyes at that idea.

"Which reminds me, I need to give her a call before we take off. If you don't mind."

I turn toward the window and watch people loading luggage into the cargo hold. I don't want to eavesdrop on Ethan's conversation, but it's impossible not to since we're sitting right next to each other.

"Yes, I'm on the plane. Still boarding," he says. "Can you ready the guest suite? I'm bringing a friend home with me. Yes, right. She's a childhood friend. Amy Casales. She's going to the wedding with me. No, I'll just use the extra seat. And can you see if Sandy has any openings tomorrow morning? Mom's taking Amy shopping. Yeah, can you make a quick call to her? Nope, that's it. Thanks, Erin-Joi."

I pour the rest of the champagne down my gullet, then wake up my phone to google Ethan. Pissy Puppy? An assistant? First class? What happened to the Ethan McNamara I used to know?

Whoa. There are a lot of results for Ethan McNamara of New Athens. American entrepreneur, game developer, and philanthropist. Founder of Chaos Labs. Currently single, no children. Damn. There are news articles about bachelor charity auctions and incubators, whatever those are. Scholarships, a foundation, and ... I stop. Either I've gotten drunk off of one glass of champagne (totally possible) or Ethan is worth ... seven point two four billion dollars?

Seven. Billion. Dollars.

He's no longer on the phone. I pivot in the roomy first class seat and hold up the screen for him to see. He shrugs.

"They're a little off, but more or less."

Wow. I really *don't* know Ethan McNamara anymore. I stare at him for a long moment. He looks pretty much the same, except for being a bit more, uh, filled out. And what might be the start of crow's feet around his eyes. Or might just be him trying not to laugh at me.

"Penny for your thoughts, Ames."

"I'm having second thoughts about this," I whisper.

"Why?"

The engine noise ramps up as the plane starts to back away from the gate.

Second thoughts be damned.

"Why, Ames?"

"You're rich."

"Uh huh."

"Like, really rich."

"So?"

"So, your friends are probably rich too."

"Some of them are. Some aren't."

"Your ex?"

"No. Her parents are fairly well off, but Everly's not rich on her own."

This strikes me as a somewhat meaningless distinction.

"I'm just a teacher, Ethan. I'm probably going to do or say something embarrassing at the wedding."

"I doubt it."

"Oh, I don't. I'm going to use the wrong fork or order some déclassé drink or something."

"Okay, the fact that you just used the word 'déclassé' in a sentence tells me you won't."

This time, I do roll my eyes. "I'm an English teacher. We know the occasional French word."

"If it's any consolation, the wedding is being held at Nautilus."

"The water park?"

"Yup."

Well, huh.

"I remember how badly you wanted that trip for Christmas," he adds.

"You made fun of me for it, too."

"Sorry."

"You didn't think anything could be better than Hersheypark."

"Well, I can't promise that Nautilus will be better. But we'll find out." He lifts my hand from my lap and gives it a gentle squeeze. "We'll have fun, Amy. I promise."

For a moment there, I think he's going to lift my knuckles to his lips. But he doesn't. He returns my hand to my lap.

"Danny originally wanted to get married at Disney World. His parents made short work of that idea."

He presses his finger to my lips. "But I have a few rules. No talking about Danny Walker on the trip. Starting now."

Well, I'm not that eager to talk about Danny, either. "What are the other rules?"

"You tell me when there's something you want to do. And when there's something you don't."

That seems easy enough.

"And you let me spend money without worrying about it."

That also sounds easy. And to most people, it probably would be. Not for me, though. I've always earned my own money. I worked through college. I was planning to work after Danny and I had kids. My mom always worked. I enjoy working. I enjoy teaching.

I open my mouth to speak, but Ethan's finger is there again, pressing against my lips.

"For this week and next, we're not going to be two middle class kids from Avondale. You're going to be the fiancée of a wealthy tech entrepreneur."

"I don't want people to think I'm a gold digger."

"What people? People you don't know? Who cares what they think?"

"I don't want your parents to think—"

"Ames. You are the last person my parents would think that of. In fact, my mother is going to be massively disappointed that we're just pretending."

"Why?"

"Because she always thought we were having wild monkey sex when you spent the night at our house."

I swear my heart has just stopped. "What? She thought we were

…" I can't even finish the thought. Me and Ethan? "Why did she let me stay over then?" My face is on fire.

"Because she likes you, Amy. She wanted you to be my girlfriend."

From above us comes the pilot's voice. "Flight attendants, prepare doors for takeoff."

As the plane begins to accelerate down the runway, Ethan's hand covers mine and I realize that I'm white-knuckling the armrest. Not because I'm afraid of flying—I'm not—but because I'm a little afraid of what I'm flying into here.

The nose of the plane lifts, followed by the wheels, and then we are airborne. Everyone on this flight is flying toward something. Home. A business trip. A vacation. New grandkids or a sick relative. What am I flying toward? I'm not sure.

I feel a soft squeeze on my hand and turn to look at Ethan. Yes, I always got the impression from Mrs. McNamara that she wanted us to be a couple, but I had no idea she believed we were sleeping together. When I spent the night in Ethan's room, we were just *sleeping*. Not together. Just next to each other. Chastely. Platonically. Because we weren't interested in each other that way. We were just two kids who had known each other since forever.

"Dollar for your thoughts," he says, smiling.

I smile back, sort of. "We don't really know each other anymore, do we?"

His smile fades and his head shakes, sadly. "No. Because the Amy Casales I used to know would never have agreed to marry Dan—" He catches himself just in time. "He Who Shall Not Be Named."

"People change."

"Not that much."

I shrug. "I fell in love with him. What can I say? He treated me like a queen. Or so I thought."

He opens his mouth to speak and I know what he's going to say —that he will treat me like a better queen. But the plane levels off and we hear the rattling of glassware as the flight attendants prepare to begin the beverage service. He closes his mouth, which is just as well. I've had enough of empty platitudes for awhile. A good long while.

CHAPTER 12

Ethan

The expression on her face is breaking my heart. I vow right here and now to treat her like a queen these next two weeks. I still don't get how she ended up engaged to that idiot. How could she possibly have fallen in love with him? Maybe she doesn't understand it herself. But it's going to be my mission to figure it out.

"So what happens when we get to New Athens?" she asks.

"We'll go to my house. Erin-Joi will have the guest room ready for you. If you're hungry, she can order in some food for us."

"You're making her wait there for us? We can order takeout ourselves."

"She lives there. It's not that far a trip."

"Your assistant lives with you?"

"She has her own wing. We don't live *together.*"

Amy cocks her head and squints her eyes in a way that is ridiculously adorable—and makes me really wish we weren't stuck in a metal tube with two hundred other people hurtling through the air at thirty thousand feet.

"Do you, like, ring her in the middle of the night for some hot milk?"

I swat playfully at her arm. "No. I'm not that kind of boss. And anyway, she'd just tell me to get it myself."

"That's so weird. Having a live-in assistant."

"Why? I'm providing someone with a good job. I pay her well, with benefits. I contribute to a retirement plan for her. She gets four weeks off a year."

"How long has she worked for you?"

"About two years now. If I was that horrible, she would have quit by now. Good personal assistants are in high demand."

"But why do you need one?"

"It allows me to get more things done in a day. More important things."

"Like design annoying games?"

"That's the only game I created and I have no plans to do any more."

"Then what do you do all day long that you need to do more of?"

"I run an entrepreneurship incubator for high school students."

"A what?"

"It's called Chaos Labs. I help high school students start businesses. We teach them about product development, business plans, marketing, all that stuff. Then, when they're ready, they get to pitch to the team for funding."

"For real? As in real funding?"

I nod. "Yup. Real money. Some of it mine, of course."

"That's really cool, Ethan. I'm impressed."

Not to brag or anything, but I impress people all the time. It means a lot to me that Amy is impressed—and not by the sheer fact of my wealth. One of the things I've learned from making a lot of money is that there are really very few people who matter in your life—and most of those people are from before you had money.

"I hope that helps make up for unleashing a foul-mouthed cartoon dog on the world."

She shrugs, but her eyes are twinkling.

The flight attendant comes through to pass out snack boxes and more drinks. Then Amy and I spend the rest of the flight gossiping about high school classmates and talking about this and that. Some of it important, some of it not. But it makes me realize what idiots we were to let each other fall out of our lives. Talking to Amy is easy. Fun.

"Is it weird being a teacher at the same high school we graduated from?" I ask.

"No. I mean, it was when I did my student teaching there. But I've been a teacher there now for longer than I was a student."

"Do you *like* teaching there?" I still can't wrap my mind around her planning to spend the rest of her life in Avondale.

"I do. I like being a teacher."

She pops a square of dark chocolate from the snack box into her mouth and lets it melt there. This is how Amy has always eaten candy—put it in her mouth and let the sugar dissolve on her tongue. I don't know the Amy who somehow managed to get herself betrothed to you-know-who, but I do know the Amy from before that unfortunate time. It could be argued that I know her better than I know myself.

"And I really wanted to be chair of the English department," she goes on. "Genevieve was fine and all, but—"

"Wait. Ms. Ludwig was still the chair? She was in that job when we were in high school."

"I know! I liked her, but she was resistant to new ideas that the younger faculty members have. There are so many things I want to do there, things we could be doing better. Things we should be doing better."

I'm struck by the passion in Amy's voice. It didn't surprise me that she chose teaching as a career. She used to go into school early every morning to tutor other students in the library. She always had a knack for explaining things in a way that others can easily understand. Unlike Charlie Gardner, who had to have been one of the worst teachers I've ever encountered. And he's the principal of Avondale High now? Talk about failing up.

I know a ton of teachers and administrators in New Athens—at public schools, private schools, elite prep schools, cutting-edge magnet schools. I could get Amy an interview tomorrow at any one of them. And any one of them would be thrilled to have a teacher like her on staff. Charlie Gardner has no idea what he's doing.

The pilot's voice comes on over the speakers, and immediately I feel the heavy drop of the plane beginning its descent. Fifteen minutes later, we touch down in a torrent of screeching wheels and shifting carry-on luggage.

In the terminal, I fire off a quick text to Erin-Joi to let her know that we are on the ground and then I log in to summon the car. I take Amy's hand and lead her toward the exit.

"Are we getting a cab?" she asks.

"No." I give her hand a gentle squeeze. I can't wait 'til she sees this. "My car is on the way."

"Don't tell me you have your own personal chauffeur, too."

"No, I do not. Nor does Erin-Joi lower herself to come to the airport to pick me up, except in the event of an emergency. And by emergency, I mean the car got stolen from the lot while I was away."

She gasps. "Maybe you should just take a cab."

"This is more fun."

Outside, the night air is warm and soft with not a trace of humidity. We walk toward the far end of the terminal, where a sign discreetly announces "SDC Pickup." There's a lone figure standing beneath the overhead light.

"Hey, Ethan," the man says just as a white car pulls up.

"Hey there," I reply. "Nice evening out."

"It is. Take care." He walks around to the driver's side, gets in, and drives off.

"Who was that?" Amy asks.

"No clue."

"He knew your name."

"Lots of people know me on sight around here." The headlights of my car come into view. "That's not the detail I thought you'd notice about that encounter."

The car pulls up and stops. The hatchback opens silently and I toss in my carry-on. Then I open the passenger door for Amy. When I slide into the leather driver's seat, her jaw is practically in her lap.

"How did this just get here? There's no driver!"

"Nope." I grin. "Self-driving car." I shift the car into drive and pull away from the curb.

Her forehead creases. "If it's self-driving, why are you driving it now?"

"The car hasn't been approved for road use yet. But owners are allowed to retrieve them from the parking lot at the airport." I leave the airport's winding road behind and hit the gas to merge onto the highway.

"Felix, open the moonroof, please." Above us, the tinted glass slides away, revealing a cloudless sky and twinkling stars. "Pretty cool, huh?"

"Felix is the name of the operating system?"

"Nope. Felix is the name of the car." She gives an unladylike snort. "What can I say? It looked like a Felix."

I see her checking out the hand-stitched nappa leather seats and carbon fiber trim. I tap a button on the steering wheel and the sound of Elgar's first symphony swells inside the car.

She pats the leather console. "If I owned a car like this, I wouldn't let anyone else drive it. Not even Felix."

"Your beemer is a pretty sweet ride."

"I'm sure it will be repossessed by—" She catches herself just in time.

"I'll buy you a new one."

From the way she laughs, I can tell she thinks I'm not being serious. But now that the thought is out of my mouth, I realize that I am totally serious. Even if her dickwad of an ex doesn't take back the BMW he bought her, I may still buy her a nicer one.

I turn Felix into the long driveway that is the entrance to my property. Lights overhead pop on, one by one, as we drive until we reach the front gate.

"Where are we going?" Amy asks.

"We're home."

She leans forward to peer through the windshield, not that there is much to see in the dark. The property is wooded between the gate and the house.

"This is your home? It looks like a state park."

I'm not sure if that comparison is a compliment or not.

"Felix, open the gate, please."

"And does Felix require you to say 'please' after every command?"

"Actually, yes." The heavy iron gates begin to swing inward. "Manners are programmed into the car's operating system."

"Do manners come standard or is that an option, like heated seats?"

I chuckle. "On a three hundred thousand dollar car, everything comes standard." I sit back and let Felix drive the rest of the way.

"Oh my god, Ethan," is all she says.

Her head swivels this way and that as the car glides smoothly through the sculpture garden and then quietly brakes to a stop at the front door. The interior lights come on, the doors unlock, and the hatchback opens.

"This is ... wow." Amy opens her door and steps out, looking up at the house. "But I was expecting something a little more modern."

"Yeah, everyone says that." I grab my luggage from the back of the car. "Goodnight, Felix." The car's headlights blink twice, then Felix drives off in the direction of the garage.

"Where's he going?"

"Felix can park himself."

Inside, Erin-Joi is out of sight, but Amy's room is impeccably prepared. A pair of women's silk pajamas is laid out on the king-sized bed, the covers turned back. In the spacious bathroom, towels are neatly folded next to an array of upscale toiletries. In the guest kitchen, a plate of cookies beckons and a pot of coffee scents the air. Erin-Joi has thought of everything. It's what I pay her for.

"Nice kitchen, Eeth."

She'll see the house's real kitchen tomorrow.

"Are you hungry?" I ask. "We can order something."

"Not really. I am tired, though. The past two days are hitting me hard right about now. Not to mention all that tequila last night." She shakes her head.

"No more drinking games for us. If you need anything, just call me. Okay?"

"Where's your room?" She looks around.

"In the other wing."

"The other wing? What is this?" She gestures at the walls and furniture.

"The guest wing."

"The whole thing?"

I nod.

"You have a kitchen in the guest wing?"

I nod again. She shakes her head.

"This is kinda unreal, Eeth."

"Yeah, I know." I give her a friendly goodnight hug, loose and quick.

What really feels unreal, though, is walking back to my wing. Walking away from her. This isn't normal—the two of us sleeping under the same roof but not in the same bed. Last night in the hotel wasn't ideal. We were both drunk on tequila, for starters. But sleeping next to her felt normal. Right. Like home.

CHAPTER 13

Amy

I open my eyes and, for a split second, I think I'm in the Avondale Hotel. But no. I'm waking up in Ethan's house. No, scratch that. I'm waking up in Ethan's *mansion.* I'm staying in the guest wing. Not guest *room,* but *wing.* It has its own kitchen, living room, dining room, and two bedrooms. It has its own laundry room, for pete's sake. It's roughly the size of my mom's entire house.

And the shower? You could fit ten people in there, if you were so inclined.

I stretch my arms and legs beneath the gazillion thread count sheets and take a deep breath. Ethan, my oldest childhood friend, is rich. As in, really freaking rich. Yes, my mom has been telling me that for years now, but I'm just now wrapping my head around the reality of it. And the source of all this wealth?

Pissy-freaking-Puppy.

That game that everyone (except for me) has on their phones. The game that, everywhere you turn, someone is playing. In line at the supermarket, in the stands at football games (last year, Danny had the announcer ask people to silence their cell phones during games, to no avail), in classrooms.

My classroom!

How am I supposed to teach to the test when Pissy Puppy is not on the test?

A knock sounds on the guest wing door.

"Come in!"

I'm expecting it to be Ethan but, instead, it's Erin-Joi, the assistant. She's carrying an armful of neatly folded clothes. She sets them on the bed.

"I laundered your clothes."

"Thank you." I'm here with only the clothes on my back, so this simple kindness makes me want to leap from the bed and kiss Erin-Joi. I doubt she would respond well to that, however, so I stay huddled beneath the covers.

"You are quite welcome. What would you like for breakfast?"

"You cook for Ethan?"

She rolls her eyes. "No, I draw the line at cooking. Ethan is in the kitchen right now. He wanted to know what you'd like. He can fix it while you shower."

I contemplate requesting something ridiculous like Eggs Benedict or French toast, but then do the responsible guest thing and ask for something simple.

"Scrambled eggs and toast would be lovely. And some coffee."

She nods primly. "Blackberry jam okay?"

I nod dumbly. This is so weird. Ethan has an assistant. I wonder whether they've slept together, which is not as far-fetched an idea as you might think. I was expecting Erin-Joi to be older—fifties or sixties—in a matronly house dress and pressed apron. Instead, she looks to be about my age and, even this morning, is wearing a crisply tailored suit.

Plus, she's attractive. I'm sure Ethan has noticed. She wears her platinum blonde hair pulled back in a severe bun, but that only serves to draw more attention to her lovely green eyes and pronounced cheekbones. I pat my face. You'd need an archeological excavation to unearth my cheekbones.

At least she didn't call me "ma'am" the way she called Ethan "sir" last night. That's one more totally surreal thing about his life. Who on earth addresses Ethan as "sir?"

When I hear the guest wing door close, I jump out of bed and carry my clean clothing into the guest bath. Ethan's guest bath is nicer than any hotel bath I've ever seen—even the nice hotels Danny and I stayed in when I accompanied him to fitness trade shows. All of our vacations were tied to a trade show—it allowed him to write off the trip as a business expense. Not that I minded. It was the sensible thing to do, financially. That was one area where Danny and I always saw eye-to-eye. Mr. and Mrs. Walker raised him to be financially responsible, just as my mom raised me.

I brush my teeth, then turn on the shower. I wasn't kidding about it being large enough for ten people. It's all glass and grey marble with a little nook cut into the wall for pricey shampoo and soap. The rainfall showerhead is big enough for two people to stand under.

This shower reminds me of another thing I was looking forward to: sexy showers with my husband. I lather up my hair with the pricey shampoo. I'm sure he and Angela christened the shower at home. Tears prick at my eyes. For a whole host of reasons.

I loved him.

I've been humiliated in front of the entire town.

I'll be moving back in with my mom. I love her—don't get me wrong—but I'm thirty-three years old. I want an *adult* life. And I had one! Then in one lousy afternoon, Angel of Albuquerque took it all away.

Albuquerque is a big city! There are plenty of men to choose from out there. In Avondale? Not so much. Who am I going to marry now?

I scrub furiously at my hair and fume over the fact that I lost the department chair job because Danny told Charlie Gardner that I was going to become a stay-at-home mom. That's not happening now, obviously.

I finish showering and dress. My makeup is back home with my clothes, so nothing to be done about that. I find a drawer fully outfitted with combs, brushes, and a salon-style hair dryer. I run the comb through my hair and leave it to air dry. It's just Ethan. He's seen me in worse shape.

When I come back out to the bedroom, he's sitting on the unmade bed with two large trays of eggs, toast, sliced melon, and coffee.

"You didn't have to wait for me."

"Of course, I waited for you." He pats the mattress. "But I *am* starving, so come eat."

Ethan is dressed in jeans and a grey button-down, sleeves rolled up to his elbows. Bare feet. He always did have nice feet. I tuck mine beneath me as I sit down. That special pre-wedding pedicure is also now off the schedule. Oh well. It probably would not have been worth the expense.

"This looks good. Thank you."

"Well, it's not the mountain of pancakes my mother used to make for us." He digs into the eggs.

I smile at the memory. "Yeah, you always did like a little pancake with your syrup."

"I'm a sugar fiend, what can I say? Speaking of my mother, she's coming by around ten to pick you up for shopping. I have to shop for a wedding gift. Then I'll meet you and mom for lunch after. Sound okay?"

I nod.

"And Ames?" He looks me in the eye to make sure I'm paying attention. "Money is no object. My mother knows that, so whatever you need to buy—you buy. Understood?"

I nod again. "Is there anything you have in mind? What kind of clothing will make people believe our engagement is real?"

"Whatever you want to wear is fine, Amy."

"Ethan, no one is going to believe that you're engaged to a small town high school English teacher. So I need to not dress like one."

"Why not?"

"Why not? What does Everly do?"

He winces at the mention of her name. "She works in alumni relations at a girls' boarding school."

"Ah. See? You went from someone who hobnobs with wealthy alumni from a private school to someone who teaches the hoi polloi at a public school."

"The only reason she has that job is because she went to school there. Honestly, she's not particularly good at it. She lacks people skills." He slathers a slice of toast with blackberry jam. "Though she did meet her new husband there. His daughter boards there, apparently."

"How old is Everly?"

91

"Our age. But her husband is in his fifties, I believe. She's closer in age to his daughter."

"I don't know, Eeth. You're way out of my league these days."

"Don't be ridiculous."

He licks a spot of jam from the corner of his mouth, which is way sexier than it should be.

I'm trying not to rag on myself here, but it's hard not to. I'm a small town teacher who couldn't even hang on to the football coach. There's just no good earthly reason why a handsome young billionaire like Ethan would be romantically interested in me. Other than possibly blazing hot sex.

Of course, that's not the case here. And I will die—literally die—if Ethan ever finds out that I'm still a virgin.

There's a knock on the door and then Erin-Joi appears in the guest wing hallway. "I cancelled all those wedding contracts, sir."

"Thank you, Erin-Joi."

"You're quite welcome, sir."

And then just as smoothly, she disappears.

"Are those your wedding contracts with Everly or ... my wedding contracts?"

"Everly and I never got to the contractual stage, so those are yours. Now you can go to the Bahamas and not worry about a thing."

"But ... how did she know who to even call?"

"I gave her your mother's number."

"Oh. Well. Thanks, then." I have to admit, it does feel like a huge weight has been lifted from my shoulders. He's right—I would have worried about the contracts the whole time we're gone. "But why does she call you 'sir?'"

Ethan laughs. "I've tried to get her to stop, but she persists." He shakes his head. "She's too skilled an assistant for me to let her go." He winks at me. "You can call me 'sir' if you want."

I clap a hand over my nose to stop from snorting coffee (probably forty dollars a pound from Papua New Guinea or someplace) all over the pale grey silk duvet cover. "I am so not calling you 'sir.'"

He feigns disappointment, then looks at his watch. "Would you like a tour of the house? We have time before mom gets here."

"Now you're making me worried. Please tell me you don't have a red room."

"What's a red room?"

"You know, a playroom. A *sex* playroom." I waggle my eyebrows.

He frowns at me, then laughs—sort of—and then frowns again. "Now you're making *me* worried." He drains his coffee and stands up. "For the record, no, I don't have a sex room."

I've never been in a sex room. Obviously! (I just saw it in that movie.) I shouldn't be feeling even the slightest bit disappointed that Ethan—in his glorious new life as a billionaire—doesn't have one. Weirdly enough, though ... I am. Just a little ... but more than I should be.

CHAPTER 14

Ethan

Does Danny Walker have a sex room?

I don't even want to think about that. Given the whole porn star thing, a sex room doesn't seem that far-fetched.

And I *really* don't want to think about Amy in a Danny Walker sex room—because there is not enough bleach in the world to wash that image from my brain. Is that the kind of sex life they had? Bondage? Whips and chains?

Granted, a ball gag would probably come in handy just to shut Danny up for a few minutes.

I shake my head as I usher Amy into the kitchen. I just don't get Amy and Danny as a couple. Danny and Angela Alessi, sure. No problem there. But Amy and Danny? I can't see it.

"Wow, Ethan."

Amy's words cut short my descent into madness over the idea of Danny boinking Amy in a red room.

"This is … over the top?"

That's pretty much everyone's reaction to my kitchen. Granted, I spared no expense. Top-of-the-line appliances. Custom cherry cabinets and marble countertops. Hand-blown glass pendants over the island. And my pride and joy—the built-in wood-fired pizza oven.

"Do you cook?" she adds, like it's the most ridiculous thing she's ever heard.

I run my palm over the cool ice white marble. "I do. When my parents come over, dad and I cook up a storm." I lead her over to the bank of French doors that lead to the patio and outdoor kitchen.

"I don't remember your dad cooking that much."

"He's really gotten into it in retirement." I laugh. "And mom is not complaining."

"Yeah, I wouldn't either."

Next, I show her the living room with the huge fireplace (stones trucked in from twelve hundred miles away) and the sectional sofa that seats fifteen. Then the home theater and my home gym, complete with a sauna for ten. (No, I've never actually invited ten people to sit in the sauna.)

"This is the door to Erin-Joi's suite. If you need anything, don't hesitate to text her."

"She really lives here?"

"Yes. But only during the week."

She laughs and shakes her head.

"What?"

"It's kind of like you have a nanny."

"Oh, Erin-Joi would say that she's the *Super* Nanny."

We take a quick peek into my suite. "Just in case you need me in the middle of the night."

"I'm sure I won't."

I refrain from pointing out how many times in the past—and not even the distant past—she has needed me in the middle of the night.

We go outside to look at the pool.

"Who is that for?"

She points at the large playground, fully outfitted with swings, a slide, a climbing wall, and a half dozen of those weird metal animals on giant springs. With state-of-the-art rubber safety tile beneath it all.

"You have kids that you haven't mentioned?"

"Just planning ahead. It was easier to install everything all at once."

She sits down on a swing. I sit on the one next to her.

"Your house is very nice, Ethan. Big, too."

"Well, it's big for one person. That's true. But I was thinking ahead. When I have a family, it'll—"

"—still be big."

I don't say what I'm thinking—which is that when I built it I thought I would be sharing it with someone by now. Everly, to be exact. If I had known that was going to blow up in my face, I might have built a smaller place. I do feel lonely here sometimes, especially on the weekends when Erin-Joi returns to her normal life. I invite my parents over all the time, but they're busy with their new life here. When I bought them their new home, they got pulled right into an active social circle. They're booked all the time. Golf, bridge, cooking classes, bus trips to the casino, concerts with aging eighties soft rock bands. Air Supply. Hall & Oates, Ambrosia.

"Remember how we used to have swinging competitions?" Amy begins pumping her legs to get the swing going.

"It's a wonder neither of us broke an arm or a leg."

She's seriously swinging now. I can feel the frame swaying around us.

"I still have that …" Her voice fades on the upward swing. "… scar on the back of …" Downward swing. "… my hip, where I had to …" Upward swing. "… get stitches in …" Downward swing. "… the emergency room."

The next time she swings past me, she launches herself into the air the way we used to do when we were kids. She stretches her arms and legs out in a spread eagle and I wince— we aren't exactly spring chickens anymore—even as I can see that she is pretty damn physically fit.

She lands it perfectly, bending her knees at exactly the right time to absorb the impact. She spins around to look at me.

"Ta da!"

"A perfect ten!"

My brain is still stuck on the sight of Amy's lean and toned legs flying through the air. Not that Amy was in terrible shape when we were younger, but she's in fitness instructor shape now—and that has to be the work of one Danny Walker.

That sticks in my craw. I know it shouldn't. Being in shape is great! I work out myself. Rather religiously, even. It's just the idea of Danny somehow making Amy over into something she wasn't before that bugs me.

My mother's voice interrupts the early stages of a fantasy wherein I am challenging Danny to a pullup contest. "Ethan, I'm here!" And then a mere beat later— "Amy, love! Oh, come give me a hug!"

An hour later, I have dispatched Erin-Joi on her mission du jour— find an engagement ring for Amy. If this were a real engagement, I would have picked out a ring myself. I am many things, but one thing I am not is a Neanderthal. I spent a ton of time shopping for Everly's ring. As in, weeks. I just don't have it in me to set foot in a jewelry store right now. I trust Erin-Joi to pick out something suitably impressive. And by "suitably impressive," I mean "will knock Everly's socks off."

Now I'm on my own. Amy and Mom have disappeared into the bowels of the Acropolis Galleria with my personal shopper, Sandy, to buy Amy a new wardrobe for the trip. That leaves me a few hours to find a wedding gift for Brad and Marissa. Sadly, I am still completely stumped as to what to give them. The problem with having super wealthy friends is that they already have pretty much everything their hearts desire.

I end up spending forty-five minutes wandering aimlessly around the mall, peering into shops and considering twenty-four karat gold flatware eggs, six-hundred-dollar scented candles, and various colorful objets d'art at ridiculous price points. I am pondering an expensive cocktail cart when Erin-Joi texts me a picture of a ring.

It's a nice ring. Lovely, really. But there's only one diamond, in a classic six-pronged Tiffany setting. (I learned a few things while shopping for Everly's ring.) There's nothing wrong with it. There just isn't anything particularly *right* about it, either. I don't want to show up to the wedding with a fiancée who's wearing an off-the-rack ring, you know?

Nope. I text back.

Five minutes later, she sends me another picture. And then another. Soon it's a flurry of texts. I veto them all. Too underwhelmingly small. Too garishly big. No to yellow gold. I want platinum.

Even though it's a fake ring whose primary purpose is to make Everly insanely jealous, I want Amy to like it as well. I'll let her keep it if she wants. She can have the gems reset into a different piece of jewelry.

Then my phone lights up with a picture of "the one."

Even in a phone picture, the diamond twinkles like a galaxy and the platinum band is studded with pink diamonds. It's perfect. Classy, but different. I hope Amy loves it.

Winner winner chicken dinner, I text back. *Is there a matching necklace and earrings, by any chance?*

Erin-Joi's reply is a gif of someone tossing money out a window. I don't care. I have more money than I know what to do with.

Toss away. And buy one for yourself.

With all due respect, sir, the last thing I want is for people to think I'm engaged to you.

I roll my eyes and mentally cross "engagement ring" off the list while simultaneously deciding against the cocktail cart. But I'm still without a wedding gift. I stroll through the Galleria, willing inspiration to bludgeon me over the head. If only the Galleria had those freestanding carts with the carnival barkers peddling odd products that no one needs. But the Acropolis Galleria is too smitten with itself to allow those.

Up ahead, I see the flashing lights of Wine Me Up. *Ah inspira-*

tion, my old friend. Rich people always need more booze. After all, you drink it and it's gone. Plus, there's bragging rights in drinking rare and precious alcohol. About a year ago, I found myself at a party where the host was liberally serving bottles of three-hundred-year-old wine. Wine that tasted as though it had been skunked for at least two hundred of those years.

I stride into Wine Me Up like a man who knows exactly what he's doing in a wine store. I don't, but I've found that money is a good substitute for knowledge when it comes to alcohol. Pay seven hundred dollars for a Scarecrow cabernet and it's probably going to be good—or if it's not, at that price, no one is going to be so gauche as to admit it. (See three-hundred-year-old wine above.)

I head straight for the champagne aisle. The salesman ignores me for a good five minutes. I get it. He's wearing a thousand dollar suit and I'm wearing jeans, a button-down with an embroidered aardvark over my left nipple, and flip flops. You'd think by now that people would remember that a plain cotton hoodie is a sign of immense wealth in some circles.

"Can I help you?" he asks eventually, in a tone of voice that conveys, "If you don't mosey on out of here, I'm calling security."

"You sure can." When faced with people like this, I sometimes lapse into the central Pennsylvania vernacular, dropping the verb "to be" and flattening my vowels. Just to eff with people. I mean, who is this guy to sneer down his nose at me? I let the pissy puppies out! He probably plays my game on his lunch break. I look him over. I doubt he's any good at it, though.

"Do you ship overseas?" I ask.

"Depends on the country."

"The Bahamas."

"Which island?"

"New Providence. Nassau."

"Yes. We are approved to do that. One bottle or two?"

"I need a case of this Krug Clos d'Ambonnay." I'm choosing this one based on the bottle, which is sleek green with a metallic navy label. It will look right at home in Brad and Marissa's penthouse. I'm sure it tastes fine. For $2400 a bottle, it should. And if it doesn't, see note above. No one will admit to not liking a $2400 bottle of champagne.

"Um, sir? A case of that will be almost thirty thousand dollars. Not including shipping."

I reach into my back pocket and pull the Black Card from my wallet. "Do you take American Express?"

"But of course." He gives a little bow.

Sure, *now* he respects me. Inwardly, I roll my eyes. I get recognized by a complete stranger at the airport, but salespeople never seem to know who I am. Anyway. I fill out the ungodly amount of paperwork needed to ship thirty thousand dollars' worth of champagne to a resort-waterpark in the Bahamas.

As he rings me up, I get another text from Erin-Joi, letting me know that she is heading back to the house with the jewelry.

Leave it in the guest wing.

Will do, sir.

I don't bother telling her that I just sprung for a case of $2400-a-bottle champagne. Erin-Joi already thinks I'm hopeless with money. I disagree with her there. I may be hopeless at many things—well, no "may" about it—I truly am hopeless at many things. But money is not one of them.

Snooty sales guy is printing my receipt when another customer enters the store. I immediately peg his suit as bespoke. It fits him to a T in a way that an off-the-rack suit never can. The sleeves are the right length, to within a millimeter, and the pants break perfectly at his shoes. He glances up from his phone, sees that Snooty Sales Guy is still with me (circling the number on the receipt I can call to take a survey and be entered to win a twenty-dollar bottle of wine), then returns his attention to his screen.

I know exactly what he's doing. He has the volume down low, but my ears are so familiar with the sounds I could hear them at a sold-out Rolling Stones concert. I bite my lip to keep from laughing. Snooty Sales Guy here is going to fawn all over this guy in a way he didn't with me.

I grab the receipt and my copy of the ream of shipping paperwork. As I pass Bespoke, I glance at his screen. "Send the wiener dog to the dog park."

Then I'm outta there.

CHAPTER 15

Ethan

"Felix. Park, please." I tap the auto-drive button and lift my hands from the steering wheel. I smile over at Amy, who's sitting in the passenger seat.

"Show off."

But she smiles back at me, which is a good sign. According to mom, Amy was a little weirded out by the morning's shopping extravaganza. I need to remind myself that she's not Everly. Everly never had any problem spending my money. Not that I minded Everly spending my money. I loved her. I really did. When I love someone, I'm happy to spend money on them.

Amy, though, is not someone who's used to having someone spend money on her. Or not *that* kind of money, anyway. Danny clearly treated her well, in that regard. The BMW. The Instagram vacations. Spending money on someone is easy. Even I admit that.

You still have to back up the money with the hard work of *actually* treating someone well. Which Danny-effing-Walker did not.

Felix glides into my parking spot next to the front door of Chaos Labs. It's my reserved spot, as indicated by the sign—which was long ago defaced by a "Tawp Dawg" sticker. The Chaos Kids—as they call themselves—walk all over me. And I happily let them.

I'd make a terrible teacher.

Amy is out of the car and staring up at the building before Felix even shuts himself off. Technically, I'm not supposed to allow Felix to self-drive, but I do in places where the odds of getting caught are low. No one is going to bust one of the city's most prominent philanthropists at his own office.

I hope, anyway.

"So this is it." I step out of the car. "My atonement for creating a game that teachers everywhere hate."

I know plenty of tech people who cashed out their businesses and then settled into lives of relative ease. Multiple homes, sailing the world, buying islands. Frankly, that all seemed like too much work to me, so I did this—started Chaos Labs, my entrepreneurship incubator. I'm mentally crossing my fingers that Amy will be impressed by it—because I want her to be impressed.

I'll be honest. It stings a little that she hates Pissy Puppy so much. I mean, everyone hates that game. It's annoying as hell. You'll get no argument from me there. But that annoying little game made a shit-ton of money and this is where I'm putting that money to good use. I'm helping develop the next generation of technology entrepreneurs (some of whom will undoubtedly go on to create more annoying game apps, but ...).

"Hate is probably understating the matter," she says.

"Loathe? Despise? Revile? Detest? Abhor? Scorn? Discountenance?"

"Definitely more than discountenance."

"The way I look at it is: someone is going to create these games. It might as well be one of my kids. Some of them definitely come from the wrong side of the tracks." Even here in New Athens—which is a thriving, well-off city—there is still a wrong side of the tracks. "Creating an app and getting into university or starting their own business is a ticket out of that."

"I'm just busting your chops, Ethan."

"I know."

That's what we've always done—bust each other's chops. The way friends do. Maybe we won't be able to pull off this fake engagement thing. Maybe it'll be too obvious to everyone that Amy doesn't see me as anything more than a friend. Why would she? She was engaged to a man who has a kinky sex playroom in his house—I can't compete with that.

(To be honest, not sure I want to compete with it.)

She looks up at the building.

"It used to be a former mill," I say.

She nods, which I of course take as an invitation to offer more information than she probably wants. It's a cool building, you know? Red brick walls, soaring ceilings, the kind of tall paned windows that light was invented for.

"I wanted a space that would be inspiring to kids, a place that was different from the school buildings they're stuck in all day."

"Yeah, most school architecture isn't that inspiring. Or inspired."

"It was sort of run down when I found it. Okay, so it was totally in need of renovation. But the city gave me a smallish grant to rehab the place and now it's a really cool former mill-slash-education incubator." I hold my hands up wide. "We've been written up in the Wall Street Journal, just saying."

"So where did the name Chaos Labs come from?"

"Originally? I intended it to be in the spirit of the Greek god, Chaos. The beginning of all things. The state that precedes creation." I put my hand on the front door's lever. "However, you'll be forgiven for thinking there was a slightly different origin story."

I take a deep breath. There was one thing I didn't realize about really cool former mills. They have terrible acoustics. The god of chaos ain't got nothin' on the demons of chaos in here. I turn the lever and the decibel level hits us like a blast the instant I push open the door. Frankly, it's amazing anyone even notices us, but the noise fades to pin drop silence almost immediately.

"Mr. M!"

"Mr. P!"

"Yo, Dawg!"

These kids have quite the sense of humor.

The first floor is one giant open space, intended to foster creativity and group work. In one corner is the Cyber Café. (Hey, I held a contest for the kids to name it and that's what they came up with.) In the center of the room are a dozen sectional seating configurations where the kids can hang out and discuss their projects informally. In the very back is a trampoline area.

"What's the insurance premium on that?" Amy murmurs.

"Hefty. But no one's gotten hurt yet. Unless you count me."

The trampoline was probably the single biggest mistake of my life. Right up to the moment I kissed Amy at the class reunion, that is.

"Hey Mr. P! Do a flip for us!"

Other big mistake? Letting the kids know that I can do flips. I tried to keep that under wraps, but I get my best ideas on the trampoline. It was only ever a matter of time before I got caught.

I kick off my flip flops, put on a pair of grippy socks, and do a few full twisting flips.

"Don't try those at home," I warn. "Or here. Your parents will kill me."

I jump down from the trampoline. Next to me, Amy quietly clears her throat. *Oh right.* I'm about to introduce her when Gavin, a tall lanky sophomore, calls out.

"What happened to your face, dawg?"

I rub my cheekbone. Forgot about that.

Then Justin, an undersized seventh grader, chimes in, because Justin always chimes in. "I thought we're supposed to settle our differences with our brains, not our bodies."

Next to me, Amy chuffs out an almost imperceptible snort.

"Right." I drop my hand from my cheek and point at Justin. "Well, I didn't hit the other guy. He hit me."

Over in the corner, The G.O.D. Squad lets out a collective gasp. As is the way of teenaged girls, they do everything collectively. I hit the turbo switch on my brain, trying to come up with the best way out of this delicate matter. I don't really want to tell the story behind the bruise on my face. Especially with Amy standing right here. If she weren't, I could maybe play it off as some macho thing, defending a woman's honor, yada yada. The kids wouldn't likely buy it, but I'd make a game attempt at selling it. But Amy is standing right here, so I tango around an explanation.

"It's okay, though. It was part of a ... a party game. At a class reunion."

Gavin laughs. "Yeah, my parents say that fights always break out at their class reunions."

"It wasn't a fight, exactly." Amy jumps in to defend *my* honor.

But Justin takes her out at the knees (metaphorically, of course). "Because you didn't fight back?"

I shrug in lieu of a sigh. "Something like that. Anyways, guys, this is my friend, Amy Casales. We grew up together. Amy's a teacher so she has eyes in the back of her head. Just so you know." I make serious eye contact with as many kids as I can in three seconds. Then I lead Amy up the spiral staircase to the second floor.

It's quieter on the second floor of the mill. Up here are the "labs," though some are more akin to classrooms, depending on the age of the students they're intended for. All of them are packed to the gills with computers, 3D printers, and whiteboards. We peek into each one as we pass.

"You have a lot of kids here, Ethan."

"School's out so the summer coding academies are running. Those are popular with parents. Teachers might not like annoying game apps, but parents appreciate the college scholarship potential." I stop in front of another room. "These kids in here are working on business plans. I hire grad students from the university to help out." I point toward the end of the hall. "The robotics lab is down there. If you hear any loud crashes, it's probably just a robot falling off the ceiling."

"Ouch."

"Fortunately, the insurance company wasn't concerned about injured robots."

We walk into my office and I close the door.

"Your mom wanted to know what happened to your face, too."

"What did you tell her?"

"That you got clocked by my fiancé for kissing me."

"What did she say to that?"

"She said it sounds like you deserved it."

"I love it when my parents take my side."

The next thing I know, Amy's fingers are touching my bruise and my heart damn near stops. It feels so damn good.

"Does it still hurt?"

"It never really hurt."

She rolls her eyes at me.

"Okay, so it hurt when he hit me. He used to be the quarterback. He's got some guns on him." Her fingers are still tracing the outline of the bruise, which is a pale shade of exorcism pea green these days. "I'm surprised the kids noticed."

"Kids see everything. Especially when it's something you don't want them to see."

She drops her hand from my cheek and it takes all my willpower not to grab it and put it back.

"But I do have eyes in the back of my head. It's true." She pretends to fluff her hair. "So who's the girl gang in the corner? They were giving off some seriously territorial vibes."

I chuckle. "Girls are sadly in the minority at Chaos, not for lack of trying on my part. Maybe a lack of effective trying, I guess. So yeah, the girls here do stick together. They also apparently never liked Everly."

"Neither did your parents, according to your mom."

I shrug. "It's beginning to look like I was the only person who liked her. Possibly I'm not as good a judge of character as I like to think."

This idea has bothered me ever since Everly unceremoniously retracted her acceptance of my marriage proposal. Being a good judge of character is important in business—how can I impart that to the kids here if I don't have it myself?

"Do the girls have a crush on you? Lord knows, enough girls at Avondale practically flash their boobs at Danny in the halls."

"No. It's nothing like that. They pretty much think I'm an idiot, to be honest. That's partly because I'm not sure how to help them with their business idea. Which is more of a non-profit. Or a crusade, really."

"Oh? What is it?"

"They've named themselves The G.O.D. Squad. Girls Online Defense. They want to fight cyberbullying and make social media a safer space for girls. And it's a great idea! Don't get me wrong. I just don't know much about starting a not-for-profit movement. I know how to develop a technology product and bring it to market. I can teach the kids how to present to potential investors, manage the resulting business, and then cash out when the time is right. The G.O.D. Squad wants television interviews and CNN and celebrities and I don't have the contacts for that."

"Well, I've survived at least a dozen of Charlie Gardner's cyberbullying presentations, but I'm not sure how useful those ever were. I do have some contacts in the health and wellness media because I used to help Da—I mean you know who—with publicity."

Wait—is she offering to help me with The G.O.D. Squad? Maybe I can get her to stay a couple more weeks in New Athens after the wedding. That would kill two birds with one stone. The other bird being that I really just want to hang with her. Seeing her again makes me realize how much I should have been missing her.

"Maybe I can pick your brains over dinner. Where would you like to go?"

"I literally know zero restaurants in New Athens. Take me to your favorite."

CHAPTER 16

Amy

A food truck? That's Ethan's favorite restaurant? At first, I'm surprised—I was expecting a billionaire's favorite restaurant to be upscale, snooty, on the two millionth floor of some glass and steel skyscraper, and with a reservations system that is completely off limits to mere mortals.

But as we walk toward Willie's ChiliMobile (which is covered in brightly painted images of chili peppers and cacti), it makes sense that this would be Ethan's favorite. The old Ethan, that is. It's parked in the quad at the University of New Athens, his alma mater. There's a long line of people stretching back from the truck's two windows. We get in line.

I'm still mulling over Chaos Labs while Ethan handles the dozens of people who materialize as if out of nowhere to glad hand and chat. Chaos Labs was more than I expected. And the kids are

111

genuinely fond of him—equal parts worshipful and busting-the-chops-of-authority.

It does atone for unleashing that foul-mouthed dog onto the world.

A little.

As the line inches forward, more people notice Ethan and come over to talk. He is unfailingly gracious to everyone. Not that I would expect anything different. I try to keep my left hand hidden behind the fabric of my five-hundred-dollar skirt. After the trip to Chaos, we went back to Ethan's house where he presented me with the engagement ring that Erin-Joi picked up this morning while I was shopping with Ethan's mom.

At least Ethan himself didn't pick out the ring. That would have been weird.

It's a gorgeous ring. Absolutely stunning, in fact. A ginormous diamond with smaller pink diamonds on the band. (I didn't even know diamonds came in pink.) But I'd rather not draw too much attention to it, especially since this wild printed skirt already makes me feel like a flashing neon sign. (Did I mention it cost five hundred dollars? Egads.) Ethan wants me to wear the ring tonight to get used to it. I didn't mention the fact that I'm already used to wearing an engagement ring. Ethan gets a dark look on his face whenever Danny's name comes up.

I don't trust my acting ability just yet. If people start coming up and congratulating us on "our engagement," I'm afraid I won't be able to pull off the con effectively. I'm not sure I'll be able to pull it off in front of Ethan's former fiancée, either.

At last, we reach the head of the line. I'm perusing the extensive menu of chili choices, when the man inside the truck shouts out, "Ethan! My man!"

I'm beginning to get the feeling that Ethan is a bit of a rock star in New Athens. Random people on the street know who he is. I mean, I've lived in Avondale my whole life and teach at the high school (for a small town, that's a high profile position). Not to mention, I was engaged to, well, you know who. Even so, there are still people in Avondale who wouldn't know me from Angel of Albuquerque. Well, maybe that's an exaggeration, but you know what I mean. The only random people who recognize me on the street are former students. Occasionally their parents, if they're the sort to come to parent-teacher conferences. Which most aren't.

Ethan's fame concerns me, to be honest. How will we pull off a fake engagement if Ethan is famous in New Athens? Or famous … everywhere? Is he famous everywhere? Pissy Puppy is certainly famous everywhere, improbable as that may seem to my teacher's brain. What if people start asking questions about the sudden appearance of a new fiancée? What if they start nosing around and discover that the sudden new fiancée is really just a recently dumped childhood friend?

"What can I do you for today?" Chili Man is smiling at Ethan like he's Santa Claus.

"A bowl of your finest Cincinnati style, extra cheese, light on the sour cream." Ethan turns to me.

"The while chicken chili, please."

"And two birch beers," Ethan adds.

The man—who is, in fact, wearing a name tag that reads "Willie"—leans toward us to get a better look at me.

"And who is this lovely lady?" he asks.

When Ethan replies, "This is my fiancée, Amy," I nearly faint. He needs to give me some advance warning on this. And maybe other people, too, because a look of surprise crosses the face of Willie the Chili Man—quickly, but not too quick for me to catch.

"You are quite the man about town," I say as we walk away with our chili and birch beers. "Even the chili truck person knows you."

"Willie knows everyone who eats his chili on a regular basis. Also, his son was one of my students at Chaos Labs. He helped his dad with the business plan for the ChiliMobile and then created an app that people can use to track the truck's location around the city. People have been known to chase it down and practically run it off the road to get their chili fix."

We walk away from the quad until we reach a pocket park with picnic tables and … sculptures? I spot the one of Ethan holding a small dog immediately. I walk over to it.

"It's a good likeness of you."

"But not of the dog."

I study the dog for a moment. "It looks like they couldn't decide between making the dog realistic or cartoony."

"That's about the size of it."

"What breed of dog is it supposed to be?"

"Pissy Puppy is of indeterminate breed. He's supposed to be all breeds. Or whatever breed you need him to be."

"That is such utter horse pucky."

He laughs and walks away from his bronze likeness. "You're right. Just like it's utter horseshit that there's a statue of me here at all. But the money I give the school helps pay for all the other, more worthy statues."

He sits down at one of the tables and opens his chili, uncaps my birch beer for me. Ethan's a gentleman like that, in the small everyday ways. Danny wasn't. I knew that all along. I just thought his other qualities were good enough to compensate. I take a bite of my chili. It's good and—if I were here eating with Danny—we'd end up discussing all the ways Danny's chili would be better. If Danny were to ever make chili, that is. He's one of those people who always thinks he knows a better way.

I'm beginning to suspect that what Danny really saw in me was a "proper wife." And his better way to do marriage was to have some action on the side. Granted, not the most original idea, but I was blindsided by the onslaught of attention he showered on me. That should have been my first clue. Instead, I thought it was a sign of true love.

Idiot.

"How's the chili?" Ethan asks.

From the expression on his face, I can tell he knows what I'm thinking about and is trying to distract me. He was always good at that—distracting me from thoughts about my dad in the hospital, from worries over how my mom was going to cope without him, from just ordinary teenage high school angst. I always thought Ethan would end up being a doctor or a therapist. Some occupation that requires that kind of intuition about other people. Instead he invented a silly game and got stinking rich.

"It's good," I reply. "Excellent, actually.

"Top ten on your all time chili list?"

"Top three, easily."

He gives me a silly thumbs up. Then he gets serious again. "I never meant for any of this to happen, Ames. I was just fooling around with game design and gave it to some friends to play. Before I knew it, it had snowballed out of control. When I was approached about selling the game, I jumped on it. Why not? Game design was never my passion."

"Is Chaos Labs your passion?"

He shrugs, which has always been Ethan's way of humbly saying "yes."

"I think what you're doing is great," I add.

"I'm still young enough that my idealism hasn't been crushed out of me by the world yet. I have all the material things I could ever want."

"Money doesn't buy everything."

"Nope. It sure doesn't. Like the grandkids my mother desperately wants. And reminds me about all the time." He drains the rest of his birch beer. "Let's finish up this chili and then go get some ice cream. I have absolutely no connection to the ice cream place, but it's great anyway."

He's right about the ice cream place. It *is* great—as in, I want one scoop of every single flavor (but settle for just a scoop of chocolate caramel swirl). And none of the young women working there seem to have any idea who Ethan is. That doesn't stop them from giggling and making googly eyes at him, despite the presence of a diamond ring-wearing (fake) fiancée.

I mean, I get it. My childhood friend—the brother I never had—has bloomed into a fine looking man. I'm not sure what that Everly woman was thinking. Ethan is handsome, rich, and also just a genuinely good guy. What more can you want? A British accent? Sure, that would be nice—but it's hardly a non-negotiable.

We leave behind the giggling girls for a walking tour of campus as we eat our ice cream.

"There aren't any more statues of you, are there?" I playfully jab an elbow into his ribs. He jabs me back.

"No. If they ever put up another one, I'll have someone take it down in the middle of the night."

I snort ice cream through my nose.

"What?"

I lick caramel swirl from my lips before answering. "I'm picturing your assistant throwing ropes over your bronze head and pulling it down."

"I'm sure there are days when she wants to throw a rope over my actual head."

"I have a hard time imagining you being difficult to work for, Ethan."

"You've never worked for me."

"You got a point there."

Still, I can't imagine Ethan being a bosshole. It's hard to imagine him needing an assistant, even. When we were kids, he was just … competent. I could always go to Ethan and he would know what to do. What to say.

He takes my hand and it feels good. Comforting—like all those times in the middle of the night when he would reach over, beneath the covers, and take my hand just as worry over my dad's health threatened to pull me under. He always knew the exact right moment—not a minute too soon or a minute too late.

Then he laces his fingers between mine, which is a step beyond "comforting." I look over at him and lift an eyebrow in question.

"We need to practice," he answers and tugs me closer to him as we walk. I nearly drop my ice cream cone.

"I don't think we need to practice holding hands." Danny and I held hands plenty during our "courtship." It was always torture for me, having that physical touch between us and not being able to take it any further. Now it occurs to me that it must have been torture for him, too—having to pretend to want to hold my hand.

"We need it to feel natural."

I let it slide. I'm not opposed to holding Ethan's hand. It does feel natural, since we've been holding hands our entire lives. I've held Ethan's hand more than I've held anyone else's, except maybe my mother's. Even the time I spent with Danny doesn't put a dent in Ethan's hand-holding scorecard.

At the same time, it feels a little weird. We're not kids anymore. I'm not a teenaged girl traumatized by her father's repeated heart attacks. Platonic friends don't hold hands this way.

Plus, my body hasn't quite gotten the message that I'm not getting married next month. That the long awaited wedding night sextravaganza is not happening. That my bridal night lingerie—a tasteful (yet sinful) confection of lace and satin—is never going to see the light of day.

Someone's phone rings and Ethan drops my hand like it's crawling with flaming cooties. I fumble one-handedly with my purse, trying to extract my phone, while also trying not to fumble my ice cream. By the time I hear Ethan answer his phone—meaning it was not my phone that rang—there is chocolate caramel swirl soaking into the five-hundred-dollar skirt.

I look around frantically for a trash can, but there are none to be found. Because terrorism. Honestly, New Athens is probably not at the top of any terrorist's list of targets. Unless their kids are glued to their phones, playing annoying game apps. Then maybe New Athens is target numero uno.

I shove the rest of the dripping cone into my mouth and start dabbing at the chocolate stain with a fistful of cheap ice cream shop napkins. Which proceed to shred and disintegrate right before my very eyes. My heart is pounding in my throat now. This is a five-hundred-freaking-dollar skirt! You know what doesn't come out of fabric easily? Red wine, blood, tomatoes, curry, and chocolate. This is why I ordered the white chicken chili and instead I've befouled myself with ice cream.

I'm spitting on my fingers and rubbing at the chocolate (which isn't working, by the way) when I hear Ethan say, "Everly." My head snaps up. It's Everly who called him? On our date? Well, okay, we're not on a date. But we are fake engaged! Which means his former fiancée should not be calling him. Especially since she's married.

Cheese Louise. I've already lost a real fiancée. Am I in the process of losing a fake one too?

I sigh and stop rubbing at the skirt. Maybe Erin-Joi knows some secret way to get chocolate out of a five-hundred-dollar skirt and then she can return it to the store for Ethan and get his money back.

I watch him as he listens to whatever Everly is saying on the other end. His expression is dark. Ethan never did have even a passable poker face. Whatever she's saying, he's not liking. There's a sour burn in the middle of my chest, like the heartburn I used to get after forcing down one of Danny's kale-rhubarb-flax seed smoothies. It could be the ice cream cone lodged halfway down my gullet. Or it could be a simple desire to rip off this Everly woman's face for daring to break my Ethan's heart.

"Sure, Everly," Ethan is saying. "Give me a call when you get there."

Or maybe not.

CHAPTER 17

Ethan

Everly has perfect timing.

Not.

Amy and I were enjoying our ice cream, holding hands, and generally just minding our own business when out of the blue Everly has to call. Now I'm no longer holding Amy's hand and she's frantically trying to wipe chocolate ice cream from the front of her new skirt.

And for what?

So Everly can tell me that she and the man she threw me over for want to invite me to dinner in the Bahamas? I was so annoyed I completely forgot to mention that I'm bringing a plus-one. But that's fine. It might be infinitely more satisfying to sucker punch Everly at the restaurant.

Oh, you didn't hear about my fiancée, Amy? See, I'm not

doomed to a lonely, solitary life with just thirty cats for company.

I shove my phone into my back pocket.

Amy looks up from the skirt and the chocolate stain she's been unable to spit-clean away.

"I'm sorry, Ethan."

"For what?"

"For ruining this skirt."

"We can wash it when we get home."

"It's a five-hundred-dollar skirt, Ethan. I doubt we can just toss it into the washer."

"Then we'll send it out to be dry-cleaned. And if that doesn't work, Erin-Joi can call the store and have them send over another."

"Did you hear the part where the skirt cost five hundred—"

I press my finger to her lips. "Yes, I heard that part. I'm happy to spend another five hundred to replace it."

Everly would not be agonizing over dripped ice cream on an expensive skirt. She would have immediately texted Erin-Joi and expected a replacement by morning. I want Amy to feel comfortable with my money, to feel comfortable with who I am now, but I also like that she isn't. I even kind of like that she despises Pissy Puppy. She knows the Ethan McNamara who had nothing, who was an awkward teenage boy who would have done anything for her.

Literally. Anything.

Someone's phone rings. I don't bother to look at mine. If it's Everly calling back, I don't want to talk to her again this evening.

"I think that's mine," Amy says. She pulls the phone from her purse. It's her old purse, I note. It's a nice enough bag, but I hope she and mom purchased a new one for the trip. After what Danny did to her, I want Amy to feel like a million bucks in the Bahamas.

"Oh hi, Mrs. Walker."

Uh oh.

"When am I coming back? In a couple weeks, I guess. Yes, I know the wedding *was* supposed to be in a few weeks. It's not happening now, though." She listens for a few moments. "No, I'm really not. I'm sorry, Mrs. Walker."

She's apologizing? Whatever the hell for?

"He should relay that message to me, himself."

Oh no no. Danny is not going to sweet talk his way back into Amy's good graces. Or her bed. I take the phone from her hand.

"Mrs. Walker? Hello, yes, this is Ethan McNamara. Yes, *that* Ethan McNamara. Yes, I understand the game is a blight on the earth. That's not what we're talking about here. We're talking about your lying, cheating scumbag of a son. No, boys will not be boys. I myself have never cheated on anyone, much less with a porn star. Yes, I get that she's a *hometown* porn star."

I roll my eyes theatrically in a vain effort to coax a smile from Amy, but she's gone back to spitting on her fingers and rubbing at the chocolate.

"No, he doesn't get a second chance," I interrupt Mrs. Walker's diatribe. "My assistant has already cancelled all of the wedding vendors." I hold the phone away from my ear to preserve my hearing as Mrs. Walker shrieks her displeasure. "Yes, you'll get a refund for any deposits you paid." I haven't actually confirmed that with Erin-Joi, but she's the kind of person who could talk a refund out of a church after the divorce.

I listen intently for a few more moments while Mrs. Walker painstakingly explains a few things to me and confirms what Adam Boyer said—that Danny's interest in Amy was spurred by his parents basically blackmailing him.

"Thanks for letting me know, Mrs. Walker. Gotta go. Have a nice evening." I hang up and hand the phone back to Amy.

"Thanks for letting you know what?"

"Nothing. Don't worry about the skirt."

Back at the house, I suggest a dip in the pool, but Amy begs off, citing tiredness. I walk her to the guest wing. I'd like to hold her hand again, but the moment has passed. Instead, I drape a brotherly arm across her shoulder.

"What did Everly want?"

"She and her husband have invited us to dinner in the Bahamas."

"Oh. Invited *us* or invited *you?*"

"She doesn't know about you yet, but you're going to be there with me so we're both going."

"I don't have to go, you know. I can fake a stomach ache or something. PMS."

"I don't want to spend an evening alone with the two of them."

"You don't think she'll catch on that we're not really engaged? The two of you were close, Ethan. How could she not?"

I'm pretty certain Everly won't notice, but there's no graceful way to explain why. She's self-centered? Not self-aware? Not inclined to deep thought? None of those explanations reflect well on me.

"Do you still love her?"

The question catches me off guard.

"No. I don't." In truth, I'm not sure I ever did. Or that Everly ever really loved me. In retrospect, I think we had one of those relationships that wasn't bad enough to leave—but not good enough to last. Inertia kept us together and then I proposed because we'd been together for a few years. Getting married was the next step, right?

"This seems like a lot of effort to make a woman jealous when you don't want her back."

She's probably right. A week ago, I cared about making Everly jealous, cared about saving face over the proposal debacle. It seems less important now. All the same, I don't want to go to a destination wedding by myself. What would I do? Sit alone by the pool and drink myself senseless while everyone else is paired off and having fun? I'd rather have a beautiful woman by my side, as would any red-blooded male.

Back in Avondale, Amy is thought of as a cute girl. If you had asked me last month, that's probably what I would have said, too. Amy Casales is cute. She's not cute, though. Not anymore. Even in an ice cream-stained skirt, Amy Casales is a tiny little bundle of beautiful.

CHAPTER 18

Amy

This seemed like a better idea from the ground. I'm sitting at the top of a three-story water slide that looks a hell of a lot steeper than it did from below. Ethan is on the water slide next to me. He looks over.

"Ready?"

In truth, no. But I'm kind of beyond the point of no return here. There's a mile-long line of people waiting behind me. I tell myself that hundreds of people have already survived this slide today and I will be just one more.

I give Ethan a smile that's way more confident than I feel and a thumbs up. "See you at the bottom!"

And whoosh! I am in freefall. Quite literally in freefall—as in, no part of my body is actually touching any part of the slide. I would say my heart is in my throat, but I'm pretty sure my heart is still back at the top, watching me plummet to some uncertain demise.

I'm not a thrill seeker, by any stretch of the imagination. Dating Danny was me going all wild and crazy. Look how that turned out.

I was worried about losing the bottom of my bikini on this slide (I've had a few close calls already today). Since my bottom isn't touching anything, that's no longer a concern. What is a concern is the speed with which the pool at the bottom is approaching. I'm hoping it's not really as shallow as it looked before.

By the time I shoot off the slide like a greased pig, Ethan is already in the water. I hit the water and immediately feel my bikini bottom wedged up into crevices I didn't even know I had. My feet find the tiled floor of the pool and I pop out of the water, sputtering and glad to be alive.

Ethan is standing in the shallow end, waiting for me. He's dripping wet, his wavy hair even wavier and shinier in the sun. Water drips from his nose and fingertips. My heart has caught up with me and is back in my chest, pounding—and not from my brush with mortality. To say that Ethan is looking a bit like a Greek god at the moment would not be an exaggeration.

His long board shorts sit brazenly low on his hips and my tailbone forgets the shock of impact from bottoming out on the slide. It's tingling again. At the sight of Ethan. *Ethan.* The boy I've known since forever. The boy who trusts me so much he asked me to pose as his fiancée, because he knows I won't go all crazy gold digger on him.

"Uh, Ames?" His eyes dart down to my hips, then quickly back up to my face.

I glance down. Yeah. The legs of my bikini bottom are up so high, I could be eye candy in a James Bond film. If it weren't for that whole "not a thrill seeker" thing, that is. I quickly tug everything back into place.

"I am not doing that one again." I climb out of the pool.

"Girl, same."

I just look at him and shake my head.

We walk along the hot pathway to the next water slide. This is our first full day in the Bahamas and we've yet to see anyone from the wedding. Not that I'm in any particular hurry. Ethan and I are having fun by ourselves, lounging by the pool and testing out all of the water rides like we're two kids.

We get in line for the Psychedelic Eel and what do our wandering eyes behold but two boys off to the side, huddled over a phone, playing a game. You might be saying, *what are the odds?* In fact, the odds are pretty good that they're playing Pissy Puppy. This is confirmed when we hear—when everyone in earshot—hears "You're in the effing doghouse!" in the annoying voice of Pissy Puppy himself.

It suddenly hits me. I turn to Ethan.

"That's your voice, isn't it?"

He grins. "Digitally altered a bit."

"Isn't it weird seeing people all over playing—" I'm about to say "playing your game," but I stop myself in case someone around us overhears. I learned that lesson in New Athens. I don't want to spend the entire week here with people gushing over Ethan.

He shrugs in a very Ethan-like way.

"At first it was. But now ..." He looks over at the boys, who are now laughing and high-fiving each other. "... it no longer feels like it's mine anymore. Nor am I sad about that. It's out in the world and it exists there, independent of me at this point."

I can't imagine being famous, even after spending several years with someone who spent most of his time imagining the kind of fame that Ethan has. Danny wants to be the biggest name in fitness. It's possible he'll get there. A complete and utter lack of shame helps in that regard. But I have no desire for it, myself. I'm perfectly happy being an anonymous high school teacher.

The Psychedelic Eel slide begins at the top of a faux pyramid and the line of people waiting moves a few steps up at a time. I can't help myself. As we climb higher and higher, I scan the crowds below for people obviously playing a game on their phone. I'm surprised by how many I see. I start counting, to distract myself from thoughts of dinner with Everly and her new husband.

There are so many ways the upcoming evening can go wrong. Everly could be a bitch to me, even though she's the one who dumped Ethan. Her husband might be the one to figure out that Ethan and I are just faking the engagement thing. I don't see Ethan behaving like a jealous harpy—he's too nice for that—but the evening might make him sad.

He's the kind of person who would love deeply. He wouldn't agree to marry someone unless he was all in on that person. I was stupid to think that Danny was all in on me. I know people were baffled by our relationship. Hell, I was baffled at first, too. On paper, there was never any reason why Danny Walker should be interested in me—much less, head over heels in love. Clearly, I was imagining the whole head over heels thing.

But that's what I want. Eventually. Some guy to fall head over heels in love with me. Doesn't everyone? I mean, I like to think I resemble Ethan in that regard. I'm either all in on someone or not in at all.

The line takes a sudden leap in progress—five steps! But my left foot has fallen asleep and I sway. Ethan's hand on my hip steadies me. Which, for some reason, is affecting the function of my lungs. My body is *very* aware of how close Ethan's body is to mine. This is not a good thing. The sudden breakup with Danny has left me hurt and confused. It would be too easy to look for solace in my oldest and dearest friend, because my oldest and dearest friend would give it to me if I asked.

What happens in the Bahamas stays in the Bahamas, right?

Except I wouldn't be able to look Ethan in the eyes once we got home. "It would ruin our friendship." That's the lame cliché brush-off people give when they want to let you down easy. But there's some truth to it, as well. How do you go back to being friends with someone after you've slept with them? You can't—not to the same type of friendship you had before. I would rather have the certainty of the friendship than the weird aftermath of a night together.

Plus, I don't want to admit to Ethan that Danny and I never slept together—especially when Danny was not abstaining himself. He took advantage of my trusting nature and desire for storybook romance. I was a fool for ever thinking I would find storybook romance in Avondale.

The line for the Psychedelic Eel wraps around the pyramid and it takes us another ten minutes before we reach the next corner.

"That looks like fun." Ethan points at a spot off in the distance.

I squint to make out what it is.

"The Savage River," he adds. His hand traces a snaking path through the air.

"Oh yeah. Now I see it."

A pale blue ribbon of water winds through the park. Here and there through the treetops, I can see people bobbing along on the park's pink innertubes. It looks like a relatively sedate ride.

"We should definitely do that one. I don't hear a lot of terrified shrieking."

We move forward a few more steps and then someone on the ground shouts, "Ethan! Ethan!"

A man and a woman in swimsuits and flip flops wave up at us. Or at Ethan, anyway, since they have no idea who I am.

"Samir! Giselle!" Ethan shouts back.

His arm reaches across my shoulders and pulls me close. We are now skin to skin, ribs to ribs, hips to hips. My tailbone is threatening to launch the macarena.

"When'd you get here?" Samir asks.

"Last night! How about you?"

"Just got in! Have you done the Leap of Death?"

Ethan gives him a thumbs up. "We survived!" He squeezes me closer. "This is Amy, by the way! My fiancée!"

I give a little wave and a big happy smile, hoping it looks convincing enough.

"Nice to meet you, Amy!" Giselle waves back.

The line ahead of us moves up a few more steps.

"Hey, you're moving!" Samir yells. "See you around, you lovebirds!"

"Who was that?"

"Samir is vice president of government relations at Brad's car company. And Giselle is one of his top programmers. They're nice. We'll hang with them at the wedding."

The line reaches another corner and I look down at the wide turquoise swimming pool below (one of twelve pools in the park, according to the hotel check-in desk). This one is a kids' pool and in the middle is a tanned, chubby father tossing his young daughter up in the air before she splashes down into the water. My throat tightens. My father used to do that with me at the Avondale town pool. My eyes tear up. Those were good years. *Normal years.* Safe years.

Then it all changed. When I was sixteen, my dad had his first heart attack. Then a second.

Then came the day when the school principal called my fourth period history teacher and asked her to excuse me from class. The principal was waiting in the hall for me and I *knew.* My dad had suffered another heart attack. I walked like a zombie to the school office, where my mother was waiting for me. By the time we got to the hospital, he was gone.

In between had been all the surgeries, all the hospital stays—all the nights I spent at Ethan's house, where his parents tried vainly to reassure me that everything was going to be okay. In the end, everything wasn't okay.

Ethan puts his arms around me.

"What's that for?" I ask.

"I remember, too. The pool."

I force a smile. "Those were good times."

"The best."

Finally, we reach the top of the pyramid and the slide's entrance. We get on a two-person innertube, me in front and Ethan in back. I barely have a chance to grab onto the plastic handles when—whoosh!—we are plunged into a dark tunnel. We careen around several curves, water spraying all around us, and then suddenly the tunnel lights up with a wild kaleidoscope of color. Behind me, Ethan is laughing and I realize that I'm laughing too. We're plunged back into darkness as the innertube whips right and left, and then the trippy psychedelic light show is back. This repeats twice more, until we shoot out into a clear passageway.

"Whoa." Ethan leans forward on the innertube. "Is that a hammerhead shark?"

On the other side of the tunnel's see-through walls swim dozens of sharks.

"I wasn't expecting this," I say. Sharks. Fun. Relaxation. The innertube floats lazily along. Danny and I traveled a good bit— mostly to fitness trade shows, but the shows were always in fun places. Florida. Vegas. Los Angeles. At the time, I thought I was having fun in those fun places. I realize now, though, that I wasn't. Not really. Danny's not really a fun sort of guy. His idea of fun is crushing the competition, whether that's a high school football team or a rival fitness studio.

Ethan's hands are on my wet shoulders. I lean back into them. Ethan was right. I did need to get away from Avondale for a little while. A shark swims up to the tube and knocks his nose against it. I laugh. I'm staring down a shark from mere inches away and yet I feel more at ease than I've felt in years.

CHAPTER 19

Ethan

"I had a blast today." I button up my new pink linen shirt and inspect my slightly sunburned face in the hotel's bathroom mirror. I match my shirt.

"So did I."

Amy is standing next to me in the bathroom, meticulously applying makeup. I know she's nervous about tonight, meeting Everly and all. Hell, I'm nervous about it, too. What if Amy thinks less of me because I once fancied myself to be in love with someone like Everly? After all, I'm apparently the only person in my life who *did* like her. I told Erin-Joi that from now on she has to give me her honest and unvarnished opinion on any woman I date. I mean, she gives me her honest and unvarnished opinion on everything else.

Amy looks beautiful in her new dress. It's a pale minty green, sleeveless and just a little bit low cut. Her legs look amazing in the new shoes, too. I shove aside the thought that she developed those amazing legs at Get Fit with Danny. Nor do I want to think about those amazing legs wrapped tight around Danny's waist, with Amy making those little cooing noises she makes when she sleeps. Of course, I have no idea whether those are the same noises she makes during sex, but she must make some kind of sexy sound and it irritates me to no end that Danny-effing-Walker knows what those sounds are.

I can tell she's feeling pretty in the new outfit. I meet her gaze in the mirror. Her eyes are sparkling and happy. For the first time since the class reunion, the tension in her shoulders is gone.

She holds up her dark waves of hair. "Erin-Joi showed me how to create a fancy updo, but I forget how to do it now." She frowns in the mirror.

"We can call her. I'm sure you won't be surprised to learn that I have her on speed dial."

"Nope. Not surprised at all."

"Or you could just leave it down." I gently pull her fingers from her hair and let the dark waves fall back to her shoulders. She picked up a little color today, too. A memory smacks me upside the head. "Remember how people used to think we were twins when we were kids? Because of our hair?"

In the mirror, her eyes check out my own dark waves. "We still look like brother and sister," she says. "You did tell Everly that you're an only child, right?" She smiles, but the sparkle is gone from her eyes.

"Stay right here. I have something for you." I go and get the matching necklace and earrings Erin-Joi purchased with the engagement ring.

"What's that?" Amy eyes the velvet jewelry boxes with suspicion.

"A gift."

She puts her hands up. "Ethan, this is ridiculous. All this stuff—" She tugs at the dress. "—you're going to have to return."

"I'm not returning any of it."

"Your assistant, then."

"Not her, either. You're keeping it."

Her eyes widen in alarm. "I can't keep all this stuff!"

"Why not?" I open the larger box and carefully lift out the necklace. I undo the tiny clasp, lift her hair away from her neck, and drape the necklace over her skin.

"Because this isn't *real*, Ethan." Her eyes are glued to the pink diamond in the center of the platinum chain.

I re-hook the clasp, rearrange her hair so it falls against her bare shoulders. "Our friendship is real."

"We're not here as friends though."

"Sure we are. If you're engaged to someone, you should be friends with them, too."

Everly and I were never friends, even though we dated for years. I didn't see that at the time, but I do now. I'm guessing that Amy and Danny were in the same situation.

"Friends don't give friends expensive jewelry."

"Erin-Joi picked this up at one of those vendor carts in the middle of the mall."

She pins me with a look.

"Okay, so not. But I can afford to give all of my friends expensive jewelry. It's not that big a deal." That's true—I *can* afford to give expensive gifts to friends, but I've never given a friend this kind of jewelry. Not even my mom, but only because she said it would make my dad feel bad. So giving diamonds to Amy *is* kind of a big deal.

I open the smaller box, then spin her around to face me. The earrings are dangly pink diamond globes on thin wires. I squint and gently poke the end of the wire into her earlobe, praying I don't accidentally re-pierce her with a new hole. After the Ice Cream Skirt Incident, the last thing I want to do is incite a Blood-on-the-Dress Affair and end up with a flustered fiancée at dinner.

Faux fiancée, I remind myself.

I carefully insert the other earring. I wish I were putting this jewelry on a real fiancée. I'm a romantic at heart. I know that's not the manly-man guy thing to say, but there it is. And I have one Amy Casales to blame for that. Being her honorary brother nurtured an outsized sense of chivalry in me. Right now, that chivalry is pounding in my chest. I meet her eyes in the mirror.

In the movies, this is where the kiss happens. It's the next logical move. I can tell she's thinking that, too. There's a lovely pink blush on her skin from her cheeks down to her sternum. And it's not *all* from the sun.

I want to kiss her. *Really* want to. Really *desperately* want to.

But I don't.

If I kiss her, the two of us will walk into the restaurant looking flustered—looking like we just banged each other silly five minutes ago and raced downstairs in the nick of time. Granted, that's exactly the look I'd love to present to Everly and her new minor royalty husband, but I don't want Amy spending the entire evening obsessing over what Everly is thinking.

Instead, I fuss with her hair for a moment, pretending to arrange it nicely against her neck and shoulders, and rueing the impulse that led me to agree to dinner with my ex.

"Are you okay, Eeth?"

Our eyes meet in the mirror. "Yeah. I'm fine. Too much sun today. I think it went to my head."

We get to the restaurant early and order drinks. I'm on my second Negroni while Amy is still sipping her first Shirley Temple.

"You can go ahead and order a glass of wine," I suggest.

"I don't want to embarrass you in front of Everly."

Seeing as I'm now on drink number two and we haven't even ordered appetizers yet, if anyone embarrasses me tonight it'll probably be me.

We're also trying to ignore the family at the next table, whose young son is playing—you know—the *game*.

"When the entrees come out, you have to put it away!" the mother hisses.

The boy ignores her.

"The tournament is tomorrow," the father says. "His game needs to be *tight*."

Next to me, Amy's eyebrows lift as if to say, *did you know about this tournament?*

I shake my head. Truly, I did not know. I mean, I knew that people do such things—hold Pissy Puppy tournaments. With cash prizes, even. Just to be clear, I am not involved in these tournaments in any way, shape, or form. I send Amy a text telling her that.

Her eyes dart over to the kid, then she thumbs me a text reply. *If only he knew ...*

I shift my chair ever so slightly to turn my face away from the family. I get recognized all the time in New Athens. Out in the wild? Thankfully, not so much. My theory is that kids don't really give a shit about who created their game obsession du jour.

"My lord," the mother says and I follow her gaze to an outlandish hat that has just entered the restaurant and is improbably attached to the side of ... Everly's head.

"Oh my," Amy whispers.

"What are those things called?" I say quietly. I know they have a name.

"It's a fascinator. It's British."

Of course it is.

Within seconds, they are upon us.

"Ethan, love!"

Everly is affecting a British accent. A bad British accent. It occurs to me how very much I dodged a bullet here.

"Up! Up!"

She wants me to stand, so I do and endure French air kisses next to each cheek. She gives Amy a cursory glance, as if Amy is some random woman I picked up at the bar.

"Ethan, may I present my husband, Lord Fletcher, Viscount of Lower Bockhampton?"

Lord Fletcher? Viscount? Should I bow or something? Kiss his ring? Seriously, I'm not sure of the protocol here.

Lord Fletcher extends his hand. I shake it. "Nice to meet you ..." I'm expecting him to offer a first name we can use. Surely, he and Everly don't expect us to call him—

"Lord Fletcher," he says.

Well, okay then.

Amy has buried her face in the Shirley Temple to hide her

amusement. Lord, I need another Negroni. Or a beer. Or an entire bottle of vodka.

Everly and the viscount take their seats, across from us. Everly looks at Amy again as if she's been expecting her to simply disappear. Amy leans across the table and extends a handshake.

"Hello, I'm Amy. Ethan's fiancée. I've heard so much about you. It's lovely to finally meet you."

The woman at the next table is still mesmerized by Everly's hat, which certainly appears to defy all known laws of gravity. Possibly a few unknown ones, as well.

Our waitress appears and takes drink orders—and not a moment too soon. I order a third Negroni. Amy has had a change of heart and orders wine. Lord Fletcher orders martinis for himself and Everly. Should I be calling her Lady Fletcher? Viscountess? When Everly said her husband was minor British royalty, I assumed that meant he was a cousin of a cousin of a cousin of a duke. Something like that.

Everly threw me over for a title. She didn't choose a husband who was richer than me. Or even one better looking. Lord Fletcher looks like a fifty-something dad. Greying hair, wider at the waist than the shoulders. I'm sure I will look like that one day, too, but Everly is only thirty years old. He's old enough to be her father.

Oh well. As long as she's happy, as my mother is fond of saying.

When our drinks arrive, I propose a toast to Brad and Marissa. It seems like an innocuous topic of conversation. That's why we're all here in the Bahamas, right? The wedding of Brad and Marissa.

But the viscount outflanks me. We clink glasses and then he says, in much too loud a voice, "So, you're the genius mastermind behind Pissy Puppy?"

The family at the next table drop their forks in unison.

"You're the tournament organizer?" the father says.

I shake my head and silently pray for Fletch to drop it. Of course, he doesn't.

"This is Mr. Ethan McNamara," he says. "The *inventor* of the game."

"Hear that?" the man says to his son, who has taken this as permission to whip out his phone again. "This is the guy who *invented* Pissy Puppy."

The kid narrows his eyes at me. He doesn't believe one word his father is saying. He takes another bite of taco and taps his phone screen.

God bless that kid. He's the reason I'm filthy rich.

The Viscount of Lower Bockhampton isn't finished yet. He fixes me with a stare. "And you sold the game for how much?"

"A bit."

"Seven point two four billion is what I read."

Man did his research before meeting his wife's ex-boyfriend. Gotta give him credit for that.

The father is still eyeing me like a besotted teenager. "So you're here for the tournament?"

"No. I'm here for a wedding. Had no idea about the tournament."

"Well, wait 'til they find out!" He nudges his son's arm, who rolls his eyes theatrically at me. I want to laugh at the kid, actually. *Dude, the cheat codes I could give you.*

I shake my head at the dad. "I don't have anything to do with the tournaments. Or the game anymore. It's owned by someone else now."

"Still, you're the inventor—"

Suddenly Amy cuts him off with a schoolteacher's efficiency.

"I'm sorry. We're here for a *wedding.*" Her crisp and authoritative enunciation cows him into silence. The embarrassed relief radiating in waves from his son is practically visible in the air.

"So how long have you two *lovebirds* been engaged?" Everly turns on me. "Ethan, I hadn't *heard.*"

Crap. Amy and I haven't really discussed our "origin story," beyond that we're old childhood friends.

But Amy rolls with it. "Two weeks!" She holds out the engagement ring for inspection. "How could I say 'no?'"

"Blimey!" Lord Fletcher yanks Amy's hand toward him to get a better look. Then he turns to me. "Looks like you spent a billion on that, eh?"

CHAPTER 20

Amy

"You didn't really spend a billion dollars on this ring, did you?" I look in horror at the diamonds on my hand.

Ethan clasps my hand in his. "Of course not, Ames. Erin-Joi would have had me committed."

We're strolling through the waterpark, aprés dinner. The pools and water slides are closed for the day, but the winding pathways are filled with couples walking hand in hand, arm in arm. Just like us.

"Do you think they bought it? That we're engaged?"

"I guess so," Ethan answers. "Honestly, I'm not sure Everly really thinks about other people much. I knew that back when we were dating. I just ... overlooked it."

We round a bend and there's another couple on a bench, passionately making out. *Blimey!* I quickly avert my eyes. The last thing I need is another reminder of what my summer was supposed to be like.

A wedding. A romantic honeymoon. Sex. Finally, sex!

Instead I'm walking and holding hands with my oldest friend and dissecting dinner with the former love of his life the way we used to dissect the day's events in high school. Who sat with whom in the cafeteria. Totally unfair questions on pop quizzes. Unfortunate outfits.

Speaking of unfortunate outfits—Ethan's ex wore a fascinator to dinner. Literally every single person in the restaurant stared at it. I mean, how could you not? It was enormous and green and plastered to the side of her head. Lord Fletcher had to keep ducking his head away to avoid getting smacked in the face with it.

"I have to say, I can't really imagine the two of you together."

Ethan nudges my shoulder with his arm. "I could say the same of you and Danny."

"Touché."

Although, in a weird way, I think more of Ethan now that I've met Everly. I was expecting some supermodel in an overtly sexy dress with perfect hair and makeup. In reality, Everly's a little plain. She seemed nice enough and smart enough, but clearly she wants a higher falutin' lifestyle than Ethan would ever want. Ethan had so much fun today on the water slides that I can easily imagine him wanting to come to Nautilus every year despite its inherent cheesiness.

I have to admit, I had fun today, too.

"I'm sorry about Everly, by the way," he adds. "I had no idea she was going to show up looking like that. She didn't dress like that with me."

"No worries."

"And Lord Fletcher, Viscount of Lower Bock-whatever? Good grief. I got dumped for that?"

I give his hand a little squeeze. "If it's any consolation, I'm pretty sure that's a fake title. I read an article once about people buying British titles. You get a few square inches of land somewhere in England and the right to call yourself Lord Whatever."

He chuckles. "What was I thinking? Proposing to Everly?"

"She must be good in bed," I make a lame attempt at a joke. I don't really want to know whether she is or not. I shouldn't care.

"She was okay."

The beach is up ahead. The moon is high in the sky and its light sparkles over the gently lapping waves. It's perfectly peaceful and ... romantic.

Of course it is.

"Was that Danny's appeal? He's great in bed?"

We kick off our shoes and walk across the sand barefoot. I don't immediately answer Ethan's question. The truth about my relationship with Danny just makes the whole Angela Alessi thing even worse. It makes me look like even more of a dunce than I already am. Nor is Ethan entitled to my deepest, darkest secrets just because we're friends.

But the wine at dinner, the zen breeze on the beach, and the surreality of Everly's fascinator have combined to make me feel a little reckless.

"I wouldn't know," I confess.

"What do you mean you wouldn't know?"

"I mean I wouldn't know."

I walk to the water's edge and let the surf swish around my ankles. The ocean water is warm and a clear azure, just like it is in the pictures. Ethan's ankles appear next to mine.

"You mean you wouldn't know because you don't have anyone else to compare him to? Or because you and Danny never had sex?"

"The latter."

"Huh." Ethan takes my hand again. "Well, I'm glad to hear he treated you like a gentleman. Or a lady, I mean." Ethan rubs his cheek with his free hand. "Next time, remind me to stop after three drinks."

Ethan's being polite. He knows as well as I do that Danny must have been cheating on me the entire time we dated. Not exactly the behavior of a gentleman.

"Don't tell anyone, please. You're the only person I've told."

He pulls me close and part of me is having an out-of-body experience right now. Like I'm floating above us, looking down at this perfectly romantic scene—moonlight, ocean, sand, two recently-jilted people gazing deep into each other's eyes. It's straight out of a sappy movie. Only what's supposed to happen next—a long, deep, screenworthy kiss—is not in the stars here.

"I would never betray a confidence of yours, Amy. I would hope that you know that by now."

His voice jams my floating soul back into my body. I drop my eyes to his chest. He's wearing a pink linen button-down shirt. Danny used to make fun of men in pink shirts. Or anything pink, for that matter. It was a pet peeve of his. Men in pink.

Ethan looks good in pink.

"And here I was worried about Danny having some special sex playroom in his basement and the two of you were doing all manner of kinky things together."

"Nope. Kissing was as kinky as we got."

"Was he a good kisser, at least?"

I sigh and try to extricate myself from Ethan's almost-embrace.

145

But he doesn't let go. "I don't know. I thought so, but hey—I live in Avondale. It's not exactly filled to the brim with worldly, sophisticated men who—"

Ethan tips my chin up and we are back to gazing deeply into each other's eyes. And then he is kissing me. And by kissing, I mean —well, I'm not sure what I mean because my brain is scrambling. My coccyx is jitterbugging. Ethan's lips are moving softly over mine. He tastes faintly of Death by Chocolate, the dessert we shared at the restaurant. He's clearly in no hurry, either. I close my eyes and give in to just how damn good this feels. After awhile, I can't stop myself. I kiss him back.

It's not until we hear voices drawing near that he breaks the kiss, out of breath, his eyes a little wilder than normal. I expect Ethan to crack a joke, puncture the bubble of romance we seem to have stumbled into. But he doesn't. He simply says, "Was he better than that?"

The next morning, we step off the hotel elevator and the music hits us like a wave we turned our backs on. It's loud, pumping, and features an unmistakable bass line of ... barking?

We haven't spoken about last night's kiss. My body hasn't forgotten it, though. My tailbone has been breaking out into a spontaneous little shimmy every now and then. In fact, I feel one coming on now.

"This looks kinda fun," Ethan says as he surveys the mob scene that has taken over the hotel's lobby. "Oh look!" He points at a giant Pissy Puppy mascot, surrounded by kids, camera flashes, and too many adults (in my opinion).

He wades into the crowd and I follow. We are back to being Ethan and Amy, besties since the Terrible Twos. In the suite last night, Ethan checked on work emails and I internet stalked Malcom Jones, the guy who swiped the department chair job right out from under me. Let's just say he has two months to wipe his social media presence from the face of the internet. The Avondale Board of Education is ruthless when it comes to pictures of teachers partying or showing any bare skin beneath the neck.

I am struggling to keep up with Ethan in the crowd, when I feel a hand grab at mine. I look down to confirm that it's Ethan's before clinging to it for dear life. At the entrance to the ballroom, there's a giant banner proclaiming, "Welcome to the First Annual Nautilus Pissy Puppy Grand Tournament!!!" A sandwich board next to the wide double doors says, "LIMITED NUMBER OF WALK-IN SPOTS AVAILABLE! TWO MILLION DOLLAR GRAND PRIZE!"

We are doomed. I can feel it in the way Ethan's hand is tugging on mine, leading me ever closer to those wide double doors.

"Just one round. Please."

I'm about to point out that, besides his obviously unfair advantage in entering a tournament for a game that HE DEVELOPED, the lounge chairs by the adult "quiet" pool will all be snapped up if we don't get there early. (We learned that lesson yesterday. The hard way.) But then my tailbone chooses this exact moment to launch into a chorus line of high kicks ... and I relent. The enthusiasm on Ethan's face is so adorably boyish, yet somehow also so freaking sexy that I can't say "no."

Inside the ballroom, he signs up at the walk-in desk. The woman manning it shows no sign of recognizing "Ethan McNamara."

"Make yourself a name tag," the woman says and hands me a tote bag filled with Pissy Puppy and Nautilus merch, like I'm Ethan's personal assistant.

Then again, what do I know? Maybe champion Pissy Puppy players have personal assistants. The game's developer has one.

"Do you worry that Erin-Joi is throwing wild parties at your house while you're out of town?"

"Nope. She's just glad to be rid of me for a week." Ethan peels off the name tag sticker and slaps it on his tie-dyed tee shirt. He wrote only his first name.

"No need to stir up trouble." He grins.

"All righty then," the registration woman says. She hands Ethan a white card with the number thirty-four on it. "This is your first tournament station. Hand the card to the attendant when you get there."

We wade back into the crowd. The music is even louder inside the ballroom, coupled with the additional noise of hundreds of people playing a video game on giant screens hung around the perimeter. And playing to win.

Well, I guess I'd be playing to win, too, with two million in prizes at stake.

As we push through the crowd, looking for tournament station thirty-four, I note that we are pretty much the oldest adults without kids here. Also that some players really do seem to have their own entourages. Or at least, people all wearing the same tee shirts in support.

Ethan easily beats his first opponent, a pimply-faced boy. No surprise there. But I am concerned that we'll end up spending all day here. Ethan can beat everyone at his own game. Who knows Pissy Puppy better than he does? I keep an eye out for the family from the restaurant. If they spot us, we'll never get to the adult swim quiet pool.

Which is where I really want to spend the day. Lying on a chaise longue, imbibing tropical cocktails, and trying not to think of the hotness that is Ethan McNamara in swim trunks lying on the next chaise longue over. Also trying not to think of last night's kiss.

My tailbone is tapping its toes again.

Ethan takes his spot next to his second-round opponent, a young girl who stands about four foot nothing in her badass miniature combat boots. Her lavender-striped blond hair is slicked back into such a severe ballet bun, my scalp is prickling just looking at it.

She gives Ethan the once-over and says, "Where's your contestant?"

"I'm the contestant. That's my manager back there." Ethan turns and smiles at me.

"You go, baby!" I shout.

The little girl's father is tattooed and bulked up in baggy camouflage pants and tight black tee shirt. Unfortunate hair seems to run in the family, unfortunately. His head is shaved on one side. Long hair brushes his shoulder on the other. I try not to stare, but he gives me some sort of death-eye look. Trying to psych me out, I guess.

Ha. *I know who your little princess is going up against. You have no clue.*

He returns his attention to his daughter. "Alright, sweetie, let's give grandpa the shellacking of his life."

The referee resets the game on the giant screen and a little timer counts down from ten in the corner. When it gets to zero, Ethan and the girl launch their thumbs into battle. I'll be honest—I'm not exactly sure what the point of Pissy Puppy is. But two minutes into the round and it's clear even to my untrained eye that Ethan is in trouble. I can tell that he's distracted by the girl's non-stop trash talking.

"Come on, Clown Boy! That's all you got? Nobody's gonna let your dogs out!"

Ten minutes later, Ethan McNamara, father of Pissy Puppy, is unceremoniously eliminated in round two of the tournament. The girl's father lets loose a string of celebratory epithets that my teacher self won't repeat here.

As we walk—okay, slink—from the ballroom, I begin to wonder about something.

"Have Brad and Marissa ever been to Nautilus before?"

"They love this place. That's why they're getting married here."

Danny has a vision board in the bathroom of his house. It was titled "My First Billion" and had pictures of yachts and Lear jets and people swimming in champagne next to private beaches. I always thought it silly, but it helped to motivate him.

"It's a little too low-rent?" Ethan guesses my thoughts.

I shrug. I don't want to criticize anyone's choice of wedding venue—and especially not when I'm here free. My ideal wedding is a small, intimate affair with no one but close friends and family around for miles. So in other words, a lovely backyard somewhere that just happens to resemble an English garden with roses and marble nymphs.

"I guess they didn't know about the Pissy Puppy tournament ahead of time."

"I doubt it, but I'm sure half the wedding party is in there playing. Billionaires like to have fun, too. We're not all caviar and Cristal."

CHAPTER 21

Ethan

The Savage River is a two-mile-long water ride with a half mile section of class five rapids, two tunnels, and a reputation for separating the men from the boys—according to the kid in line in front of us. Said kid is maybe nine years old so I'm not sure whether he considers himself to be one of the men or one of the boys.

"How many times have you done this ride?" Amy asks.

"Sixteen times today!"

Suddenly I feel like such a slacker.

The kid proceeds to show us his ride-related injuries (skinned heels and elbows, an assortment of bruises) and offer us tips. "Don't resist the rapids. That's when you capsize. Just go with the flow. Watch out for little kids. They tend to panic. Don't get behind any pregnant women. It'll take you all day just to complete one lap."

Amy thanks him for the advice, but he has one more bit of sage wisdom to impart—with a serious nod of the head.

"Don't forget. This is The *Savage* River. It's not a lazy river."

"Duly noted. Are you here for the tournament?"

His head bobs up and down.

"How'd you do?"

"I made it through to the final round tomorrow."

"Wow. That's awesome."

"How'd you do?"

I love how he assumes I'm there for the tournament, too. Not everyone is biased against grandpas playing game apps.

"I got iced in the second round."

"That's harsh, dude," he says. "Sorry."

"You must be pretty good to make it all the way to finals. That last level is the hardest."

"I know." He shrugs. "I have to be at the top of my game tomorrow. I need that two million dollar grand prize."

He says it so matter of factly that I have to inquire further. Why does a kid his age need that kind of money? College tuition? Buy his parents a house? Impress a girl? (In my experience, the ladies are not that awed by Pissy Puppy.)

"Why's that, bud?"

"My little sister is sick. My parents stay near the hospital in Dallas. My older brother takes care of me. Which sucks, if you know what I mean."

I nod. "I can imagine." I look around for sucky older brother, but don't see anyone who particularly fits the bill. "You aren't here by yourself, are you?" The airlines wouldn't let a kid his age fly from the states to another country alone, would they?

"Nah, my brother and his girlfriend are around somewhere. I can take care of myself, though."

This strikes me as true. He is one poised little kid. "Well, good luck tomorrow."

"Thanks, dude."

We watch the boy climb onto an inner tube and get whooshed away by The Savage River's opening current. I snag an inner tube for us and hold it steady so Amy can climb on in her one-piece swimsuit that somehow manages to look like less fabric than your average two piece. I cannot fathom why my mother let her buy that. Yes, I'm enjoying it, but so is every other red-blooded male at Nautilus. I scowled at twenty guys, at least, on the walk between here and the hotel. *Back off. She's my fiancée.*

Fake fiancée, but they don't need to know that.

I climb onto the tube behind her and we drift toward a narrow, stone-walled channel.

"Did you let her win?" Amy asks.

"Hell, no."

"So grandpa really did get shellacked."

I give her a friendly smack on the thigh. "If I were a lesser man, I'd say that was the most utterly humiliating thing I've ever experienced." I leave my hand on her thigh and hope she doesn't notice. Her death grip monopolizes the inner tube's handles, so I need *someplace* to rest my hands.

"Well, it's not like you need the prize money."

"True. I do not."

For the first ten minutes, The Savage River does not seem all that savage. In fact, it's really pretty placid, placid enough for me to relax and simply enjoy the feel of Amy's body resting against mine. I try not to stare over her shoulder at her nipples poking against the fabric of her swimsuit. I'm still stuck on the idea of my mother standing by while this suit was purchased. Or maybe that was the point? No matter how sexy it is, every time I look at it I'm going to think of my mother?

It is one damn sexy swimsuit.

Instead, I stare at the hundred or so inner tubes, bobbing and swirling around the wide pool ahead of us, like a bunch of pink Cheerios in a bowl of milk. I return to happily contemplating Amy's nipples—my mother be damned—when I hear, "Mac! McNamara, I say!" In a British accent.

It's Everly and Lord Fletcher, His Royal Highness Viscount Whatever, on a Cheerio about a hundred feet away from us. Everly is waving frantically at us, like she's drowning—or maybe she's just trying to shake off Lord Fletcher's hand, which is clamped over her left boob.

I give a lame wave, happy that there is no easy way for them to reach us, short of walking across the flotilla of inflatables between us and them. Then I lean forward and press my lips to Amy's neck.

"Hey," she says. But she doesn't pull away.

"Just making it look real." I kiss her neck again. Her skin tastes of chlorine and sunscreen. In other words, delicious. And she still has that Amy smell, a scent I doubt I'll ever forget. It's been imprinted on me since childhood.

She twists on the inner tube and puckers up, gamely playing along. I don't even think twice. I don't even bother to look and see whether Everly is still watching. Or any impressionable young children nearby. I don't care. I kiss Amy the way I've wanted to kiss her all day. Deeply, passionately, like this kiss is going to lead somewhere.

By somewhere, I mean "bed." Which is not where last night's kiss on the beach led.

Unfortunately, we are stuck on a listing inner tube on a not-so-savage artificial river in the Bahamas. There should be some way to get off this ride in the middle. She never did answer my question last night—whether I'm a better kisser than Danny Effing Walker. It shouldn't matter. I'm confident enough in my kissing prowess. No one has ever complained, at any rate. Not even Everly, and she complained about a lot where I was concerned. I mean, how could Danny kiss her like this and then not sleep with her? That's not the Danny Walker we grew up with.

Amy's hand brushes the front of my swimsuit, lightly—accidentally, I'm sure. But instantly, I'm hard. I break the kiss before she accidentally discovers how turned on I am. The kid from the line floats by on his tube. He gives me a hearty thumbs-up and a theatric wink. I wink back and watch as he gets swept into the crowd of Cheerios ahead, which are now funneling toward the left side of the lagoon.

"I believe those are the rapids ahead of us."

Amy points to a spot where the pink Cheerios jam up and then, one by one, get sucked into a narrow cavern of white water. There is appropriate screaming.

"We're gonna get soaked," I say.

"Mmm hmm. That's the point of a water ride. Getting wet."

Minutes later, we are whisked into the white water where our inner tube bounces and spins in alarming fashion. Amy is white knuckling the plastic handles. I am white knuckling Amy. I take back what I said earlier about The Savage River being placid and relaxing. Evidently, the designers of the waterpark were simply lulling unsuspecting patrons into complacency.

Up ahead of us, a tandem inner tube collides with a wave and goes ass up, unceremoniously dumping its riders into the water. Amy and I are soaking wet already. A minute ago, I was trying to think down an erection. Now my manhood has retreated so far it's probably hanging from one of my ribs.

I hear a yelping noise nearby. It's the same yelping noise Everly makes when she has an orgasm. Before I can look around to see if Everly is, in fact, having an orgasm on The Savage River, the savage river wells up beneath us and sets our inner tube to spinning. It's a little like watching my life flash before my eyes—yes, there's Everly. And Lord Fletcher, grinning and shouting, "bloody 'ell!" And the young boy who stood in front of us in line, the one with the ill sister. He's alone on his inner tube and his face is not that of a kid having fun. I want to reach out and pull his tube toward us, but that's impossible. The cavern we're in has narrowed even further and every few seconds another wave blasts down on us. People are in the water, swept downstream without their inner tubes.

"Hey, Mac!" Someone shouts in a British accent and I'm thinking that I don't know Lord Fletcher well enough for him to have a nickname for me when suddenly, Amy is gone from the inner tube. In a split second I'm gone, too, and flailing underwater. I pop back up to the surface and spot Amy, her hair drenched and matted to her head. I wave, but she doesn't wave back. There's a look of horror on her face.

"Are you okay?" I shout at her, but she can't hear me over the roar of the water and the screaming. I realize she isn't looking at me. I turn to follow her gaze. The little boy is in the water, too, his face even more panicked than before. He drops below the surface, pops up, drops again. He's drowning.

I launch myself through the rapids. No easy feat, given that the water is now filled with people and empty inflatables. I grab at him, but his skinny arm is slippery and he falls away as another wave gushes through. I grab again, this time getting a fistful of swimsuit. I yank him to me, and wrap my arms around his shoulders.

"I can't swim!" he cries.

What the hell is he doing on this water ride if he can't swim? And where the hell is his brother? The Savage River is clearly meant to be exhilarating in a mildly dangerous way—if you're a decent enough swimmer. But if you can't swim, The Savage River is truly dangerous.

"Hang on to me." I grab an unoccupied tube as it sails past my head and we let it pull us downstream until we are past the range of the whitewater machine. And just like that, the water is calm again.

"You okay, bud?"

He nods, his eyes reddened from the chlorine. We float through what is supposed to be a dark cave. On the other side is light and Amy hanging off an inner tube, waiting for us.

"We're almost to the end," she says. I feel the boy's body relax a little against mine.

My feet come into contact with the floor of the pool and I walk us over to the faux stone wall.

"What's your name?" I ask the kid.

"Ted."

He wipes his nose roughly with his forearm and there's something in the gesture that kicks me in the heart. This is a tough little kid. I look around to make sure no one is in earshot, then lean down and look him in the eye.

"Well Ted, can I give you some advice for the tournament tomorrow?"

He shrugs. I know what he's thinking. Advice from a guy who lost in the second round? Ordinarily, he would have a point. But.

"I know something about the game that very few people do." Because I don't tell many people. The ones I have told are here in Nautilus for a wedding, not the tournament. "I have an in with the developer."

His interest is piqued now. I go on. "When you get to level twenty-nine—the final level. Got it?"

He nods solemnly.

"There's a candy dish on the table. Know what I'm talking about?"

He nods again.

"Hidden behind the candy dish is a pile of dog poop. You have to smash the dish, pick up the poop, and fling it at Pissy Puppy. If you hit him, the level immediately ends and you win."

He narrows his eyes, considering.

"I know it sounds crazy," I add, " but if you make it to that final level, give it a try."

"Oh, I'll make it to the final level." His cockiness is back.

"Just trust me on it, okay? It's guaranteed to work. Every time. Smash the dish. Fling the poop."

"Smash the dish. Fling the poop. Got it."

We fist bump.

"And stay off The Savage River from now on, bud."

CHAPTER 22

Amy

I'm standing on the hotel balcony while Ethan showers. After a day where we seemed unable to shake Everly and her husband, we're opting for room service and dinner in private. Or in hiding, depending on your point of view.

After The Savage River, we ended up having lunch with them, then drinks poolside, then racing them several times on a side-by-side water slide. That Ethan and I lollygagged our way down the twisting, turning slide apparently was not enough of a hint.

I have to say, if I'd known we'd be spending this much time with Ethan's ex, I probably would have stayed in Avondale. I assumed we'd be keeping more distance from Everly.

Eating in the room isn't going to be some huge deprivation, however. Ethan booked, like, the penthouse suite. It makes me wonder whether this is actually the honeymoon suite and Ethan snatched it right out from under Brad and Marissa's nose. Except Ethan would never do something like that.

I would totally stay in a suite like this on my honeymoon. The balcony looks out over the ocean, turquoise blue water as far as the eye can see. Below me, couples stroll on the sand in the early evening sun. A card in the suite's bathroom reminds us to take advantage of the opportunity to watch the sun rise in the morning (with mimosas and pain au chocolat, ring extension 5569 to order before ten p.m.).

I go back inside and ring extension 5569 because why the hell not? This is the only time I'll ever stay in a place like this, and Ethan keeps bugging me about spending his money.

There's an enormous floral arrangement on the coffee table and I lean over to smell the roses. Maybe the hotel got mixed up and thinks we're a honeymooning couple? There are certainly a lot of them around in the park. You can spot them from a mile away. They're holding hands, shoulder to shoulder and hip to hip, not an inch of daylight between them. Their eyes are a little glassy, like they're not even noticing the rest of the world around them—or like they spent all night awake, making love, and then watching the sun rise.

You know, the way I wanted to be on my honeymoon this summer. I wanted to be majorly sleep-deprived because Danny and I were boinking our brains out. Yeah, I was really looking forward to having sex. I've heard so much about it! LOL. I've got a drawer full of sexy lingerie from my bridal shower back in Avondale. Danny didn't even give me a chance to deploy any of it on him. If he had, maybe he wouldn't have needed Angel of Albuquerque. Why go out for hamburger when you have steak at home, right? Isn't that what they say?

Oh, who am I kidding?

Ethan's head and bare shoulders appear from behind the door to the main bedroom. "Is the food here yet?"

I shake my head and try to deny the fact that I'm picturing what is behind the door. Is Ethan totally nude? Is there a fluffy hotel towel wrapped around his waist? Boxer shorts? Even in high school, Ethan was a boxer shorts kind of guy.

My tailbone is shimmying like a backup dancer for Tina Turner.

"Why don't you shower then? I'll listen for the door."

I grab my things and hurry into the bathroom, still steamy and smelling of shaving cream. The shimmying is getting to be ridiculous. I'm not attracted to Ethan and he's not attracted to me—even if that kiss on The Savage River felt like the kiss of two people who are attracted to each other.

I'm just consumed by horniness because I've spent the past year and a half thinking about having sex with Danny and now I've been jerked back to the "I'll probably die a virgin" stage.

I turn on the water, wait for it to get hot, and step into the shower. It's a big walk-in shower with two rainfall showerheads. I shampoo my hair and try to just enjoy the pleasures of a rainfall showerhead without ruminating on the fact that these things were designed to be enjoyed by two people who are having sex. Which Ethan and I are not.

He's probably good at sex. Ethan would be considerate and gentle. He'd be a real gentleman. Case in point—not once did he put the moves on me when we were teenagers and I was sleeping in his bed. Granted, I was often crying on those nights.

I doubt crying would have stopped Danny, for example. He would have at least tried. Of course, he never tried with me in high school. He had no idea I even existed. He admitted as much once after a few too many poker night beers.

"Are you sure we went to high school together, babe? Because I just don't remember you."

And damn if I hadn't actually tried to make him feel better over it. Like he really cared that I was pretty much the only girl in Avondale who was completely invisible to him during his horny high school daze?

This doesn't exactly cheer me up. The most considerate boy in Avondale didn't want to hook up with me—nor did the least considerate. I lather up a fluffy hotel washcloth. Maybe I *should* ask Ethan to sleep with me, relieve me of my virginity. He would do it, I'm pretty sure, just to be nice. It wouldn't be horrible, either. Ethan's a good kisser and my body has been so primed in anticipation of *finally* having sex this summer. It could work.

Ugh. What am I thinking?

I can't be sexually attracted to someone I've seen in a diaper.

Yet … after that kiss on The Savage River today, my body was definitely sexually attracted to … something. I turn and dial the water temperature all the way to cold. Does that whole cold shower thing work? I'm about to find out.

It's okay, at first. Bearable. But then the water gets *really* cold, like tiny nails of ice shooting from the rainfall showerhead. I squeal and quickly turn off the water entirely.

Yup. A cold shower definitely works. All I can think of now is a warm towel.

A knock sounds on the bathroom door. "Are you okay, Ames?"

Apparently, the universe can't be content with letting me think of warm towels.

"I'm fine!"

I hope he doesn't open the door to double check. When the door remains closed, I reach a cautious hand out to grab a fresh towel and dry off. I'm combing out my wet hair when I hear other voices in the suite. Our dinner must be here.

I hurry to dress in yet another of my brand new outfits—this time, a lemon yellow sundress with green slices of lime embroidered along the bodice. It's a dress that screams, "This is Amy, a friend! Just a friend! Seriously, just a friend!" There is nothing sexy about it, which is why it spoke to me on the shopping trip with Mrs. McNamara. She, on the other hand, was intent on dressing me like a forties pin-up girl.

Out in the suite's living room, a round table with a white tablecloth has been wheeled in. Big silver domes cover the plates and a bottle of wine with an expensive-looking label sits in a bucket of ice. It looks like a movie set.

"Let's eat on the balcony," Ethan suggests. He's dressed in shorts and a Nautilus tee shirt purchased from the gift shop downstairs, which we ducked into to avoid the rabid girl who beat him at the tournament. "Cute dress," he adds.

We carry our salad plates out to the small (romantic!) table on the balcony. Ethan goes back for the wine and glasses. He shakes out a giant white napkin and meticulously lays it across my lap. He holds up a large peppermill like he's wielding a weapon.

"Some freshly ground pepper, milady?" He peppers my salad, then uncorks the wine, sniffing the cork. "Notes of eggplant, feta cheese, and gummy bears." He pours an inch of wine into a glass and hands it to me.

I feign seriousness as I sip the wine. "I'm sorry, sir, but I'm tasting Swedish fish, not gummy bears."

He rears his head back in wide-eyed mock horror, then lifts the bottle to his lips and takes a swig. "Eh, you could be right."

Gummy bears or no, the wine is delicious and we polish off the bottle through salads, sea scallops and risotto, and a loaf of fresh-baked bread that is airier and tastier than any bread has a right to be. Ethan clears the table and calls down for dessert and another bottle of wine.

I lean back and stare up at the sky, streaked with pink and lavender. It's a perfect evening. The food was great. Ethan was funny and charming. I'm a little buzzed from the wine. The idea of asking Ethan to sleep with me, just to dispense with my virginity once and for all, is starting to make a little sense. I trust Ethan, after all. He's nice enough to agree (probably) and too nice to lord it over me later. He might even be better in bed than Danny is. Maybe it's a good thing he dumped me! I can have sex with someone better!

By the time Ethan returns to the balcony with the second bottle of wine and a large slice of red velvet cheesecake to share, I've made up my mind to ask him. Proposition him, I believe is the technical term. I take a bite of cheesecake and think about the best way to phrase my proposition—"Ethan, let's bang" sounds a little blunt—when an obnoxious computerized voice begins blaring.

"This. Is. A. Fire. Emergency. Please. Evacuate. The. Building. Immediately."

"You have got to be kidding." Ethan peers over the edge of the balcony, looking for signs of the fire emergency. I don't smell any smoke, just clean salted ocean air.

"This. Is. A. Fire. Emergency. Please. Evacuate. The. Building. Immediately."

"What do you think?" He leans further over the railing. "Should we wait it out?"

"Umm. I'm a school teacher. I believe I'm required by law to get everyone out of a building when a fire alarm goes off." I stand.

"I think only firefighters are required to do that."

"Be that as it may." I am already inside the suite and scooping up a room key. The sound of a fire alarm throws me into autopilot. I have to bite my lip to keep from shouting, "Everyone out! Single file! Orderly, please!"

I wave to Ethan, gesturing him to come on. I can't leave the room until everyone is out. He lingers. *Oh good grief.* I can get thirty surly teenagers out of a room in under thirty seconds, but not a sexy billionaire?

I mean, a *not* sexy billionaire. I can't believe I was about to proposition *Ethan*. Saved by the bell—err, fire alarm.

"Ethan! Come on! We have to take the stairs, you know." And we're on the twentieth floor.

That seems to light a fire under his ass, pardon the pun.

I practically drag him like a surly teenager from the room and down the hall to the stairwell.

"I'm sure this is just a false alarm," he says at floor nineteen.

"Better safe than sorry." It's not until we hit floor seventeen that I realize the odd sensation beneath my feet is because I'm barefoot. "We left our shoes in the room."

"We did—"

"But we're not going back! You can afford to buy us new ones, if necessary."

"Is this a bad omen for Brad and Marissa? The hotel catching on fire the night before the wedding?"

"Only if they're superstitious." Personally, I'm not. Though what *is* a bad wedding omen is walking in on your fiancé eating a porn star for lunch. Throwing the hoagies only added to the bad karma, I'm sure.

At floor thirteen, we finally encounter other guests running down the stairs. They are all wearing shoes, though one guy is wearing two *different* shoes and his wife/girlfriend's top is on inside out. Maybe this is their fault. Their amorous activities set the bed on fire!

By the time we reach the ground floor and limp outside, the Bahamian fire department is allowing people to go back in. *Figures.* I collapse onto a teak bench beneath a tropical-looking tree.

"My feet are killing me."

Ethan collapses next to me. "We should have waited it out. Probably one of the punks from the tournament pulled the alarm as a joke."

"People who play video games obsessively are terrible people."

"The worst," he agrees and wraps an arm around my shoulder, scooting me closer until our thighs are touching. Immediately, my tailbone starts up with the chicken dance. Maybe it's not too late to proposition him? As long as we don't do it standing up, that is. My feet really are killing me. I rest my head on his chest, but the moment is short-lived.

"Ethan!"

It's Everly.

"Evs!" Ethan calls out.

Evs? Like Ames? That he has a nickname for his ex shouldn't surprise me. Nor should it *hurt.* But it does. And reminds me that Ethan was in love with this woman—and not so long ago. The two of them were having sex regularly (I'm assuming). Ethan was making tender love to her, because Ethan is just that kind of guy.

Everly skitters over in her platform sandals.

"Where's—uh—Lord Fletcher?" Ethan asks.

Everly plops herself down on the other side of Ethan. I scootch away from Ethan's thigh. This is awkward.

"Oh, Jasper," she sighs. "I don't know. He went off to get something or other and hasn't come back yet."

"He's missing all the excitement," Ethan deadpans.

Meanwhile, I'm stuck back on "Lord Fletcher's first name is Jasper." I get unstuck quickly enough because Jasper is running toward us, out of breath, his shirt untucked, and looking very un-British-like. I'm more convinced than ever that his title is fake and purchased off the internet. If not, he's completely ruining my idea of royalty.

"Everly, love! I've been looking everywhere for you!"

"I was in the room, waiting for you. Did you get what you needed?" Everly is looking pointedly at Jasper's empty hands.

He looks down at his hands, as if he's suddenly remembering that he has hands. "Oh. No. They didn't have it." He looks back up at her. "But you made it out of the hotel!"

This is getting even more awkward. I'm guessing Jasper was at the pub, slamming back pints of Guinness, perhaps to get away from Everly. I wiggle my bare feet. "Well, I hope they've turned the elevators back on."

I stand. We've spent enough time with Everly and Lord Fletcher today. We ate dinner in the room expressly to avoid running into them again and now here we are. Fortunately, Ethan takes the hint and stands, too.

"Time to get back to what we were doing before we were so rudely interrupted." Ethan scoops me up in his arms. "We'll see you at the wedding tomorrow." He turns and carries me to the hotel lobby.

"I can't believe you just insinuated that we were having sex."

"Why not? You're my dearly beloved—and super hot—fiancée. Of course, we'd be having wild monkey sex in our hotel room."

The thought of Ethan and Everly having wild primate sex should be halting the wild monkey dance my tailbone is doing. But it's not. The thought of Ethan-Everly sex is cancelled out by the feel of his strong arms beneath my thighs and the whisper of his breath against my bare shoulder. My nipples are so hard, they're about to start firing like fembots.

The elevators are running again—at least one thing has gone right today. Ethan carries me onto an empty car.

"I can probably make it the rest of the way. Your arms must be getting tired."

"You're not that heavy, Ames. Besides, odds are this elevator is going to stop on a floor and my ex will be standing there with her Lord Fletcher-Jasper. I'm not sure what the name protocol is there. Nor do I particularly care."

"That does seem to be the way our luck is trending today."

"Well, just in case. I want to be prepared and look like two lovers who can't wait to get back to their suite."

He kisses me. And I'm pretty sure it's not just the movement of the elevator that's making me swoon. He's a good kisser. A consistently good kisser, too. Every time he's kissed me, it's been an amazing kiss. I forget about my sore feet. My tailbone is doing a sexy striptease and slinging its shirt around like a lasso. Sure, there's that little voice reminding me that Ethan and I shouldn't be kissing at all. Certainly not this often. And certainly not like *this*.

Ethan's lips aren't tentative or testing. Neither are mine, I realize, as our teeth touch. I'm kissing him back in a way I never kissed Danny because I never wanted to tempt him away from his determination to wait for our wedding night. I *wanted* to tempt him, seduce him, bang his brains out like every other woman in Avondale had. But I didn't want to seduce him and have him regret it later.

I was an idiot for—

My thoughts of Danny and idiocy are interrupted by Ethan's tongue, which is now caressing my tongue in a way that has halted my tailbone in its tracks.

My tailbone is on fire, along with everything else in the general vicinity.

The elevator doors open with a melodious chime and we break the kiss. Ethan carries me (breathless, hot and bothered) down the hall and sets me on my aching feet just long enough to tap the key card on our door. Then he swoops me back up again and carries me into the suite.

The words are out of my mouth before I even know I'm going to say them.

"Will you sleep with me?"

CHAPTER 23

Ethan

Am I dreaming? Are my ears functioning properly? Am I drunk on that kiss? Because I think I just heard Amy Casales utter the words I've fantasized hearing since I was in high school.

Will you sleep with me?

Maybe she just means sleep-*sleep* with me. As in share a bed. Platonically. But I have to be sure, so I say—in all my eloquence— "What?"

"Will you have sex with me? Hook up?"

Okay. Now that that's cleared up. I set her down gently onto the plush hotel carpet. She's flushed. One skinny strap of her dress has slipped off her shoulder. Her lips are ... still inviting. So all it took was one passionate kiss in an elevator? If I had known that, I would have searched high and low for an elevator in Avondale.

"I'm tired of being a virgin, Ethan. I'm thirty-three years old, for crying out loud."

Wait. What?

"Wait. What?" I hope I didn't just say that twice. Amy's a virgin? There is no earthly way. I know she said that she and Danny never did the deed, but frankly I'm still having a hard time imagining that. Danny Effing Walker not availing himself of a willing woman?

"I told you Danny and I never ... and I never did before, either."

Whoa.

I take her hand and lead her into the bathroom, where I begin filling the giant jetted tub.

"We're taking a bath?" Amy looks back and forth between me and the gushing faucet.

"We're soaking our feet."

"Oh."

The disappointment is loud in that one, quiet word. For a split second, I start to lose my resolve. I take a deep breath.

"Amy, I can't take your virginity. You should give it to someone who—" I was about to say "who loves you," but I stop myself. *I* love her. I've always loved her. This realization smacks me on the forehead and then boxes my ears, for good measure. "—to someone whom you love," I say instead.

"I trust you, Ethan."

"That's not a good enough reason to sleep with someone."

"People do it for less."

She's got me there. I've slept with women for less of a reason than that.

"I just want to know what it's *like*. I've been waiting all these years and I was *so close*. My wedding night was almost here. And now ..."

She lifts her legs over the side of the tub and sits on the edge. She pulls up the hem of her dress so it doesn't get wet, which doesn't exactly help my resolve. Because I cannot be the first person she has sex with. Yes, yes. If we had hooked up in high school, she would have been a virgin then. I would have been a virgin then too. But I'm not now. And suddenly, that seems like an important distinction.

"And now, it's not," she ends.

I sit down on the other side of the tub and dunk my feet in. "Danny never deserved you. You will meet a man someday who will make love to you the way you should be made love to."

I have spent hours—no, probably years if you total it all up—thinking about this moment. The moment where I have a chance to make love to Amy Casales. I have to say, this is not how I envisioned it going.

"I'm horny *now*, Ethan. Not someday."

I watch the warm water swirl around my ankles. We could sleep together tonight. And it would be fine. It would probably be amazing, even. But I don't want to take advantage of her in her current heartbroken state. Story of my life, huh?

"And I know it won't be some big passionate thing, Eeth. I just want to experience it. People hook up with friends all the time."

The thing is, *I* want it to be some big passionate thing. Not a meaningless hookup. And I don't want *her* first time to be—in her eyes—just a friend hookup. A pity fuck.

"I can't, Ames. You deserve better."

"I was going to sleep with Danny."

This is true. Still.

"You deserve better than both of us."

She kicks a foot through the water, sending a spray of hot water my way.

"Fine. Forget I asked. But you're going to feel bad when all the eulogies at my funeral extoll my lifelong purity."

I splash her back. "If you're still a virgin at fifty, I will hook up with you."

"Gee, that's generous. How about thirty-five?"

"Forty-five," I counter.

"*Thirty*-five."

I can't believe we're negotiating the age at which we'll finally have sex with each other.

"Thirty-eight and that's my final offer. I'm giving you five years to lose it," I say with mock sternness.

"Fine. Deal."

We shake on it.

CHAPTER 24

Amy

I thought I could handle this.

Now I'm not sure.

We're sitting on the pretty white chairs on the beach with a hundred or so other guests. There's a light breeze tickling the ends of my hair. Beyond the rose- and seashell-festooned wedding arch, turquoise water rolls up to the sand in white ribbons of surf. Above the horizon, pillowy clouds hold up a perfect blue sky.

You couldn't ask for a nicer day for a wedding.

My wedding was supposed to be like this. Hawaiian beach. Rose-festooned wedding arch. (I loved the seashell idea, but had visions of them blowing off in a gusty ocean wind and pelting the guests.) A harpist playing Pachelbel's Canon in D. Danny standing by the minister in his sharp black tux, waiting patiently—expectantly—for the wedding party to make their way down the aisle and into position before my grand entrance. Me waiting in the fairytale dress and satin shoes with their sensibly chunky low heels (better for walking on sand), listening acutely for my musical cue, the switchover from Pachelbel to Israel Kamakawiwo'ole's "Somewhere Over the Rainbow."

Mrs. Walker was adamantly opposed to the song, but Danny and I loved it. It reminded us of our first trip together to the National Functional Fitness Club Owners Conference in Miami, where we danced on the beach to that song. Mrs. Walker got her way on most everything concerning the wedding (we were honeymooning gratis at the Walkers' Maui timeshare, so our leverage was not good), but not the processional song. Danny put his foot down on that.

I take a deep breath, fighting back tears. I shouldn't be sad, I know that. Danny turned out to be a royal dick. I shouldn't be throwing myself a pity party at someone else's wedding. But I'm sad for myself and the thought of having to start all over again exhausts me. Dating again—in Avondale, where the dating pool is more like a kiddie pool. Back to being a teacher, waiting for the English chair to retire, and teaching to the test.

Ethan's hand squeezes mine. "You okay?" he whispers.

I nod, not wanting him to see the shine in my eyes or the way I'm biting down on the inside of my cheek. I focus my attention on Brad and the groomsmen, all dressed in white linen shirts, tan linen pants, and brown leather flip flops. They look effortlessly cool, like laidback rich guys. The bridesmaids are draped in sleek gowns of rose-colored silk, their hair perfectly curled, their eyes perfectly lined and mascara-ed.

Mrs. Walker and I had chosen similar gowns, but in navy silk, and neat chignons for hair (again with the potential ocean gusts). I pull my phone from my tiny macramé wedding purse and text my mom.

Can you take the dress to Goodwill? Maybe someone else can get married in it. It's a gorgeous dress. Someone else should wear it on their fairytale day.

Of course. How's the wedding?

Waiting for the bride. I snap a discreet picture of the wedding arch and send it to her.

Ooh pretty! See you when you get home. Love you! XO

Love you too, mom.

"Everything okay?" Ethan asks again.

I nod. "Just asking my mom to donate my dress."

"Oh." He touches my wrist. "I'm sorry, Ames. Do you think that if I hadn't, you know, at the reunion, then all that other stuff wouldn't have happened either?"

I've actually given this some thought. If Ethan hadn't kissed me at the reunion, would Danny maybe not have taken up with Angel of Albuquerque? As appealing as that idea is—that my relationship with Danny was perfect up until the minute Ethan McNamara planted one on me during a stupid party game—I know it's not true. All the signs were there before. I just hadn't seen them. Didn't want to see them. I wanted to believe that someone like Danny Walker could be so head over heels in love with me that he would practice celibacy until we got married.

(Wall, meet head.)

Danny Walker? The kid who used to have sex in the parking lot before first bell? That Danny Walker?

Yeah, right.

My powers of self delusion are pretty impressive, you gotta give me that.

"No, I think he was probably cheating on me all along." I thread my fingers into Ethan's. He lifts our hands to his mouth and lightly kisses my knuckles.

"We're engaged," he mouths and winks.

I give him a chipper smile. I appreciate his friendship, his steadfastness. In the cold light of this morning (okay, the balmy tropical light), I was glad he declined to sleep with me. And even gladder that he made no mention of it. He's too good a person to tease me about it, even. He'll make some woman a fine husband. I bet the day will come when Everly regrets dumping him in favor of Lord Fletcher.

Meanwhile, Pachelbel's Canon drones on.

"What's taking so long?" Ethan murmurs.

Brad is waiting. The minister is waiting. The wedding party is waiting. The flower girl and ring-bearer (who are totes adorbs) are waiting, albeit not as patiently as the adults. Although … now that I really look at Brad, I can see a tightness beginning to form around his mouth. His jaw looks a little clenched.

"Maybe Marissa couldn't fit into the dress," Ethan jokes quietly. "She's been eating for two."

"What?" I mouth. "She's …?" I glance down at his stomach.

He nods. "But no one knows."

"You know."

He shrugs. "Only because my mom guessed and Brad confirmed it when I asked. He's over the moon about it, but his parents don't want it announced until after the honeymoon."

"Well, maybe that's it, then." Though, as a former future bride, I doubt that Marissa hasn't been trying on the dress every twenty minutes, just to check. "Maybe she has a touch of morning sickness." Pregnancy and wedding jitters? That would do it.

The guests are growing restless, and Brad looks as though he is trying to communicate telepathically, first with the maid of honor—though what's she going to do? Leave her place and run back into the hotel? Then with his mother, who is studiously ignoring him.

Even the harpist seems to be getting tired of Pachelbel's Canon droning on.

Suddenly we hear an anguished cry and turn en masse toward the sound. Everly is on the weathered wooden walkway that leads from the hotel to the beach. She's moving in fits and starts toward us, a yellow fascinator bobbing off the side of her head until at last it detaches. She bats it away with a manicured hand. Her matching yellow sheath is too slim and narrow to allow her to properly run, so it's like watching a movie in slow motion.

I'm confused as to why she's attempting to run, in the first place. She's a bit late for the wedding, but this entrance only makes that more obvious. I glance around. Come to think of it, I haven't seen Lord Fletcher yet either.

Everly stops her hobbling and leans down, yanking off her heeled sandals and tossing them into some nearby bushes. I'm starting to get a bad feeling about this. As she comes closer, my bad feeling is confirmed. Her face is tear-streaked, dark mascara raccooning beneath her eyes.

Pachelbel's Canon stutters to a stop.

Yeah, really bad feeling.

"Jasper!" She cries out and stumbles to a stop.

I feel Ethan's thigh clench next to me. I look around for Everly's husband, but there's still no sign of him.

"Marissa's run off with Jasper!" Everly collapses onto the sand. The assembled guests gasp.

Wait—what? I thought Marissa and Brad were pregnant! Ethan must have misinterpreted. I look back at Brad standing next to the wedding arch. The expression on his face is stricken. Devastated. Ethan hadn't misinterpreted. Not only is Brad being left at the altar by the bride, but his unborn child is leaving, too. I don't even know the guy, but my heart is breaking for him.

"Oh, god," Ethan whispers.

Marissa's mother jumps up from her seat and runs toward the hotel. Around us, our fellow guests are glancing around nervously. Furtively. No one seems to know what to do. This is one of those situations you hear about, but never actually witness in real life. Even Brad looks frozen in place, his feet rooted to the ground, unsure what happens next. I'm guessing he's hoping to wake up a minute or two from now and discover himself lying in bed in his hotel room—all of this just a terrible dream.

Meanwhile, Everly is wailing and clutching at fistfuls of sand.

Ethan leans into my ear. "Amy, I gotta go help her. I'm the only one here who knows how to calm her down." His face is apologetic.

I make a little shoo-ing gesture with my hand. "No worries. Go help her."

I'm sure Ethan still has feelings for Everly. How could he not? A decent guy like him? He wouldn't fall out of love that quickly. If Lord Fletcher really has run off with the bride, that frees up Ethan and Everly to get back together again. There's an annoying stabbing sensation in my chest. I make a mental show of ignoring it. This is terrible for Brad, obviously, but good for Ethan. As his friend, I should be glad for him.

Brad is on the verge of tears as the minister tries to comfort him, leading him gently away from the scene of the crime. It's obvious the minister has done this before. I guess I'm glad I found out about Danny's cheating *before* we got married. Canceling a wedding is easier than canceling a marriage, to be sure.

Guests wearing stunned expressions rise from the pretty white chairs and make their way around Ethan and a distraught Everly on the sand. My heart goes out to her, even as my mind toggles through the potential ramifications of this. I jiggle the enormous diamond that's suddenly heavy on my ring finger. First my real engagement got broken. Now my fake one is getting broken, too.

After a few more minutes, he helps her to her feet and she leans heavily on him as they walk toward the hotel. The other guests begin to clear out, but I feel no urgency to move. I sit with my feelings, which are a jumbled up mess right now.

Ethan will tell her that we aren't really engaged. That I'm not really his fiancée. I'm just Amy, the girl he's known forever. Those are all things he *should* tell her, because that's the truth and Ethan is honest that way. I'm beginning to feel bad that he and I were pretending to be engaged to fool her. It's a very un-Ethan thing to do.

Or maybe I no longer know Ethan as well as I used to. We haven't seen much of each other in recent years. He's changed. He's a billionaire, for starters, while I'm still as poor as ever on my teacher's salary.

I'm sad. That's the main thing I'm feeling. But not sad because Ethan and Everly will get back together now. I'm sad because for the past week I've had Ethan's friendship back. And that's been nice. I can be myself around him. Let myself have fun. I can even proposition him, have him shut me down cold, and our relationship is still okay.

My whole life has been upended since the class reunion. I lost my fiancé, wedding, honeymoon, honeymoon sex, and my future as Mrs. Danny Walker. But I regained my best friend.

And now I've lost him again.

CHAPTER 25

Ethan

It takes me nearly an hour to calm Everly enough to walk her back up to her hotel room. Fortunately, Lord Fletcher has already packed his things and vamoosed. Which disappoints me, actually. I was rather looking forward to punching the guy in his insufferable viscount face.

There's a bottle of wine in the room fridge. I open it and pour Everly a large glass. "Here, drink this."

"I can't believe he would do this to me!"

There are all kinds of things I could say to that, but I hold my tongue. My goal here is to get Everly settled into her room for awhile and then go find Amy.

"What would you like from room service?"

She waves off my question in favor of a big gulp of chardonnay.

"I can't eat right now! I have to find Jasper! Why would he leave me?"

I can think of a few reasons, but the bigger question is why would Marissa leave Brad? And for Everly's husband, of all people? Brad is a bonafide billionaire and genuinely nice guy. Hot as shit, too. Or so the ladies say.

"I'm going to order you room service. You can eat it later, if you want."

Everly stalks into the bedroom and begins yanking open drawers. "All of his stuff is gone! How can he do this to me?"

I call down and order her a Cobb salad, a side of bread sticks, and strawberry sorbet. Everly doesn't eat chocolate. That should have been the first sign that we were not, ultimately, compatible.

"Am I still Lady Fletcher?" Everly wails from the bedroom.

The melodrama is all coming back to me now.

I walk into the bedroom. "Evs? Your food will be up in twenty minutes. I'm heading out, okay?"

"Why, Ethan, why?"

I take a deep breath. "I don't know, Everly. I'm sure things will all get sorted out in the morning." I am not, in fact, sure of this at all. In fact, I rather doubt it. No point to inflaming the situation at the moment, though. I give her a quick hug and am almost to the door when she calls out.

"What happened to my shoes?"

I mentally run through the past hour and realize that I can't remember her wearing shoes. They weren't on her feet when I picked her up off the sand.

"I need my shoes!"

"I'll buy you a new pair," I say and let myself out.

I no sooner close the door than my phone vibrates with a text. It's Brad's brother. *We're in the bar.*

CHAPTER 26

Amy

I look around. I'm alone now, except for the hotel staff who have swarmed in and are beginning to fold up the chairs and dismantle the lovely wedding arch. I want to tell them to stop, to save it for another wedding, but that's silly. That's just my ingrained thriftiness speaking. The white roses will be wilted, their edges tinted brown, by this evening. I hope they save the seashells, though.

I stand up and head for the hotel. I might as well go change out of this dress I bought for the wedding. It's gorgeous but—as much as I'd love to walk around in it all day—without a wedding, I'm a tad overdressed for Nautilus. I'll get the receipt from Mrs. McNamara and return it. Ethan will insist that I don't, but I can't see myself wearing it again.

It'll remind me of this trip and I'm not sure those are memories I should dwell on in the future. This past week has been a freak intermission in the movie reel of my life. Three days from now, I'll return to Avondale, maybe get a part-time job for the rest of the summer, and then make the best of things in the fall with Malcolm Jones in the job I was all but promised.

Life could be worse.

I see a flash of metallic silver in the bushes. Everly's shoes. She was so distraught, she forgot them. I climb into the bushes to retrieve the silver sandals, the branches clawing at my arms and legs as I go. I end up with a map of angry red scratches, but I have the shoes. I look at the label on the insole. Christian Louboutin, same as Angela Alessi's shoes that I tossed in the toilet at Danny's house. I hook my fingers through the silvery ankle straps and continue on my way, the sandals swinging by my calves as I go.

Inside, the hotel lobby is jammed with people again. There's a new sandwich board by the ballroom's flank of open doors: Tournament Awards Ceremony! 4pm! It must be close to four o'clock now. The wedding was scheduled for three. The crowd is pushing me toward the doors and I don't resist. I'm curious to see who won. I hope it's not that foul-mouthed little girl who shellacked Ethan in the second round.

The gaming consoles and giant screens have been cleared out, save one screen at the front of the ballroom. That's all I can see—I am packed shoulder to shoulder with the people around me. Instinctively I hug tighter my tiny wedding purse with my phone and room key.

"Ladies and gentlemen!" a voice booms from the speakers.

I train my eyes on the giant screen. A man has taken the stage, wearing a tuxedo that is printed all over with images of Pissy Puppy. I manage to squeeze my phone up in the three inches of space between me and the woman in front of me and snap a grainy picture. I know Ethan will want to see that suit.

"The first annual Nautilus Pissy Puppy Tournament has been a smashing success! We had over two thousand contestants who played nearly ten thousand rounds. How about a round of applause for them?"

The man points his microphone at the crowd. "And can I get a—"

"Who! Let! The! Dogs! Out!" The crowd breaks into a chant. The large crystal chandeliers hanging from the ceiling begin to sway and I begin to worry.

"All righty then," the emcee goes on. "On to the winners. Well, you're all winners in my book!" He laughs. "No, not really. There's no respawning in Pissy Puppy. No participation trophies, either. We have one winner. The rest of you are losers." He laughs again. The crowd titters along uncertainly.

I'm glad Ethan is not associated with this. He'd be aghast that there is only one winner. I get the backlash against participation trophies, but second and third place isn't unreasonable, is it?

"Our winner fought valiantly and fended off all comers. He displayed a coolness under fire that Napoleon would have envied. If Napoleon were still alive. Which he isn't! Because he was a loser!"

"Who! Let! The! Dogs! Out!"

"But our winner today is no loser. No sirree. He is the First Annual Nautilus Pissy Puppy Tournament Grand Champion! He will take this win with him throughout his life!" The emcee squints off to the side. "Come on out here, Theodore Fernsby the Third!"

I realize I'm holding my breath in anticipation. I let it out and an involuntary shiver runs down the spine of the woman in front of me.

"Sorry," I whisper. Either she doesn't hear me or she's ignoring me. It's entirely possible that it's the latter. The crowd is focused on the giant screen like we're all in some dystopian thriller and Theodore Fernsby the Third has just won the dubious honor of being sent to a penal colony island and dropped off to fight for his life.

I wait for an adult to stride across the stage and pick up the giant gold trophy and giant cardboard check made out in the amount of two million dollars. Instead, it's a child. Theodore Fernsby the Third is the boy Ethan rescued from drowning in The Savage River. The one whose sister is in the hospital.

Well, good. He seemed like a nice kid. A bit full of himself, but nicer than the girl who shellacked Ethan. Nicer by a country mile.

Theodore is plainly nervous, up there on the stage with the freakishly grinning emcee. I'd be nervous too—the guy is too creepy by half. Theodore's hair is slicked back and his Nautilus-branded tee shirt is tucked tightly into the waistband of his jeans. I'm guessing the brother's girlfriend dressed him. I look at the giant trophy and giant check and wonder how a kid the size of Theodore is supposed to carry those off stage.

The emcee extends his hand and gives poor Theodore a gripping handshake that practically lifts him off the floor. "So what is your secret, lad? Pissy Puppy players everywhere want to know the key to winning."

The contrast between the nervous Theodore on the stage right now and the almost cocky kid we met in line yesterday is stark. But if I've learned anything in my years of teaching, that's how kids are.

"Well …" he starts. The emcee shoves the microphone in his face. "Lots of practice, I suppose."

The emcee turns to the crowd and rolls his eyes. "Bo-o-r-r-ing!"

He points the microphone at the crowd. Half of the assembled mob around me echoes his "bo-o-r-r-ing" while the other half barks "Who! Let! The! Dogs! Out!"

Does Ethan even understand what he unleashed on the world? It's not just that his game is the bane of teachers' existence everywhere—it's that millions of people are spending time on it when they could be doing something more constructive. Something worthwhile. Like ... lying on a Caribbean beach, drinking rum, and listening to the sound of waves lapping at the shore.

Or ... playing with their kids in a pool, tossing them up into the air and watching them laugh and shriek as they splash back down.

Every single person in here should be outside with their kids, enjoying the sunshine and the ocean and the death-defying water slides. I want to charge the stage and rip that microphone out of that smirking emcee's hand and shout at the crowd: "Life is short! Play with your kids today! You could have a heart attack and die tomorrow! No, really! You could! Kids, get your parents out of here!"

I don't get it. Maybe I'll never get it.

Theodore grabs the microphone and holds it up to his mouth. "It takes lots of practice and ..." he pauses for dramatic effect, "... fling the poop!"

I turn and squeeze my way out of the ballroom as the crowd chants, "Fling! The! Poop! Fling! The! Poop!" These folks can do what they want, but personally I'm going outside to enjoy the sunshine. In the room, I change out of my expensive new dress and into a swimsuit and shorts. I toss a book, hat, and sunscreen into my beach bag and then add Everly's shoes—in case I run into Ethan. He can return them to her.

I slide my feet into my also new—but not expensive—flip flops. I

189

had to draw the line somewhere—and, really, who needs expensive flip flops? What could a high falutin' designer's imagination add to simple flip flops?

I'm on one of the walking paths through the park when Ethan calls.

"Hey there," I answer.

"I'm so sorry about this." Ethan immediately launches into an extended, rambling apology.

"Don't worry about it. I'm headed to one of the pools. Don't know which one yet. Wherever I can find a free chair, I guess."

"I'm headed to the bar to check on Brad. I'll come find you."

"Okay." I'm a little disappointed that Ethan isn't coming to find me sooner, but I understand. Brad is his friend and he just had the shock of his life. "Oh, hey. You'll never guess—" But Ethan has already hung up.

I drop the phone back into my beach bag and circle four pools before finding two open lounge chairs by a pool shaped like a dolphin. Cute. I wave my Nautilus wristband at the towel shack and pick up a couple towels. I spread one each on the chairs. I'm not sure what the park's policy is on saving chairs, but my fiancé—fake fiancé, I mean—has been consoling the woman he *actually* proposed to so I feel entitled to an exemption. I'll wait for someone to challenge me on it.

Then back down, of course.

I'm slathering myself with sunscreen when my phone rings again. It's my mother.

"Sweetie, how are you?"

"I'm fine. What's up?"

"Well, I heard about the wedding. I wanted to make sure you're doing okay."

"You heard about Brad getting left at the altar? How?"

"Ethan's mom. Word travels fast."

"Huh. Sure does." Even across international waters.

"Are you okay?"

"Of course. It wasn't my wedding, mom. Ethan is with Brad in the bar now."

"Ah. That's good."

"And he was consoling Everly for awhile. It was her husband who ran off with the bride."

"Everly the witch?"

"Yeah. Well, I'm not sure she's really a witch. Not compatible with Ethan, to be sure, but ..." I don't finish the sentence. Plenty of people fall in love with completely incompatible partners.

Case in point: one Amy Casales.

"I'm just hanging out at the pool." A waiter approaches. "Can you hang on one moment, mom?" I order a frozen strawberry daiquiri. "Sorry, mom. I really need a drink and I didn't want the waiter to pass me by."

"Totally understand. Has it been a good trip otherwise?"

I consider for a second. "Yeah, it's been fun. We haven't died on any of the water slides yet, anyway. Although there was a big Pissy Puppy tournament here. Did you know people do things like that? Compete for cash prizes over a stupid game?"

"Nothing surprises me anymore, Amy. But you're young. You should still be surprised by things."

The waiter returns with my daiquiri and we hang up. I take a sip and close my eyes. This doesn't have to be a bad day for me. Danny used to say that. "Just because other people are having a bad day doesn't mean it has to be a bad day for me."

He was chock full of those self help sayings. It's a thing at the fitness conferences he goes to—getting a roomful of people to stand atop their chairs and shout pithy motivational slogans. I used to think it was silly, but maybe there's something to it. Danny is relentlessly forward-thinking. Which is not a bad thing, necessarily. Maybe Charlie Gardner should have us do that at faculty meetings. "Just because we're teaching to the test doesn't mean we're not teaching!" Or something. Though I doubt Charlie has that much positivity in him.

Next to me, the other lounge chair creaks. I open my eyes, expecting—hoping—it's Ethan, come to find me. It's not. It's Everly. So much for pithy motivational sayings.

Her eyes are red, her cheeks splotchy. But she's calm. I don't see any weapons on her.

I flag down the waiter. "Another strawberry daiquiri?"

I have no idea whether Everly likes strawberry daiquiris, but in my world everything is improved by a strawberry daiquiri. Everly fumbles in her bag for her wallet. I wave off the twenty dollar bill.

"Ethan won't mind if I buy you a drink or two."

"Thanks."

"Oh!" I set down my own daiquiri and retrieve her shoes from my bag. "I pulled these out of the bushes for you. I didn't know your room number, but I figured Ethan could return them later. But here you are."

She takes the shoes and drops them onto the tiny patch of concrete between us.

"Nice shoes," I add.

"They were a gift from Ethan."

Ouch.

I look at my cheap flip flops, also a gift from Ethan.

"I guess Ethan has told you," I say and take another sip.

"Told me what?"

"That we're not really engaged."

"You're not?"

I shake my head.

"Could have fooled me." She glances at the large diamond on my ring finger. "Why not?"

"We're just friends. I had a bad breakup recently and he thought I could use a week away."

Everly lifts her daiquiri in toast. "Join the club." She takes a big sip. "But wake up, girl. He worships the ground you walk on."

I roll my eyes. "Yeah, in a friends-since-we-could-crawl sort of way."

She rolls *her* eyes. "No, in a he-wants-to-throw-you-on-the-bed-and-shag-you-blind sort of way."

I roll my eyes again. We're in an eye rolling contest, apparently. "He's had plenty of opportunity to do that." I cringe inwardly. That sounded kind of mean. This is his former fiancée I'm talking to. And probably soon-to-be future fiancée.

"He's too much of a gentleman to take that opportunity until you give him the green light."

I think of the flashing neon green light I gave him last night. Ethan is too much of a gentleman to take that opportunity from me, period. But this is not a conversation his former and current fake fiancées should be having.

"He adores me. But that's not the same as being in love."

"He never looked at me the way he looks at you, is all I'm saying." Then she rolls her eyes again for the win.

CHAPTER 27

Ethan

When I get to the bar, Brad is blitzed. To put it nicely. Not that I fault him for that. I may have had a drink or two myself the night Everly shot down my marriage proposal. In retrospect, I dodged a major bullet there but that night? Yeah, it stung my pride.

The hotel bar is all dark wood and glowing gold lights. The chairs and stools are covered in burgundy leather and brass accents. It's an uber-masculine setting—filled with men in loud Hawaiian print shirts, preppy shorts, and flip flops. Even in their linen pants and shirts, Brad and his groomsmen are overdressed by a mile. Me? More like two miles. I'm still wearing the dress shirt and tie I put on for the wedding. The tie coordinated with Amy's dress (my mother thinks of everything).

The groomsmen have commandeered a large table in a corner of the bar. They grab an extra chair and shoehorn me in.

"How's Evershly?" Brad slurs.

My heart goes out to him. On the list of awful things that could happen to a rich guy—a genuinely *nice* rich guy—inviting a hundred of your friends and business colleagues to a destination wedding and then getting left at the altar is near the top.

"She's fine."

He nods. Brad is the kind of guy who would be concerned about Everly. After all, she got publicly humiliated today, too.

"At least she dumped you before you got to the altar," he adds.

A lesser man might take that as a bit of an insult. I chalk it up to the alcohol speaking. My dad used to say, "Ethan, every morning I wake up and say, 'whatever happens today, don't be the lesser man.'" Apparently, he still says it to this day. God bless my mother. A lesser woman would have smothered him with a pillow by now.

"Believe me, I know how lucky I am."

"She give you the ring back?"

I nod. "Yup."

"That's good." He nods solemnly. "You spent, like what? Thirshty thousand dollars on it?"

"In that ballpark."

"I spent sixty-five on Marissa's ring. Plus—" He thinks for a moment. "Almosht two hundred grand on the wedding."

Brad's brother claps him on the shoulder in sympathy. I flag down a waiter and order a draft.

"Where'sh Amy?" Brad asks.

Brad and I have been friends since our college days at the University of New Athens. He knows who Amy is, that she's a childhood friend of mine. Does he really believe that Amy and I are engaged now? He's been busy with wedding stuff since we landed in the Bahamas, so I have no idea.

"She's hanging out at the pool," I answer. "I told her I needed to spend some time getting shitfaced with you."

He nods again and I am reminded that nodding excessively like a wise old sage is one of Brad's drunk tells. "She'sh a good woman. You two should elope."

Brad's facial control is too lax with alcohol for me to discern whether he's being serious or not.

"We were considering that," I say. Not really, of course, but it's an appealing idea. Skipping all the wedding nonsense and just going straight to the honeymoon. My mother would kill me, naturally, if I deprived her of all the wedding nonsense. Amy's mom, too.

Not that they need to worry. We're both only children and thus suffer from an overdeveloped sense of responsibility toward our parents.

"Well, it could be worse," the best man chimes in.

I'm wondering how that could be. Getting left at the altar is pretty bad. Sure, it's not the absolute worst thing that can happen to a person, but right now it feels that way to Brad. Then I remember that Marissa is pregnant. So scratch what I just said.

"Did you hear about the guy who waited until his wedding night to have sex?" Dirk, the best man, is about to make a bad situation worse, I fear. "Got to the honeymoon suite and his bride turned out to be a dude!"

Yup. Worse.

We all sit in hushed silence as we imagine that moment. The waitress returns with my beer just in time for Brad's brother to declare, "This calls for shots."

And more shots, as it turns out. I stop after two and staunchly resist the pleadings of the guys. I had too many Negronis the other night at dinner and the evening ended with me kissing Amy on the beach like we were about to have sex for the first time. Too much tequila could easily make me lose my cool like that again.

Even though I want to lose my cool like that again.

The guys are still trying to make sense of the poor man who discovered on his wedding night that his bride was a dude, trying to game out all the possible scenarios that might lead to that. It makes me think about Danny and Amy waiting to sleep together. I'm pretty certain Danny wasn't worried about Amy being a dude. I remember the pictures on Danny's Facebook feed—Amy on the beach in a tiny bikini.

He played her for a fool. Some might say that Everly played me for a fool, but I'd disagree. We had a genuine relationship. I might have been more in love with her than she was with me, but I don't believe she was using me. I just didn't transform into the person she hoped I would. Which was British royalty, apparently.

And definitely we slept together. Personally, I don't think anyone should get married without taking the car for a test drive, so to speak. (Yes, I know this analogy doesn't really work with self-driving cars like Felix.)

"Was Evershly good in bed?"

I eye the third shot of tequila that's been sitting in front of me, taunting me.

"Apparently not, if her husband ran off with another woman!" The table laughs awkwardly at Dirk's lame attempt at a joke. I shoot eye daggers at him. Dirk and alcohol have never been a good combination.

"Actually, she was pretty good." I rise to the challenge of defending Everly's honor. How good someone is in bed depends a lot on how good their partner is. I've spent enough time around Dirk, for example, to know that he's probably a selfish prick in bed.

I am not a selfish prick. I may be as clueless as the next guy in many ways, but I always care about my partner's pleasure. I care about my own, too, of course, but the lady comes first.

Another round of tequila is ordered and the conversation quickly devolves from there into war stories of worst sexual experiences. They're going around the table, one by one, each guy trying to outdo the other in some kind of weird reverse competition we're all going to regret in the morning.

I slam back a third shot of tequila and pay the tab on my way out.

CHAPTER 28

Ethan

After casing just about every swimming pool in the park, I finally come across Amy at the Dolphin Dreams family pool. She's stretched out on a chaise longue, two empty daiquiri glasses on the table next to her. Her eyes are closed, her oversized sunglasses pushed up to her hairline. She's wearing a simple black two-piece swimsuit. The bottom is a high-waisted granny panty thing, which shouldn't be at all alluring but is.

Alluring as all get out.

I grab a towel from the towel shack and stroll over. I lower myself onto the empty chaise next to her as quietly as I can. I can't tell whether she's napping or not. My eyes rake over her outstretched body. My lips tingle with the desire to plant a kiss on her stomach, right above the alluring-as-hell granny panties.

I don't, of course.

But I really, really want to.

I'm getting hard just thinking about it. And that complicates what is already a more complicated situation than I expected this to be. I've been half in love with Amy since I was old enough to comprehend that there could be "special" feelings between a boy and a girl. Now would be the perfect time to finally act on those special feelings—if only she hadn't just been dumped by her dickwad of a fiancé.

I should have foreseen that attending someone else's wedding was going to be difficult for her. Of course, that was going to dredge up unpleasant emotions. Why didn't I see that beforehand?

At least Danny doesn't have any bad sex stories to share about her. Although I wouldn't put it past him to make up some if he were to find himself in a bar situation that called for it. Thinking about Danny Walker deflates my hard-on. He's good for that, at least.

I admit, I was caught off guard last night when Amy propositioned me. Obviously, it's an appealing idea—finally getting to sleep with the woman of my dreams (and there have been many, many dreams over the years, let me tell you). All day, I've been alternately trying to talk myself into and out of it.

"That chair is saved, by the way," Amy says without opening her eyes.

"Oh. Okay. I'll move along, then."

Her eyes snap open, followed by an eye roll. "It's saved for you."

I smile and touch her nose with my fingertip. "You need to get something on that nose. It's getting a little pink."

She leans over the edge of the chair.

"I'll get it." I rummage through her bag and come up with a tube of sunscreen. I squeeze out a drop and gently rub it onto her nose. It leaves a faint white sheen. Yes, I'm dying to slather this tube of sunscreen all over her body, but my hard-on is returning.

She reaches behind the chair and pushes it into an upright position. "I gave Everly her shoes back."

"Thanks. Where were they?"

"In some bushes. How's Brad?"

"Drunk off his ass."

"Understandable. I guess I should be glad I caught Danny with Angela Alessi before the wedding. Saved me from running down the aisle, screaming about my husband-to-be absconding with a porn star."

"I would have picked you up and carried you back to your room."

"I know you would have."

The waiter stops by and I order two glasses of water with lemon.

"I don't recall getting a save-the-date card, though," I add.

"I didn't think you would want to come."

The waiter returns with the water and I hand a glass to Amy. "Actually, it would have been me running down the aisle, screaming, 'I object to this union!'"

"We deleted that line."

"I would have done it, anyway."

She gazes out at the pool, where parents are playing with their kids, kids who are having the time of their lives. Amy and I had terrific childhoods, the kind of childhood I want for my own kids. I know so many people with fractured families, estranged siblings, divorced parents. But we had great parents. Believe me, I know how lucky I am.

Everly's family is pretty formal. Just wealthy enough to be

overly pretentious, but not wealthy enough to evade insecurity over it. I used to wonder how we were going to reconcile our vastly different ideas of family and home and childhood.

With Amy, I wouldn't have to. It's so easy to picture us here again in the future, with kids we're tossing up in the water. Little dark-haired kids, a boy and a girl. Or two boys. Or two girls. Doesn't matter to me as long as there's more than one. I don't want an only child. It worked out okay for Amy and me—we were like siblings. But you can't count on that kind of friendship. What we had was special.

Hell, I can even picture us here with our parents on one big family vacation. The four of them could hang out at the casino during the day, babysit for us in the evening while Amy and I go on a romantic date and have hot hotel sex without the fear of being interrupted by nosy dark-haired children.

You could have had hot hotel sex with Amy last night.

"That kid won the tournament," she says.

"The one we met at The Savage River?"

She nods. "Theodore Fernsby the Third."

I laugh. "Quite a name there. Well, good for him."

"What did you say to him yesterday after we survived The Savage River?"

"I gave him the secret to making it through the final level."

She turns to look at me, her eyes wide. "Seriously? Isn't that kind of cheating?"

"Only if someone finds out. So don't go all teacher honor code on me and snitch."

"Cross my heart."

"Besides, did you really want that little girl to win?"

She makes a horrified face. "Was that a real possibility, do you think?"

"Oh yeah. She was good. But I'm glad our little Theodore the Third was better. I look at it as my good deed for the week." In addition to comforting Everly.

There's another good deed you could do.

I shush the voice in my head.

"So what was the secret?"

"You remember that old candy dish my parents used to have in the living room? Well, they still have it, actually. They moved it from Avondale. I think it qualifies to be a McNamara family heirloom at this point."

"The cut-glass one with the peppermint candies?"

"That's the one. I put it in the final level. Behind it is a pile of dog poop. If you smash the candy dish and fling the poop, your opponent immediately dies, the game ends, and you win."

"Uh. Hmm. Umm. What does your mom think of that?"

"She's horrified. So horrified that she shows the candy dish to every person who sets foot in their house." My eyes are twinkling.

"You're incorrigible, Ethan McNamara."

"That's my name. Don't wear it out."

She smacks me lightly on the thigh, which perks up another part of my body. The most incorrigible part, to be exact.

A lifeguard's whistle sounds. It's time for the twenty-minute pool break for kids.

"Want to get in?" I nod my head toward the dolphin-shaped pool.

"Sure."

I kick off my flip flops and strip off my tee shirt, then take Amy's hand to help her up from the chaise. The water is cool but pleasant. I jump in and immediately go under water to acclimate myself all at once. Amy does what she's always done—sit on the edge and dangle her legs first before gradually easing into the water.

"It's not bad!" I call out.

She nods. "Just give me a minute."

The water depth is four feet at this end of the pool. I dive under and glide over to her. I pop up and whip my head back and forth, spraying her with water.

"Eeth! You always do that."

It's true. I always did that when we were kids. In the summer, our mothers would pack a cooler of peanut butter sandwiches and juice boxes and the four of us would spend the day at Avondale's town pool. I can still see the old, worn plaid blanket my mother would spread out for Amy and me to sit on. She and Mrs. Casales sat in lawn chairs while they read magazines, often out loud to each other.

I was always impatient with the amount of time it took Amy to get in the pool and finally pinch her nose shut and dunk her head. It never made sense to me since she was a strong swimmer. That's Amy in a nutshell. Good at many things, but cautious in her approach to life. Her father's death made her even more cautious. Life can all go wrong in a heartbeat. Unfortunately, she was one of those kids who had to learn that early.

That's where Amy and I are different. If the lifeguard can blow the whistle and end the kids' pool break at any moment, I'm not going to wait. I'm jumping in right away to take advantage of whatever time I have.

I put my hands on her knees and gently push them open to make room for me. Her gaze on me is steady. She doesn't protest. I put my hands beneath her armpits and lift her off the wall. Immediately, her legs wrap around my waist to keep her torso out of the water.

This is not helping my incorrigible parts.

I carry her out to the center of the pool, trying to ignore the nearness of her breasts, the softness of her still-dry hair, the sweet scent of sunscreen that takes me right back to all those long-ago summers. Carefree summers—before there were marriage proposals to be rejected, job promotions to lose, fiancés taking up with porn stars.

I slide my hands around to her bottom, to better support her weight. I'm at full incorrigibility now, even underwater. From the look in her eyes, I know she feels it. I'm pressing right against her lady parts.

My holy grail. (Forgive the blasphemy.)

"You need a cold shower," she says quietly.

I give a rueful little smile. "If a pool isn't doing the trick, a shower won't, either."

"I offered."

I can hear the note of hurt in her voice—and it's like a taser to my heart. If I had to hurt every single person in the world except for one, that one would be Amy. If I had to hurt every single person in the world to save Amy from hurt, I would do it. Without a second thought.

"I was stupid," I say.

"We've established that already. Years ago, really."

I give her bottom a gentle squeeze. I'm taking liberties here, possibly dangerous ones given that her very fit thighs are wrapped around my hips. She's biting her lip to hold in check a smile that is flitting around her lips. I want to latch my teeth onto that lower lip and free it, then kiss the living hell out of this woman.

"I'm talking about years ago. I was stupid for letting us lose touch."

"It happens, Eeth. We went to different schools. Your parents moved away. You moved away. We were friends as kids because our parents were friends. It was convenient."

"I don't believe that." Because our friendship is decidedly inconvenient right now.

She gives a little shrug and just that tiny movement makes Mr. Incorrigible's eyes roll helplessly back in his head. We weren't best friends simply because we lived on the same street and our parents were friends. We grew up in a small town. Those conditions existed for every other kid in Avondale.

Pushing our friendship further carries risks. I acknowledge that. I try not to make decisions based on the whims of Mr. Incorrigible. If we head down this path and it doesn't work out, we might end up hating each other. (Though I doubt it.)

If Mr. Casales were still alive, I would ask his permission to officially court his daughter. I'm certain he would say, "yes." He would trust me with her. But he's not here and I can't. So I do the next best thing.

I look past her face and the lovely lips I want to bite and kiss, devour into oblivion. The coast is clear.

"Do you trust me?"

She nods.

I shimmy my hips to loosen the grip her legs have on me. (Mr. Incorrigible is pleading for mercy now.) I move my hands from her derrière to her hips. Her eyes widen and she realizes—too late— what I'm about to do. With a mighty heave of my arms, I toss her up into the air and watch as she splashes down into the water ten feet away. Momentum dunks her beneath the surface, then she pops out—her hair wet and plastered to her face like dark seaweed.

I'm in trouble now.

She shoves the seaweed hair out of her eyes and charges me, splashing all the way. Just as I knew she would. Just as she did back in the Avondale town pool after I'd sneak up on her and give her a World Champion Wedgie. Through the torrent of water coming my way I can see her laughing.

When she reaches me, I pull her up against my chest. I am mentally running through my options when the lifeguard's whistle sounds again. We are surrounded by rapid-fire explosions of water as tiny bodies cannonball into the pool. I choose a not-altogether-random option.

"Let's go upstairs."

CHAPTER 29

Amy

In the elevator, Ethan pushes me up against the wall and kisses me. My tailbone is in a state of shock due to this sudden turn of events.

Also because we're not alone in the elevator.

There's a pride of pre-teen girls huddled in half-horrified/half-fascinated silence in the corner. When the elevator stops, they shuffle off. Once they're all in the hall, one of them shouts back, "Get a room!"

Ethan breaks the kiss long enough to shout back, "Got one, ladies! But thanks for the tip!"

"Ethan," I murmur as his lips crush mine once again. "They're kids."

"Yes, Ms. Casales. I'm headed to detention straight away."

The elevator arrives at our floor just in time. Ethan's fingers were beginning to toy dangerously with the tie of my swimsuit top.

I'm straightening the cup when he scoops me up into his arms and sets off down the hall at a fast clip.

"Are we really going to do this?" I ask.

"By this, you mean 'hook up?'" Ethan's face is flushed and not from the sun.

I nod.

"No, we are not going to 'hook up.'"

I can practically hear the air rushing out of my hopes.

"We are going to do every last thing I've ever fantasized about doing with you, ever since I was old enough to ... well, since before I was old enough to really be thinking about such things."

"Umm, what day do we check out?"

We've reached our suite already. Ethan holds me in one arm while pressing the key card to the door in the other. He hip-bumps the door open.

"Okay, so maybe not *everything*. But we're going to make a sizable dent in the list."

He drops the key card on the floor and continues on into the bedroom, where we tumble onto the mattress in a jumble of arms and legs and lips.

Desperate, hungry lips.

He cups my face in his hands. "First thing I've fantasized about doing is kissing you without feeling like I shouldn't be kissing you." He runs his thumb over my bottom lip.

"You should definitely be kissing me." I'm certain we are both going to regret this in about half an hour, or however long this is going to take. How long is sex supposed to last? In the movies, it's always twenty seconds of kissing and blurry thrusting. So maybe more like sixteen minutes, if we split the difference.

He leans in, and my heart well and truly stops. Finally! I'm going to have sex! In sixteen minutes, I will be a real, grown-ass woman. Then his head rears back. My heart restarts, grudgingly. Ethan is regretting this already.

"You never answered my question the other night."

"What question was that?" It's hard not to pout here. I mean, honestly. How hard should it be to lose my virginity? In sex ed, they made it sound harder to keep than to lose.

"Whether I'm a better kisser than Danny."

He's got performance anxiety? Even though he knows I have literally nothing to compare him to? For reals, I don't even care whether this is going to be good sex or not. I just want to do it and cross it off my list.

"Yes, you're a better kisser than Danny. But I don't want to talk about him right now." Because I don't! Danny could have been doing this with me, but he wouldn't—so screw him.

"Neither do I." He presses his lips together in a hard, tight line. "No more mention of he who shall not be named."

Then his lips open and cover mine … and oh, it's glorious. Something vibrates deep in my body, and it's either the air conditioning kicking on or Ethan moaning. No one has ever moaned about me before. Dann—he who shall not be named—kind of more groaned. Groaning means "I'm in agony because I have a hard-on, but I'm not going to let you have it."

Moaning is—

"Ames. Stop thinking." Ethan nibbles at my jaw.

"I want to remem—"

"Let me do the thinking for now." His words fill my mouth and the vibration settles into a low rumble.

Ethan's kiss is soft at first, exploring, asking permission. His fingers tangle in my wet hair, angling my head into better position.

I'm kissing him back, hungrily. Kissing is the one part of this I'm familiar with.

The rest? Totally uncharted territory for me. Danny and I never made out on a bed. I've never been beneath Danny's body the way I'm beneath Ethan right now, with just the skimpy fabric of my swimsuit separating our bare skin.

"Ames?"

I moan into his warm breath. My hips are doing this rolling sexy backup dancer move, completely independent of any conscious direction on my part.

"If you don't stop thinking about him, I will turn this car around." His fingers slip from my hair to the back of my neck, where my swimsuit top is tied. "Kissing you while you think of someone else is not on my list of fantasies."

"Sorry—"

He sucks my lower lip into his. "Shhh. Just sit back, relax, and enjoy the trip."

He undoes the top tie on my swimsuit. Then the bottom tie. He tugs it off my chest and tosses it aside. He sits back and just looks at me, his expression one of awe, almost.

"Did you ever used to sneak a peek at me?"

He smiles. "I was a teenaged boy. Of course, I tried to sneak a peek now and then." He runs a finger from the base of my neck, down my sternum, and between my breasts. "Oh hell, Ames. There were nights when I stayed up for hours, just watching you sleep." He touches my nipple. "Why do you think I nearly failed trig in eleventh grade?"

His thumb is slowly twirling my nipple and it feels so good I'm about to pass out.

"Close your eyes."

I do, and give in to the delicious feeling of Ethan touching my breasts. Just when I think it can't get any better, something warm and soft closes over my hard nipple. I suck in my breath as his tongue circles it over and over. My hips are about to explode with lust.

He switches to the other breast and sucks gently, rhythmically drawing the ache that is between my legs up to my ribs. I used to imagine this, with my vibrator cranked up to eleven. My imagination was pathetically lacking. This feels so much better than even my wildest fantasies.

I open my eyes and watch him, watch his lips work around my nipple. He knows I'm watching. After a few more minutes of this— this heavenly bliss!—he lifts his head. His eyes look as dazed as mine feel.

"You okay?"

I nod.

"Okay if I continue?"

I nod again. "What's next on your list?"

His grin is downright diabolical.

He kisses his way down my stomach and runs a finger beneath the elastic of my high-waisted swimsuit bottom.

"This is way sexier than it should be." He slowly tugs it down over my hip bones.

"Your mom thought it would look cute on me."

"My mom is often wrong."

The swimsuit bottom is sliding down my thighs and I hold my breath. Ethan is about to see what no man has seen before. Am I ready for this? I hear the soft thump of fabric landing on the floor. When he nuzzles his nose between my legs, my eyes roll back in my head.

"Ethan." The word is so quiet even I can barely hear it.

"That's my name, don't wear it out." He nuzzles some more.

Ethan. Ethan. Ethan. I do a quick practice run in my head. I used to practice saying Danny's name when I masturbated with my vibrator. Now I'm terrified that it will be his name that flies off my lips at the wrong moment. I practice thinking *Ethan. Ethan. Ethan.*

His—*Ethan's!*—warm breath sends a slow, rolling shiver up my spine. I feel his hands push my thighs a little wider before settling firmly on the points of my hip bones. Am I really about to let him do this? Am I ready? Should I stop him before—

"Stop thinking."

The words are spoken in so un-Ethan-like a tone that my attention immediately snaps from the ceiling to his head between my thighs. He's looking at me—his eyes dark, his expression deadly serious. He doesn't look like Ethan anymore. Or not any Ethan that I know, at any rate.

"Stop. Thinking."

There's a command in his words that I've never heard from him before. My heart stops. We really are moving past "Amy and Ethan, friends" here. Maybe he was right, after all, in saying "no" to this yesterday. Am I ready for the consequences of this? What if we can't go back from being "Amy and Ethan, fuck buddies" to "Amy and Ethan, friends?"

"Speak now or forever hold your peace."

His lips are hovering oh so close to right where I want them to be. Where I'm dying for them to be. My thighs are actually quivering against his cheeks.

"Please, Eeth."

"Please, yes?" His breath caresses skin that is so on the edge, my toes are curling. "Or please, no?"

"Please, yes."

At the first, slow touch of his tongue on my skin, my body nearly combusts. Vaguely, I register the sensation of his hands pressing harder on my hips, holding them in place as he ravishes me, teases me, brings me to the brink over and over before finally tipping me over into a panting, bucking, gasping freefall of pleasure.

Ethan. Ethan. Ethan.

At least I got the name right.

I look around the room. Things should look different, right? I'm seeing the world with new non-virgin eyes. But it all looks the same, except for the torn condom package on the nightstand, my swimsuit lying inside out on the floor, and the man lying next to me —who is now more sexy beast than adorable (if sometimes annoying) childhood playmate.

"Was it everything you imagined it would be?" Ethan's eyes are still closed.

"I thought you were asleep."

"Just resting my eyes."

"Do you need a cigarette or something?"

"Do you have a cigarette?"

"No."

"Looks like I'm shit out of luck, then."

"I think this is a non-smoking room, anyway." I bite my lip to keep from laughing.

"That, too."

He opens his eyes and rolls onto his side, facing me. "You didn't answer my question."

"Yes, it was everything I imagined."

"Liar."

I smack his bare hip lightly. His cock twitches. I tell my hips to ignore that.

"Okay, so I originally imagined it with someone else. What about you?" I'm not sure I really want the answer to this, but reciprocity seems called for.

"Yes, you are the person I originally imagined this with." He catches my hand before I can smack his hip again. He threads his fingers into mine.

"I'm getting the sense that you are a little, uh … pervier than I realized, Mr. McNamara."

He squeezes my hand. "Oh Ms. Casales, I am way pervier than you realize."

He winks theatrically and suddenly I collapse into a fit of laughter. Unladylike wheezing laughter. Between tears, I manage to get out, "I can't believe … you … thought … *he* … had … a sex room!"

He pulls me closer and works a leg between mine. My hips are doing some slow stretches and warm-up kicks.

"Pretty sure every man wants a sex room."

He takes my hand and places it on a certain stiffening part of his body. "And how do I compare here?"

"Oh, Ethan. You are not going there."

"Just between friends?" The twinkle in his eye says he's joking. "You never felt him beneath his clothes?"

"Yes, but—" My words are interrupted by Ethan waggling his eyebrows at me. We are back to "Amy and Ethan, friends." "He felt huge. Ginormous, really. I mean, it's a good thing we never slept together. It probably wouldn't have even fit."

We are both laughing hard—like "Amy and Ethan, friends" if "Amy and Ethan, friends" were naked and wrapped up in each other's bodies and trying to ignore the fact that one of us is hard as a rock again.

By "one of us," I don't mean "me."

We calm down, eventually, and Ethan's concern is genuine when he asks, "But seriously, it was okay?"

This is why Ethan will be an amazing husband to some woman someday. And why Everly is out of her freaking mind if she lets him go again.

"It was perfect, Ethan. Thank you." I run a finger down the center line of his chest, tracing a path between all the lovely muscles he didn't have when we were kids. "But if you want to hit the minibar and drink yourself blind so you don't remember it in the morning, I won't be offended."

He cranes his neck to look at the alarm clock on the nightstand. "It's eight o'clock. What I really want to do is hit up the dinner reservation I made for nine o'clock."

Dinner sounds like a good idea, now that we've reverted to being friends again. I rush into the shower. I'm lathering my hair when the glass shower door opens and Ethan gets in. Naked.

As one does in a shower.

My soapy hands instinctively cover myself—one hand trying in vain to cover my breasts, the other over my hips. He removes my hands.

"Kinda late for that. It'll be faster if we shower together."

My glance drops. He's hard again.

"Ignore that. It has a mind of its own. It's just excited that it finally got to see the object of its original sexual fantasy."

I rinse my hair. "Do you always talk about your penis in the third person?"

He rubs the bar of soap over his chest. "I have more control over it if I think of it as a separate entity. In theory."

He washes his hair, then hands me the soap.

"I can't believe we just slept together." I wash quickly.

"Shhh. We'll discuss it at dinner. Give the diners next to us a cheap thrill."

I spin around to rinse the soap from my skin. When I complete the wash cycle, I end up breasts to chest with Ethan, water running over both our heads. His erection bobs against my belly, firing up the ache between my legs again. Is that normal? Having sex and then, not fifteen minutes later, wanting to shove someone against a wall in the shower and do it all over again?

It's a question I don't get to ask—because Ethan is shoving me up against the shower wall and kissing the ever-loving hell out of me.

CHAPTER 30

Ethan

When the elevator doors close, I loosen my tie and take it off. Fortunately, we are the only people on the elevator. I wrap the tie around Amy's head.

"What are you doing?"

"I want you to be surprised."

"By the restaurant?"

"Yes, silly. Just trust me on this." Her cheeks are still flushed from the bit of naughtiness back in the shower.

The elevator bumps to a stop and the doors open. I take her hand and lead her into the busy hotel lobby. We get a few looks, but I flash a genial smile and keep going. Really, this isn't any weirder than a few thousand people flying all the way to the Bahamas and then spending hours inside playing a silly game that a college kid developed in his spare time.

(Okay, so occasionally I cut class to work on it. Don't tell my mother.)

We make it through the lobby and outside without hotel security questioning us. I have a few hundred dollars in large bills stuffed in my pocket, just in case. Bribery is not beneath me. Not where Amy is concerned.

"Watch your step," I caution as we reach the wide set of stairs leading from the hotel's back veranda into the waterpark. I veer us to the left so we can take one of the perimeter walking paths. The park is more heavily shaded here, the only light shining from small lanterns hung discreetly in the trees.

"How far is the restaurant?" Amy asks. "It's not in the hotel?"

"It's not far." I give her hand a squeeze and she squeezes back.

"I'm starving."

"Common side effect of sex."

"I read that somewhere." She laughs softly. "Actually, it was in an article my mother texted me. Fourteen things you need to know on your wedding night. Have a healthy snack ready for later."

"Isn't that what room service is for?"

"Or some mysterious restaurant?"

I let go of her hand so I can drape an arm across her shoulder and pull her into me. "Fourteen. That's an oddly specific number."

"I know, right? I was never sure whether that was a high number of things one needs to know, or whether fourteen is too low."

"Well, feel free to try out any of the fourteen on me."

She laughs again. "You're a good sport, Ethan."

I know she views what just happened between us as two old friends hooking up, as me doing her a favor by relieving her of her virginity once and for all. But that's not at all what occurred. Not for me. I've always been in love with Amy. Even as kids, when she seemed to me to be part fairy princess, part witch. I was awed by and scared of her, all at the same time.

I'm not scared of her anymore, obviously. But she is still a maddening mashup of adorable princess and sexy witch—and I am certain she has no idea that she is both of those things. Everly did me a huge favor by dumping me. Danny, too. Maybe I'll send him some hot stock tips to thank him.

No, what happened in the room tonight—and then again in the shower—was not merely two old friends indulging in some post-breakup fuck buddy fun. And now that I've had a taste of Amy, I'm not interested in stopping at just one night.

The paved walking path ends at the beach. I stop. "We should take off our shoes here." I kick off my leather flip flops and Amy does the same. I loop both pairs over my free hand as we step onto the sand.

"We're getting pretty far from the hotel."

"Mmm-hmm."

Ahead of us is a white cabana with a cozy round table and two chairs inside. Waiting just beside it is a waiter and the hotel's top sommelier with the bottle of wine I had Erin-Joi order earlier. (Erin-Joi is far more knowledgeable about wine than I am.)

"Welcome, sir," the sommelier says.

I untie the blindfold, roll it up, and stuff it in my pants pocket. Amy looks around, surprise written all over her face.

"We're eating on the beach?" She glances around again. "By ourselves?"

I pull out one of the chairs for her. "Our own private restaurant."

I watch her processing this as I take the other chair across from her. The waiter opens the large cloth napkins with a flourish and covers our laps. The sommelier uncorks the wine with extraordinary gracefulness and pours a tiny amount into a stemless glass.

"The Connor Cellars pinot gris," he says as I lift the glass to my nose and sniff, pretending to know what I am sniffing for. I nod in what I hope is an agreeably sage way and take a small taste. "Excellent." He fills our glasses.

I also catch the amused smile flitting around Amy's lovely lips. She knows I am so full of shit right now. And I love that she knows it—and that I don't have to pretend to be someone I'm not. I'm a doofus guy who lucked into a lot of money. I don't know much about wine or yachts or antiques—the sort of stuff people expect a billionaire to be into. I like to think that I'm interested in the things that my younger self would be fascinated by right now, even without all the money.

The waiter turns and nods at someone in the distance. A moment later, two salads and a basket of freshly-baked bread is brought to the cabana. Black pepper is grated and then everyone disappears, leaving us alone on the beach.

"You set this up just for us?"

"Just us. No Pissy Puppy fanboys. No exes. No minor royalty."

"And the hotel agreed to this?"

"Well, they're not doing it for free."

"How much is 'not free?'"

I lift my glass of wine and belatedly she does the same. We clink without making any specific toast. That might be bad luck. I'm not sure. I sidestep her question, though. It doesn't surprise me that she is uncomfortable with my wealth. Sometimes, I'm uncomfortable with it. You can take the boy out of Avondale, but you can't take Avondale out of the boy.

"And if someone pulls the fire alarm in the hotel ..." I shrug. "... it won't interrupt us at all."

We tuck into the salads and bread, with the sound of the ocean lapping at the shore instead of canned restaurant music. Amy pays close attention to her arugula and shaved parmesan. I worry that she's embarrassed by what just transpired between us.

"I have another surprise for you tomorrow."

She looks up from her concentrated study of wild greens and transparent slivers of cheese. "Oh yeah? What is it?"

"If I tell you, it won't be a surprise."

She rolls her eyes at me.

"You seem a little sad."

She pushes salad around with her fork. "Just a little down at the prospect of going home. Going back to reality. Before I know it, it'll be time to get ready for the new school year."

"So don't go home right away. Stay in New Athens for awhile."

"What would I do there?"

"Hang out in the city. I can fly your mom down. My mom would love to hang out with the two of you."

She seems to consider the idea, but I can see my argument is not yet compelling enough.

"You could be my date for a charity bachelor auction that I regrettably agreed to participate in."

"A date for a bachelor auction? Isn't that an oxymoron?"

A team of waiters appears to clear our salads and replace them with a platter of BBQ shrimp. Amy's eyes are making grabby hands at the shrimp, and finally she smiles again.

"Thank you."

She has loved BBQ shrimp since we were kids and our families went to the local seafood joint together, sitting outside beneath a patio umbrella and gorging ourselves on the all-you-can eat buffet.

"Or you could help me out at Chaos Labs," I resume our earlier conversation.

"How could *I* help?" She pops a shrimp into her mouth and then licks seasoning from her lips. Which makes BBQ shrimp way more tantalizing than normal.

"I need help with The G.O.D. Squad. I really want to see them win funding from the board at the end of the summer, but they're doing something completely different from anything we've funded in the past."

She closes her lips around another shrimp. I've never given much thought to the lives of shrimp, but right now I would really like to be one.

"Can't you just give them the funding? Make an executive decision?"

I shake my head. At least, I think I'm shaking my head. It's possible I'm nodding instead. I'm still somewhat dazed and distracted by Amy polishing off BBQ shrimp.

"Everyone on the board has an equal vote. Mine doesn't count for more. The winners need to have truly earned it. I don't want Chaos Labs getting a reputation for handing out participation trophies."

"I'm just an English teacher, Eeth."

There goes the last shrimp. Does it realize how lucky it is? How envious I am of it?

"I couldn't even get a girls' mentoring program off the ground in my own high school."

"So here's your chance. What else did you do for Danny's business, besides get him press coverage?"

"I hired a graphic designer to redo his logo. The original one was a pair of sneakers with a barbell in one hand and a smoothie in the other."

I cringe.

"And I rewrote the web site, which previously sounded like it was written by a sixteen-year-old boy hepped up on Viagra."

"You have a head for business."

"Don't even say it."

I think it anyway. *And a body for sin.*

My private army of waiters returns with our entrées—buttery sole meunière, buttery mashed potatoes, and buttery glazed baby carrots.

"You're going to have to carry me back to the room after all this."

A certain part of me twitches at the prospect of carrying Amy back to the hotel room, tossing her onto the bed, and ravishing her the way she just ravished all those shrimp. I opt for a slightly different angle of negotiation.

"If I carry you up, will you stay in New Athens for a bit?"

She slides a forkful of sole meunière into her mouth while she weighs my initial offer. I am prepared to raise the stakes, if necessary. I've also decided that I no longer wish to be a BBQ shrimp. I now aspire to be a filet of sole.

"I guess I could stay for a few days."

We finish our buttery entrées, the bottle of wine and then half of a second bottle, the dessert platter (because what's the point in being a billionaire if you can't have all the desserts?), and coffee—and then I carry Amy back to the room. It was my nefarious plan to slowly and sweetly make love to her the way she should be made love to. The way one Mr. Danny Effing Walker surely would not have if their wedding had proceeded as planned. Alas, we are both a little tipsy and overstuffed with butter and sugar. We fall asleep about two-point-three seconds after our heads hit the pillows.

I awake to morning sun on my face, momentarily confused because I can feel that my flip flops are still on my feet. Also I'm fully dressed and smell of butter. This is not how last night was supposed to end. Maybe we made love on the beach and fell asleep on the sand?

Now that's a lovely thought.

I pat around with my hands. Nope, no sand. I'm surrounded by high thread count sheets. And the soft background noise is air conditioning, not the gentle back and forth of ocean waves. I roll onto my side and snuggle into the warm body next to me. At least one part of my original plan held. Amy and I did sleep together— although more literally than I wanted.

She is still fully dressed in her sexy one-shoulder top and a skirt that is bunched up around her thighs. One slender foot is bare. From the other dangles a sandal with skinny straps. I kick off my flip flops and nudge the sandal from her foot.

She stirs.

I snuggle closer and drape an arm over her body. I'm stirring too, if you know what I mean. The planned activities for the day don't begin until eleven o'clock. Plenty of time to make up for last night and the part of "sleeping together" that was prevented by our actual sleeping.

"Good morning, sleepyhead," I whisper into the curved bone of her ear.

"Nnnn. Unnnhh. Ppsshhh."

I believe that translates as, "Good morning, you hunkahunka burning love. Ravish me before breakfast."

Okay, so I'm paraphrasing a bit.

I lean back to escape Amy's flailing hands, patting herself down for any possible wardrobe malfunctions. This is exactly what she did all those mornings in high school when she awoke in my bed. Her hand seems to get hung up on the lack of clothing on her left shoulder, patting frantically and rubbing around for a strap. I still her hand.

"Your top only has one shoulder."

"Oh." I feel her body relax into the mattress. "I forgot."

"Good morning, sleepyhead."

"I heard you the first time."

"Just checking." I pull her closer. Desire hums through my body like the first sip of morning caffeine. How many mornings in my life have I opened my eyes and wanted to pull this woman in close? Too many to count. Sleeping with her wasn't the motivation behind inviting her to the Bahamas, but now that we've crossed the rubicon … I don't want to go back.

"What made you change your mind?"

I know what she's talking about, but I quickly weigh the pros and cons of pretending I don't.

"Be honest," she adds.

Honest. That was one thing I always tried to be when we were kids. When her dad was in the hospital, I never said, "Don't worry. Everything will be fine." Even though everyone else was telling her that. I didn't know whether everything would be fine. Instead, I let her talk and cry and worry. I made sure she did her homework and studied for tests. I made her hot chocolate with extra marshmallows.

And in the end, everything wasn't fine. But I took care of her. I protected her.

"Tell me, Eeth."

"At the bar yesterday, Brad and the guys were trading worst sex stories."

She wriggles in my arms to face me. "And you needed one?"

"If I did, you didn't exactly give me one last night."

She rolls her eyes.

"I didn't want you to end up in some guy's worst sex story," I go on. "I'd rather your first time be with me. And your second." I run a thumb along her lower lip. And her third and her fourth and her ...

"Well, thank you, Eeth. I thought it was pretty great, to be honest."

Her words have me on the verge of kissing her again.

"I mean, I was three parts terrified to five parts embarrassingly out of control horny or whatever the ratio was."

"That was definitely a new side of Amy Casales for me." I slide my hands down to her bunched up skirt and pull her tight so she can feel how hard I am for her. "Out of control horny." I suck her earlobe into my mouth and her little gasp of pleasure inspires me to keep going. "Not a new side of me, though. I spent my entire adolescence in an out of control horny fog for you, Ames."

"No, you didn't."

"Oh yes, I most certainly did." I slip my hand beneath the hem of the bunched up skirt and toy with the elastic on her panties.

"You never did anything about it."

"Because when I found myself fortunate enough to have you in my bed, you were generally distraught and in need of my friendship more than my lustful teenaged desires." I stroke the warmth between her legs and her breathing skips a beat.

"So was it everything you expected?"

Does she realize how hot the fire she's playing with is? Because it's not as though all those years of pent up teenaged lust just disappeared. It's been suppressed and is now on the verge of being released. Explosively released. As in I may not be able to stuff the genie back into the bottle explosively released.

I dip a finger into her wetness and stroke her wall. "We've merely scratched the surface of my fantasies where you are concerned." Time is slowing down around us, catching up to us.

"Tell me about these fantasies."

"Easier just to show you."

"So show me."

I hook my leg between hers and patiently stroke her. She's getting wetter and wetter, which is making me harder and harder. I have so many fantasies about making love to Amy Casales—and have had them for so long—that it could easily take years to run through them all. I could kick myself for wasting all this time on other women when I could have been with Amy.

Her eyelids flutter. This is what I want to see—what Amy looks like when she gives herself over to pleasure. To my pleasure. I slide her panties off and patiently bring her to the brink over and over.

"You're torturing me," she pants.

I change the pressure and angle of my stroke, and she falls apart before my very eyes. I watch the waves of pleasure wash over her face and roll down her spine, her back arching up from the bed. It's the loveliest thing I've ever witnessed. I could spend all day making her back arch that way. All day? Who am I kidding? I could spend the rest of my life.

CHAPTER 31

Amy

"Is that the surprise?" Automatically I lower my voice since we are in the hushed atmosphere of Sparadise, the awkwardly named spa at Nautilus. We are in some sort of staging area—a purple and pink mood-lit room with mysterious hallways branching off like a traffic roundabout. A small figure with one of the spa's enormous white towels wrapped at least twice around his waist is disappearing down one hall.

Theodore Fernsby the Third.

"Well, that is quite a surprise," Ethan murmurs. "But no, the spa itself was the surprise. Figured we both needed it."

For the record, I'm feeling pretty relaxed already this morning even though the coffee from breakfast hasn't had time to kick in yet. But Ethan's morning wakeup call—aka Ethan's morning wood—was the most relaxing thing I've ever experienced. Even my mind is relaxed.

Ninety percent of it anyway.

Ten percent is jabbing at the rest, shouting, "It's just pheromones, idiot! Endorphins! The intoxication of being on vacation! You are not falling for your oldest childhood friend!"

Except I am.

I think.

Maybe.

Possibly.

Things feel different this morning. Different good or different bad? That's what I'm worried about. Are we about to mess things up here? Or take them to the next logical level? Or are we just scratching an ancient itch that we were fated since birth to scratch?

Probably that last one. Ethan is such a good guy that he can probably sleep with an old friend and not have it ruin the friendship.

But can I? I'm the emotionally unstable one here. The lunatic who actually *believed* that Danny Walker loved her when really it was just—

"Do you think Danny wanted me because I'd be a respectable, prim and proper wife?"

A look of startlement detonates on Ethan's face.

"I don't know, Ames. Probably? But he was wrong about that." Ethan's lips capture mine in a deep kiss that is wholly inappropriate for the Sparadise waiting room. He kisses me for a full minute before adding, "You weren't so prim and proper this morning."

My face flames, then threatens full-on ignition when Ethan caresses my cheeks.

"I love that I can make you blush." His breath tickles my ear.

"And that I could make you come so hard that you couldn't remember my name."

"I couldn't remember my own name."

My tailbone is twitching spastically like Charlie Gardner dancing at last year's faculty holiday party.

"Sign of a great orgasm," Ethan adds.

I sigh. It *was* a great orgasm. The second one was pretty great, too, with Ethan hell-bent on a third when room service arrived. Probably a good thing or I wouldn't have the leg strength to be standing here right now.

"Maybe I'll dm Danny on Facebook and let him know how un-prim and proper you really are."

"McNamara party of two! Sixty-minute couples massage with the Sparadise Sensual Oil Blend!" Amazonian twins—a man and a woman, each at least six feet tall—are waiting for us at the head of one hallway. The other guests in the staging area avert their faces as we walk past. You'd think they just announced that we're heading into the Sparadise BDSM Dungeon with patented Kinkometer.

(That wasn't on the menu of services, by the way. I'm making that up.)

We follow the Amazons down the long hallway, past door after closed door.

"I wonder what service Theodore is here for?"

"Shhh!" The female Amazonian twin hisses at us over her shoulder. "Silence is part of what makes this relaxing."

Ethan and I give each other the side eye.

"Sorry?" he mouths.

"Shhh!"

Okay, so Amazons have eyes in the back of their heads. Good to know. I hope little Theodore has nicer spa attendants.

The Amazons lead us into the last room on the left. Inside are two side by side massage tables covered with plush white fabric that looks like velvet. The lights are low and scented candles flicker around the perimeter of the room. Hidden speakers emit the sound of waves crashing gently into shore.

I relax. This is going to be great, as soon as the Amazons leave and the masseuse and masseur arrive. We were told there would be one man and one woman … I'm starting to get a bad feeling about this. There is one Amazon man and one Amazon woman. Please, god, let these not be the—

"You may disrobe now," Amazon Woman says. Amazon Man has opened a teak cabinet and is lining up bottles of scented massage oils.

I wait until Ethan shrugs off the thick monogrammed Sparadise robe before taking off my own. Amazon Woman points to two hooks on the wall behind us.

"Same sex or opposite sex?" she barks.

Before I can even process what she's asking, Ethan replies, "Opposite, please."

Twenty seconds into the massage, I understand why Ethan made that choice. Amazon Man is far less, uh, aggressive with me than Amazon Woman is being with him. I mean, it's still not relaxing for me because I'm concerned about Ethan, but she would have left me bruised and sore. I try to focus on the background noise, the gentle waves crashing softly into the shore, but even with my face buried in the donut pillow I can sense the energy coming from Ethan's table. And it's not good energy.

Amazon Man is working on a knot in my lower back. I lift my head and say, "stop." You could hear a pin drop in here. Well, if it weren't for the gentle waves. "Stop," I say again. "I'm out." I push myself up to a sitting position and pull the towel up to my armpits. Amazon Women glares at me and then leaves the room in a huff.

I'm about to apologize to Amazon Man, who is still standing there, but I catch myself in time. There is nothing for me to apologize for. I'm not enjoying this and I don't wish to continue. I'm done with being Doormat Amy.

I hop down off the table and Ethan follows suit. Amazon Man is tapping furiously away at a tablet.

"Your next service is the Couples Mud Bath with Sparadise Sea Salt Seaweed Volcanic Mud."

I'm beginning to entertain the idea that the Amazon twins are not actually human, but just really well done robots.

"Take us there, please," I say in the same tone of voice I use when saying, "Pencils down" during standardized testing.

He leads us through the maze of hallways to a small, private room with a double-wide tub of mud in the center. There are no Amazonians here. Rather, the attendant is a tiny woman, wizened and wrinkled, who looks to be approximately five hundred years old. A witch, perhaps? I'm about five seconds past the point of being surprised by anything today.

Witch Woman gives us plastic shower caps for our hair. Not exactly a romantic couples thing, but we snap them on. She nods silently at our Sparadise robes, then at two hooks on the wall. After hanging up my robe, I step into the tub, expecting my feet to sink to the bottom. Instead, the mud is spongy and firm. I carefully lower myself onto it, not entirely trusting the odd, un-mud-like surface.

Ethan has barely settled in when Witch Woman begins shoveling mud onto our nude bodies. I have to say this is not what I was expecting. I had pictured a hot tub, only with mud.

When we are slathered neck to toes, the old woman leaves,

closing the door behind her. We are blissfully alone and I hope it stays that way.

"Are we allowed to talk, do you think?" I turn my head to look at Ethan. The mud slides against my cheek.

"Sorry about that."

"Not your fault."

"I'll take you to a nicer spa when we get home. New Athens has some really wonderful ones."

"You've been?" With Everly, I assume.

"There are a couple I haven't tried yet."

Of course, Ethan can read my mind.

I turn my face back to the ceiling and watch the programmed lights and shadows play across its surface. The crashing waves have been replaced by a melancholy hand pan. I'm going to miss Ethan when I go home to Avondale. And not just because of the glorious sex. (Yes, this morning was absolutely glorious.) I'll miss that, too, of course. None of the sex advice articles my mother has been forwarding to me for the past year really did the act proper justice. It was for sure better than I was expecting.

It was also for sure better than sex with Danny would have been. I'm certain of that. For starters, Danny would never have said *we've merely scratched the surface of my fantasies where you are concerned.* My first time with Danny probably would have entailed him fantasizing about porn stars while he was inside me.

Yuck.

Angela Alessi is welcome to him.

"This feels strangely good," Ethan says.

"It does." The mud is warm and slick on my skin.

"What are the therapeutic benefits of this again?"

"She didn't say." Literally, Witch Woman said not one word to us. "But I imagine it has something to do with our pores."

I feel a disturbance in the mud force between us and then Ethan's muddy hand clasps mine. I turn my head back to him and there is a tender look in his eyes that I never saw from Danny. Is this really happening? Are we really—finally—falling for each other?

After half an hour, Witch Woman returns to help us out of the slippery mud and hose us down. We are then shunted off to another room, where we are wrapped with thick hot towels and instructed to lie down on teak beds. Above us, wind chimes trill in the air conditioning stream.

"This is the first relaxing thing we've done," Ethan says.

"I believe this is the spa treatment that helps you recover from the other spa treatments."

His foot nudges mine. "I'm sorry about this, Amy. I'll make it up to you when we get home."

When the towels run out of heat, we get up and make our way back to the dressing room. I try not to think about the fact that "home" is two different places for us.

We run into Theodore Fernsby the Third at one of the many poolside restaurants dotting the waterpark. He's sitting alone at the bar, drinking what I hope is a virgin mocktail.

"Hey there, Ted." Ethan stops at the bar. "Are you waiting for your brother?"

"Nah." Ted takes a long draw on his glowing orange drink. He's back to his pre-Savage River attitude. "I ditched them after breakfast." He pulls a phone from his pocket and shows us a long string of text messages. "They had security looking for me, but I paid off the guy."

"Oh yeah?" I can't tell whether Ethan's glance at me is one of amusement or alarm. Maybe a little of each. "How much did that take?"

"I told him to fling the poop."

Ethan high fives him. "Good for you. Why don't you eat lunch with us? We've got a table ready." A waitress is hovering patiently a few feet away.

Ted flags the bartender to settle up his tab, but Ethan cuts him off. "Put it on mine," he tells the bartender.

"Sure thing ... Mr., uh, McNamara."

"I knew it was you!" Ted says as we follow the waitress to our table. "You're the inventor of Pissy Puppy."

"So why didn't you say anything the other day?" Ethan gestures to the waitress, indicating our need for a third place setting.

"I didn't want to be an annoying fanboy."

"Ah. Well, thank you for that. Annoying fanboys are the worst. Although adult fanboys are the absolute worst."

"Lucky for you, my brother has probably given up on finding me and is boinking his girlfriend by a dumpster somewhere instead."

I kinda love this kid.

Ethan leans down next to Ted and pulls out his phone. "Let's take a selfie for you to show him later." Ted's face lights up like a winning slot machine. Ethan hands his phone to Ted. "Text it to yourself."

After a moment's hesitation, Ted does and thens hands the phone back.

"Great," Ethan says. "Now you have my number, too. Call me anytime. But treat it like the poop. Don't fling it around willy nilly. Got it?" He fixes Ted with a deadly serious look.

"Got it. I'll guard it with my life."

"Well, you don't have to go that far. I can always get a new number if your life is truly in danger. Like, say, you interrupt your brother's dumpster diving."

I hide my face in the giant drinks menu to stem my laughter.

"Is that your girlfriend, Mr. McNamara?"

Ethan pulls the menu away from my face. "This is Amy, my *fiancée.* We were here for a wedding, but my ex-girlfriend's husband ran away with the bride so it got cancelled."

Ted lets out a low whistle. "Sounds complicated."

"I don't know the whole story yet, but my guess is that it'll end up being simpler than we suspect."

The waitress returns to take our drink orders. Ted orders another Sand in the Crack ("virgin, please"). Ethan and I stick with sparkling water.

"So wait." Ted leans forward. "You were here for a *wedding?* Not the tournament?"

"Nope."

"Why not?"

"Well, it would hardly be fair for me to enter a tournament for a game I created."

"But you did enter. You got iced in the second round."

I duck behind the menu again. The lunch options are what you would expect from a poolside café. Sandwiches, burgers, salads, chicken fingers.

"Well, that was a spur of the moment decision. One I regret, to be honest."

"So you just threw your round?"

I'm trying to guess what young Ted will order from the menu.

"No, I got legitimately beat. I was distracted by my opponent's purple hair and viciously foul mouth."

"Dude! That's the girl I beat in the final round! I flung the poop just like you said and she lost!"

Ethan is looking at Theodore Fernsby the Third with a look akin to something like adoration. "Ted, when I get home, the first thing I'm going to do is set up a college scholarship fund for you. Anywhere you want to go, anywhere you get in—I'll pay for it."

I lower the menu to look at Ted. Ethan is playing with fire here. Kids latch onto promises and remember them long after the adults who rashly make them have forgotten. But Ted looks suitably skeptical. His cockiness probably hides a kid who is used to disappointment.

We eat lunch. Ted orders the same half soup-half salad combo that I order. We collectively agree to pass on dessert and Ethan scribbles his signature on the bill.

"You seem like a smart fella, Ted."

Ted shrugs in mock modesty.

"But you don't know how to swim."

Ted's face falls. "Yeah, my dad keeps promising to teach me. But my sister has been sick and all ..." His bottom eyelids brim with sudden tears.

"Well, my man, if you don't have any other plans for the afternoon, I'd love to teach you. Between your brains, my inside knowledge of swimming, and Amy here's official teaching expertise, I'm sure we can have you swimming like a fish in a matter of hours."

And just like that—whatever hope I had of not falling irretrievably in love with my oldest childhood friend is now officially gone.

He's always been my best friend. Turns out he's amazing in bed. And now he's going to teach a kid we just met how to swim. In the spa, I was dipping my big toe into the idea of falling in love with Ethan.

Right now?

I just dove in headfirst.

CHAPTER 32

Danny

(not the hero of this story)

The music is pumping so hard I can feel the bass inside my head. Fifty pairs of sneakers pound the floor in unison. Well, most of them anyway. In any class, there's always two or three people who have no sense of rhythm, can't count out a simple four beats. Even so, the studio is rockin'. The class is getting to that point where it's less an exercise class and more a communal … coming together. You know—spiritual. Something that flows through your body and your blood, sweat, and tears to touch … your soul. You get what I mean?

A class at Get Fit with Danny is a spiritual experience. Like sex. I'm pumped from the Future of Fitness trade show in Vegas yesterday. My brain is filled with new ideas. And Angie is right—pole dancing is the next fitness craze. Well, probably not, actually. But I'm def adding it to the schedule at Get Fit with Danny. With a little training, she can teach it. Plus, it's a class I want to watch. That alone is reason enough to add it to the schedule.

I added barre because I thought it would be fun to watch, but those women are so damn serious about it. And they all end up with thighs that could crush a guy's head. Even Amy did.

Hell, I can probably sell more memberships with pole dancing, too. *Guys, join Get Fit with Danny today and you can watch all the pole dancing you want—at no extra charge!*

Or maybe I *should* charge extra for that? Most of my friends would pay for it.

Wait.

If I was in Vegas yesterday at Future of Fitness, then ... I'm probably not in Avondale, watching a Boogie Butt Dancercise class.

I check my eyes. Yup, both closed. So I was dreaming Boogie Butt. But the pounding is still in my head. Not a good sign.

I open one eye, cautiously, not sure where I am. I'm lying on a bed, but it's not my state-of-the-art memory foam mattress at home. Of that, I'm sure.

I sniff the air. Angela's perfume. And sex. Whoa. There's a whole lotta sex smell in this room. I'm still in Vegas. Whew. I had a bit of a panic attack there for a minute. Worried I was about to find myself waking up in Hawaii next to Amy. I mean, yes, I was looking forward to banging her on our wedding night. (I was subsequently looking forward to banging Angie in Hawaii every night of the trip formerly known as the honeymoon, but my parents said no dice. No wedding, no honeymoon at their timeshare.)

Now Amy Casales is still on the list of Women in Avondale I Haven't Banged. Most of the other women are my friends' mothers, so Amy was one of the few on the list I had a legitimate chance of crossing off. Not that I'm giving up on the mothers just yet. Especially Zach's mother.

I stare at the ceiling and listen to Angie snore. Amy's no great loss. (No mom and dad, she really isn't.) It was mostly the virgin thing that appealed to me. The thought of being her first was a total head rush. But the sex would have been tame compared to me and Angie last night ... hooboy, we rocked the rafters. I thought that fucking upside down was just CGI in her movies, or the cameraman turning the camera upside down. Turns out it's real! Damn. No wonder we got blitzed—and the throbbing behind my eyes says we definitely got blitzed. Or maybe that happened before the sex. Last night's a little fuzzy. But I remember fucking upside down! I am one hundred percent sure that happened!

I hear a buzzing. Is that my head or my phone? I open my other eye and gingerly turn my head to look at the alarm clock. Only nine o'clock. That means it's six o'clock on the east coast. Too early for anyone to be calling. Nature is calling, however, so I get up to piss.

I'm washing my hands when I see it. The pounding in my head stops for an instant, then takes up worse than before. I dry my hands and hold the left one up to the mirror, just to check. Yup. It's in the reflection, too. A ring.

Specifically, a wedding band.

Not as nice a one as the band I purchased for the wedding to Amy. This one is downright cheap. Definitely not something I would purchase unless I was under the influence ... oh shit. The pounding in my head makes that sting beat drummers play at the end of a joke.

I tiptoe back to the bed. Angie is still snoring, so I carefully peel back a corner of the duvet. (That stain will wash out, I hope).

Damn.

Damn damn damn.

And triple damn.

There's a matching cheap ring on her finger, too.

There is no effing way. I know people joke about getting drunk in Vegas and waking up married, but … that's just a joke, right? That doesn't really happen.

Please tell me that doesn't really happen.

My head is pounding worse than Boogie Butt now. My phone is buzzing nonstop, too. It takes me several minutes to locate it. It's in the mini-fridge, along with Angela's panties.

I'll figure that out later.

I wake up the phone, expecting another pissed-off message from my mother. Instead, I watch in horror as voice mail notifications appear rapid-fire. Is the world ending? Stock market crashing? I scroll through a few texts.

Dude! You're trending on Twitter! Congrats!

Just saw my newsfeed! You rock!

My brain is trying to process the fact that people I actually know —IRL—are on Twitter at six in the morning.

Yo, you're famous!

Well, it's about damn time. I tap the Twitter app and run through the trending topics. Good news—Get Fit with Danny is, in fact, trending. Bad news—so are some other things.

Oh shit.

CHAPTER 33

Ethan

I corner my mother in the kitchen of the new home I bought for her and dad. As soon as the plane touched down, Amy and I were greeted with a text from Erin-Joi informing us that the pleasure of our company was requested at dinner. But no mention was made of the fact that dinner turned out to be a "dinner party." With guests.

My mother is stuffing more mushrooms on her giant granite-topped island. I lean my elbows on the granite and pop one into my mouth, which immediately garners me a light smack on the hand. Then she pushes an appetizer plate my way. I load it up.

"So. You told people Amy and I are engaged?" I pop another stuffed mushroom into my mouth.

"No, I haven't told anyone."

I lift one eyebrow.

"Seriously, Ethan. I did not tell a single soul. You two were just pretending."

"Right. And no one saw you shopping with Amy?"

"Not that I know of."

"Well, then why are all of your friends here under the impression that Amy and I are engaged?"

"Word got out."

"Well, what am I going to do now? Amy and I aren't really engaged."

"I don't know. You could do worse than Amy, you know."

"Yeah, I almost did."

"True." She wipes her hands on her apron. "Word is out about that, too. Marissa left Brad at the altar for Everly's husband?"

I convinced my parents to sell their house in Avondale and move here because, like a good son, I missed them. Clearly, I didn't think that decision all the way through—because now I have parents who are plugged into every last grapevine in the city of New Athens.

"And he's a viscount?"

"A fake viscount, I believe."

"But does he have a fabulous accent?"

I don't understand this fascination women have with "fabulous" accents. My father still has his flat, nasally central Pennsylvania accent. As far as I know, that's not why my mother fell in love with him.

"Brad has a fabulous bank account," I point out.

She rolls her eyes. Like a fabulous bank account is something women sneeze at.

"And why can't you invite me and Amy to dinner yourself, instead of having Erin-Joi relay the message?"

"Because I like talking to Erin-Joi. She always says something that makes my day."

"Something about me or about life in general?"

"Both." She sets about making another pitcher of sangria. "Oh, Ethan. Lighten up. You just got back from a vacation in the Bahamas. Did you and Amy not have a good time?"

"We had a great time."

"Then why are you so cranky?"

"I'm not cranky."

She quirks an eyebrow at me. Yes, I got that from her.

And also yes, I am cranky. In one week, Amy goes home to Avondale unless I can convince her otherwise. We spent the entire flight home discussing the fact that our friendship took a turn on this trip. I want to see where that goes. I believe she does, too, but her overdeveloped sense of responsibility is getting in the way. She says she has the new school year to get ready for. Even though I told her I can get her a job at literally any school in the greater New Athens metro area. By lunchtime tomorrow.

"Ethan, love. Not everyone wants you to fix their life."

"What?"

"Maybe Amy doesn't want you to get her a teaching job in New Athens."

"Did I just say that out loud?"

"Yes, you did."

Great. Just great. Now I can't even tell when I'm thinking and when I'm talking.

"Falling in love will do that to you."

I smack my forehead. "Stop listening to what I'm thinking!"

"Did you and Amy sleep together on the trip?"

Dear lord, please tell me I didn't say *that* out loud.

"The lord has better things to do. But no, you didn't. I just have eyes, that's all."

I sigh and pull out one of the barstools that ring the island.

"Have you told her how you feel?"

"Sort of."

"What does 'sort of' mean?"

"It means I told her I'd like her to stay in New Athens. But she has a life in Avondale. Such as it is."

"Well, sweetheart, that's part of your problem right there. Belittling her life. She has a job and friends there. Her mother lives there."

"I can move Mrs. Casales here."

"And Mrs. Casales would probably love that. But you can't go rearranging other people's lives with your money, Ethan."

Tons of people ask me to rearrange their lives with my money all the time.

"They're not the people you want in *your* life, though. And no, you didn't just say that out loud. I'm your mother."

"You can read my mind," I mutter.

"I know how you think, that's all. And I know you want to take care of Amy. But maybe she prefers to take care of herself." She pours me a glass of sangria. "Is it true that Amy dumped that awful girl's shoes in the toilet?"

"Yes, she really did. How did you hear about that?"

"I spoke with Amy's mom a few days ago."

"She'll be glad to have Amy home again."

"I'm sure she will. She also wants to see her daughter be happy." Mom pours herself a glass of sangria and sits on the barstool next to me. "What's your hesitation in telling Amy how you feel?"

"We're both on the rebound from other relationships. And the usual. If it doesn't work out, it'll ruin the friendship."

"You and Amy haven't been in touch for years, so I'm not sure how that applies."

"Harsh, mom."

She pats my hand in an irritatingly motherly gesture—irritating because she's right. Amy and I hadn't spoken in years. It took a damned class reunion and a stupid party game to change that. I'm about to defend myself anyway when Amy bursts into the kitchen, her bare feet sliding across three feet of imported Croation tile.

"Amy, love!" My mother speaks first. "Has Ethan here ruined your friendship yet?"

"What? Um, no?"

"What's up, Ames?"

"There's an impromptu Pissy Puppy tournament going on in the living room and your expertise is requested."

"Did you tell them that I got my ass handed to me in the last tournament?" I plaster a gracious smile on my face to mask my supposed crankiness—Pissy Puppy paid for this house, after all—and head out to the living room, leaving Amy alone with my mom. Possibly not the smartest thing I'll do all day.

Felix drops us off at the front door. Erin-Joi left the lights on for us before retiring, in addition to putting Amy's things in the guest wing. I'd rather Amy sleep in my wing, but I was too tired to explain the situation.

Inside, the house is quiet except for the low roar of the air conditioning. I'm hit with a flash vision—me coming home from work and being rushed at the door by a dozen kids. Well, okay, maybe not a dozen.

"What did you and my mom talk about while I was refereeing my dad's friends?"

"Avondale. *My* mom. Weddings. That I should make an honest man of you."

"I think you should, too." At least there's one thing my mother and I are in agreement on.

I open the door to the guest wing master bedroom. On the bed are two sets of matching pajamas—plaid pants and tee shirts. Amy doesn't notice those, though. She's mesmerized by a long gown hanging on the door to the walk-in closet. It's a silvery swath of sequins, like a mermaid's tail. Matching silver heels are arranged beneath it.

"What's this?" She gently fingers the sequins.

"Looks like Erin-Joi procured a dress for you to wear to the bachelor auction. But you can go shopping for something different, if you don't like that one."

"It's gorgeous. Maybe you should marry Erin-Joi."

"She has a boyfriend. And a surprisingly low tolerance for me, actually."

"Why does she work for you, then?"

"She takes a sadistic pleasure in torturing me? Plus, I pay her well."

"This would be a lot to get used to." She walks around the spacious room. "The huge house. An assistant. The talking car." She turns and gives me a small, rueful smile. But she's thinking about it, and that's enough to send my heart soaring into the stratosphere.

"We could buy a smaller house," I counter. "I can pay Erin-Joi not to work for me. I have other cars. Although Felix might get jealous and stalk the other cars."

"Seriously?"

"No." I put my arms around her. "Well, at least I don't think so. Felix will grow on you, in any case." I pull her in close and desire spikes in my loins. And my spine. And my toes. In every part of me. But mostly in my brain—because all I can think of right now is how well and truly my life is going to suck without Amy in it.

"Ames—"

"Eeth—"

We both speak at the same time, our words tripping over each other.

"Sorry," she says. "What were you about to say?"

I was about to launch into the mother of all sales pitches, but my own mother's recent admonition stops me. I want Amy and I'm willing to rearrange my life in any way necessary. But I want to hear what she has to say first.

"You go ahead," I say.

"I do need to go back to Avondale for a bit. I need to put my affairs in order there. I can't leave Charlie in the lurch and scrambling to find a replacement on short notice. But I could come visit on weekends and ... maybe you could come visit me ... and ... we could take things slow?"

I want to box my ears to make sure I'm hearing correctly. She wants to give *us* a try? The next thing I know, she's kissing me, stretching up on her tiptoes to reach me. I lift her up, she wraps her legs around my waist, and then I promptly lose my balance and we fall over onto the bed, wrinkling the neatly folded matching pajamas in the process. Which Erin-Join must have purchased and put there, but I can't think about that right now.

Amy wants us to give this a try!

I take over the kiss, our tongues tangling to match our tangled limbs.

"We can take it as slow as you want," I murmur into her soft lips. (Though we've known each other for literally decades, so how much slower can we go?)

"We don't have to take it slow tonight."

Honestly, I think I'm dreaming—because Amy's hands are fumbling with the button and zipper on my shorts. Mr. Incorrigible isn't making this any easier by getting harder than is humanly possible and twitching like he's being tased repeatedly. I'm trying to remember what kind of clothing Amy has on, so I can figure out how to get her out of it. My hands find a zipper and I tug, then I'm inside what I think is a dress—but who the hell cares at this point? Dress, blouse, straitjacket—all that matters is that my hands are on her bare skin, touching, caressing, worshipping. Mr. Incorrigible has been freed from my shorts and is right now enjoying some soft caresses of his own.

"You went commando today?" Amy says as her fingers tease the mister.

"I'm an optimistic man. What can I say?"

I can't think of anything to say, actually, as Amy begins to relieve me of my clothes—and then to undress herself. Somehow, while my brain is otherwise occupied with thoughts of my current great fortune, I end up flat on my back with Amy straddling my hips.

A very naked Amy.

I think this is Fantasy Number One Hundred and Seventy Four: me looking up at Amy beautifully unclothed, my hands running up and down her torso, my thumbs twirling her pert nipples.

"One hundred and seventy four?"

"I didn't just say that out loud, did I?"

Her bemused expression tells me that I did.

"I was young back then. It took me awhile to get up to the kinky channels."

"You'll have to tell me about the first hundred and seventy three sometime."

"Be my girlfriend, Ames, and we can act out each and every one."

My hips jerk suddenly. Mr. Incorrigible is saying, "enough with the chit chat."

"I agree," Amy says and leans over to kiss me. She kisses the hell out of me and then rides me until my eyes roll back in my head.

CHAPTER 34

Amy

The G.O.D. Squad is explaining their proof of concept to me—a younger cousin in a neighboring town who tried out for the school's chamber singers despite having a terrible singing voice and was then mercilessly roasted for it, both in school and online. The G.O.D. Squad responded with an avalanche of memes on the value of trying new things and pushing oneself out of one's comfort zone, as well as videos (oh so many videos) of people singing terribly.

"We even got Wrath to make one!" A girl with fierce red braids taps the table with her perfectly manicured green nails to emphasize this point.

"Wrath?" I ask.

There's a moment of disbelieving silence before Red Braids rescues me. "Wrath. The singer?"

I nod. I have no idea who Wrath the Singer is, but it doesn't seem like an important point. The point is they managed to get someone famous to join in the campaign. The girls are impressive, if a little terrifying in their zeal. They are true believers in what they're doing.

I take another large swallow of hot, black coffee. Ethan and I stayed up too late last night. Oh hell, who am I kidding? We never even went to sleep. We stayed up all night making love over and over. My body is exhausted and sore in a most delicious way.

Now we're at Chaos Labs, where Ethan is truly in his element. The minute we walked in, his energy changed. This is his baby, his creation. I'm spending the week helping The G.O.D. Squad develop a plan for world domination. They want nationwide media coverage and a large scale recruitment campaign. Also, they want to win funding in the August Fund-Off competition. As the only girls' team at Chaos, they are majorly invested in beating the boys.

Totally understandable.

I watch Ethan as he moves from group to group in the large open space. There are students huddled around a communal computer. Kids kicked back on comfy sectionals as they discuss coding and business plans and marketing strategies. Two kids are brainstorming on the trampoline. He gives his full, undivided attention to every single kid. I don't know whether he's a natural born teacher or not, but he's definitely someone who naturally cares deeply about others.

The more I see of Ethan in his adult life, the more my heart is in freefall. It's not just because of the blazing physical chemistry between us—honestly, I did not see that one coming. No pun intended. He's built something special here at Chaos. The kids plainly worship the ground he walks on.

He's at a loss, though, for how to help The G.O.D. Squad. Their plan is to mobilize a network of girls to drown out bullying and bad social media and emotionally support girls to help them get through it. I'm not sure how much help I'll be, either—my years of teaching (not to mention the past few weeks of my life) have left me a little cynical about the goodness of people in general. But it's a worthy idea, so I'll give it my best shot this week.

"Ms. Casales?"

"Yes?"

"Is it true that you and Mr. McNamara are engaged?"

As a cynical high school teacher, I should have foreseen this.

"Not yet, no." I see their eyes glom onto the ostentatious diamond engagement ring on my finger. "It's a friendship ring."

"But you're in love? You two aren't just old childhood friends."

"Well, we're both."

The group collectively cringes, then launches into a discussion of boys they went to kindergarten with and the "sheer impossibility" of dating any of them.

"Is it true he got iced in the second round of a Pissy Puppy tournament?" Red Braids again.

"I don't think he was trying to win, really." Ethan said he was, but I feel the need to defend his manhood in front of the Chaos kids. I glance around to make sure he's not within earshot, but he's disappeared.

My phone rings. I dig it out of my purse to check the number. It's a New York number I don't recognize. A robocall about my car's warranty, probably. As soon as I drop the phone back into my purse, it rings again. Massachusetts. Then another call. Los Angeles. Dallas. Minneapolis, Phoenix. What the hell? Is it really *that* important to scam me into a fake car warranty? Danny's number suddenly appears in the mix. Oh hell no. I should have blocked him. I turn off the ringer and lay the phone on the table next to me.

But the screen continues to flash with text notifications. What on earth is going on?

Then a text from Danny. *I'm sorry, Amy. I really really am.*

Too late, dude. My fingers are itching to text back with the news that Ethan and I stayed up all night making love. Does Angel of Albuquerque spend all night *making love* to Danny? Doubtful.

I sweep the phone from the table and into my purse. The girls have fallen silent. My teacher spidey senses are on full alert. They're looking warily at me. I glance down at my top to see whether there's a giant rip in the fabric and my bra is showing.

Nope.

Clothing still intact.

Then the swearing begins.

"Hoover dam fudge rockets shiitake … shrooms!"

It's Ethan's voice. As far as kid-friendly cussing goes, this is pretty lame, but it's enough to shut down all activity among the kids. They all look nervously at one another.

We hear several more "shiitakes" and then a loud shattering crash, like someone just threw a large object across a room.

"I think Mr. McNamara is upset," one of the girls says quietly.

The other girls glance from their phones to me and back again.

"I'll go see what's up."

I hurry up the stairs to where Ethan's office is. I knock on the closed door.

"Not now, please!"

I open the door and step inside, then close the door behind me. There's a laptop lying on the floor in a puddle of glass. Ethan's shirt is torn down the front and his lovely, wavy hair looks like someone attacked it with a rake. And I'm surprised to see Erin-Joi. I had no idea she was even at Chaos this morning.

"I need the bodies buried, Erin-Joi. BURIED. As in never to be found. And call Jack D. I want this down *immediately*. No, not immediately! *Yesterday!*"

Erin-Joi is as cool as a cucumber, pardon the cliché. Her prim and proper linen sheath dress is not even wrinkled, let alone torn.

"I think you should probably call Jack yourself," she says.

Who's Jack? And what does he have to do with all this swearing and the broken laptop on the floor?

"Eeth, what's going on?" I have a feeling I probably don't really want to know, but last night I told this man I loved him. And now he's raging like a banshee in his office. Which is so not like any version of Ethan that I know.

Erin-Joi shoots me a look that says exactly that—you don't really want to know what's going on here—but I'm thinking I outrank her currently.

"You're trending." He rakes his hands through his hair again, like he's trying to pull it out by the roots.

"What do you mean I'm trending?"

"On social media."

I look at him blankly.

"You're *trending.*"

"I don't know what that means, Ethan. I'm not really on social media. I'm a teacher. I can't live my life online."

He points at a large computer on his desk, still intact. I lean in to peer at the screen and scan a list helpfully named "United States Trends." There's a candy brand trending. A pop song that's just released. An actress no one has thought of in at least a decade. Then I see the first one.

#Pole dancing.

Pretty sure Ethan doesn't pole dance.

#Get Fit with Danny.

Ok-a-a-y.

#Amy.

My heart stops. My lungs stop. My brain is on the verge of shutting down, too. This can't be happening. I'm not even on social media! I have literally no social media accounts! Not even for the purposes of "liking" the stuff Charlie Gardner posts on the Avondale High School accounts.

"Ames." The warning in his voice is clear.

But I do it anyway. I click on the hashtag. I click on the video. There's a woman pole dancing in a Get Fit with Danny tee shirt. Her abundant—and clearly unrestrained—breasts bounce and sway beneath the thin cotton. (Danny was too cheap to get the next grade up.) She spins around the pole and there is lettering on the back of her teeny tiny satin shorts. The video is too grainy to read the lettering (plus, the lettering is too small—I told Danny that), but I know what it says. "I GOT THIS ASS AT GFWD" on the left cheek. On the right cheek is the studio's phone number.

I recognize what this is. The video was made at a fitness trade show. I used to go to them with Danny all the time. There were always booths set up where you could get a quickie demonstration and mini lesson on whatever the next big thing in yoga or group exercise was going to be. You could try your hand at stuff like pole dancing or boxing or the mirror.

But I still don't get why Ethan is seething like a rabid squirrel over it.

Then the camera zooms in on the pole dancer's face. My face. I'm watching myself pole dancing in a video that is getting "likes" at a rate of about fifty per second. Except I've never pole danced before in my life. Not even in a quickie lesson at a trade show. (Not that Danny didn't try to talk me into it a few times.) It's my face on someone else's body.

WTF?

The woman flips upside down and begins swiveling her hips around the pole—and I finally recognize her.

Angela Alessi, she of fucking-upside-down fame. It's Angel of Albuquerque's body with the face of Amy Casales, mild-mannered high school English teacher.

My legs are shaky all of a sudden. There's a field of black encroaching on my vision from both sides.

"I think I'm going to faint," I squeak.

I faint.

When I come to, I'm lying on the sofa in Ethan's office, Ethan and Erin-Joi peering down at me, their faces looming large in my fuzzy vision.

"How long was I out?" I've never fainted before in my life and it felt a lot more dramatic than I would have guessed.

"Twenty seconds?" Erin-Joi guesstimates.

"I have to leave." I push myself up to a sitting position.

"And go where?" Ethan says.

"Home. You can't have me around here." The hurt look on his face is breaking my heart. "You can't have me seen here at Chaos Labs."

"What? Why not?"

"You've put too much into this place. I don't want to ruin it."

"Amy, you're not going to ruin Chaos."

I shake my head sadly. "As soon as parents find out about this, they'll pull their kids. Is there a back entrance I can leave by?"

"Ames. You don't have to leave. I'm going to get this taken care of."

"It's already out there. You can't rewind time. I have to go."

"She's right," Erin-Joi chimes in. "She needs to leave. Soon."

Erin-Joi retrieves my purse from downstairs and then we both climb down the fire escape to the back alley, where Felix is waiting for us. Erin-Joi gets in the driver's seat. She is too much of a take-charge person to let a car do the driving. We ride in silence for miles while I book a flight on my phone and then call my mother to pick me up at the airport in two hours.

Erin-Joi is the one to speak first. "Why would she do this to you? She already has your ex, right?"

I stare out the window as the streets of New Athens thin out to suburbs and then countryside as we get closer to the airport. I shrug. "She was always one of the mean girls. I guess some people don't outgrow that. Also, I threw a pair of her shoes in the toilet. That could be it."

"What kind of shoes?"

"A pair of black fuck-me pumps. Christian something or other. Red soles."

"Ah. Expensive shoes."

"That's what I've been told. I should replace them. I should never have thrown them in the toilet. Besides, she did me a solid favor by stealing Danny."

"Sounds like it."

I sigh. "No chance I'll be able to find those shoes in Avondale, though, Maybe online?"

"I'm sure I can find a pair in New Athens and ship them to you."

"Thanks, but I need to pay for them myself. Karmic restitution or something."

"You can reimburse me. What size does she wear?"

"I don't know. I didn't look before chucking them in the loo."

CHAPTER 35

Ethan

I stand at the window and watch as Felix drives away with Erin-Joi and Amy. I still don't think she needs to leave. I own Chaos Labs and there is no way a pissant like Danny Effing Walker and his porn star girlfriend can ruin it.

When Felix is out of sight, I proceed to clean up the laptop I smashed in a fit of pique.

Okay, so a temper tantrum.

I dump the remains of the laptop into the wastebasket beneath my desk. The noise from downstairs is a dull hum instead of the usual loud roar. I need to go down there and address the kids. For starters, I preach about how "cool, calm, and collected" is the way to go—and they just heard me go ballistic. And then *after* starters, I'll address what is happening to Amy online. I make every kid sign a pledge of honesty and ethical use of technology on their first day at Chaos. In return, I am honest with them.

The boys have mostly gone back to what they were doing before, but The G.O.D. Squad is a buzzing hive of activity. Elana is standing on a chair like a conductor before an orchestra, her copper red braids swinging emphatically as she speaks.

"First, we wrest control of the Chaos Labs social media accounts from Mr. McNamara."

"Hello. I'm standing right here."

She gives me a quick glance. "We know." She turns back to the girls.

"Then we get her former students involved."

"How do we find them?" Madison asks.

"Her high school has to have a Facebook page." Elana turns to me again. "Where does Amy teach?"

"Avondale High School. In Pennsylvania."

"Got it!" Madison waves her phone in the air.

"We can reach out to people who have liked the page. Mr. Mac, what subject did Amy teach?"

"English."

"Perfect. Everyone has to take that."

Damn. When the girls talked about world domination, I thought they were merely employing hyperbole for rhetorical effect.

"Next, we need to get a hashtag trending on Twitter. Any ideas?"

I realize my jaw is hanging open in amazed awe. I'm touched that they are working on this on behalf of Amy. At the same time, I'm a little terrified.

The girls toss out a dozen or so hashtag ideas before settling on "what I learned from Amy." Sounds appropriate for a teacher. I pull out my phone and log into the Chaos Labs account. I am going to be the first to post.

Patience. Compassion. Love. Heart emoji heart emoji heart emoji. #what I learned from Amy.

"That's lame."

Fourteen girls are looking at me, phones in hand. I shrug. "It's the truth."

"What exactly is your relationship status?"

"Amy said you two are not, *in fact*, engaged."

So much for that pledge of honesty. Strictly speaking, I haven't signed one. Just the kids.

"We aren't engaged *yet*."

"What about the gram?" Emma asks.

"Right. How many followers are you up to these days?" I duck to avoid getting whipped with one of Elana's braids.

"Twenty-three-point-six million." Emma is beaming like the sun at the equator.

My eyes nearly fall out of my head. 23.6 *million?* For a teenage girl? I squint at Emma. Is she somehow famous and I've just been clueless? (Entirely possible.) I take a quick peek at Chaos Lab's "gram." Okay. Let's just say we're south of one thousand followers. Note to self: don't get on The G.O.D. Squad's bad side.

"We don't have a bad side, Mr. Mac."

Clearly, I'm still thinking out loud.

"Do you have any photos of Amy?"

"I have a few recents from the trip." Not all of them appropriate for the day's purposes.

"Text them to me."

I forgot how bossy girls can be. Amy was never bossy. But I

do as Elana commands and send her a few pictures from the Bahamas. Amy in the dress she wore to Brad's ill-fated wedding. (Not the picture from the mud bath.) Amy on the beach in her minty green dress. (Not the picture of Everly's, uh, hat.) Amy mugging for the camera next to the Pissy Puppy tournament sign. (Not the one of Amy in her granny panty swimsuit. Wet granny panty swimsuit.) A selfie of Amy and me at the airport.

That earns me a chorus of "awwww."

"You two are totes adorbs."

"Do people still say that?"

"No."

Why do I get the feeling that I've just been hit with some major teenage shade? But the girls move on.

"Jaya! Courtney! We need to commandeer your TikTok accounts."

This is exhausting.

I check in with the rest of the students, then return to my office to call Amy's number. She doesn't answer. I had a feeling she wouldn't. Still, it hurts. It takes me back to high school—and not just for the sheer juvenile pettiness of what Angela Alessi is doing. It takes me back to all those nights when I tried to comfort Amy while her parents were at the hospital, even though I knew that nothing I could say or do would really bring her peace.

I want to be with her now. Be by her side. Punch Danny Effing Walker's lights out. I owe him for the class reunion anyway, when he punched me and Jack dragged me out of there before I could retaliate.

I text Amy. *Just so you know, The G.O.D. Squad is on your case. Everything will be okay.*

I get a thumbs-up emoji in reply. Well at least she's not ghosting me.

By the time I get home in the evening, I'm completely wiped out. Mostly from watching The G.O.D. Squad work their phones. Honestly, Danny and Angela are outmatched, outwitted, and outclassed by these young women. I made a few strategically placed phone calls myself, but every time that damn video was taken down it popped up somewhere else.

In the cavern that passes for my living room, I find Erin-Joi watching television and texting faster than seems humanly possible.

"Have you seen this one?" She jabs a finger in the direction of the television.

I stop to watch. "Yes. Unfortunately." It's the not-award-winning "Angel Does Albuquerque." "I can tell you how it ends."

"That's okay."

"Umm. Why are you watching it?"

"I need to estimate her shoe size."

"You can do that just by watching?"

"Sure. I'm comparing her foot size to his. Then I'll look up his height on a film web site along with the expected average shoe size for a man his height and go from there. I'll include a gift receipt, just in case I'm wrong."

Erin-Joi is rarely ever wrong.

"You know, you're probably the only person who has ever looked at their *feet* while watching this movie."

"I am aware of that."

"And why do you need her shoe size anyway?"

"I think what happened today can be traced back to Amy throwing this woman's shoes in the toilet. Which—I will say—must have been a very satisfying moment and one I surely would have succumbed to myself."

I sigh. "Is that all this is? Angela Alessi is breaking the internet with Amy over a damn pair of shoes?"

"They're pretty expensive shoes. I'm texting every store in New Athens and asking which sizes they have in stock right now."

"Put it on my credit card."

"She specifically asked me not to do that."

I sigh again. "Do you know how utterly impotent I feel right now?"

She chuckles. "I don't think the glow in Amy's cheeks this morning was the result of spending a week with an impotent man."

CHAPTER 36

Amy

I'm on day five of Operation Lay Low. I'm lying in bed in my child-hood bedroom, staring at the ruffled yellow curtains that are way cheerier than I currently feel. The snooze on my phone goes off and I try to stretch some motivation into my limbs. My mother is in the kitchen, according to the coffee, bacon, and pancakes I'm smelling. She's been a champ this week. Except for the incident yesterday, where she nearly ran down Angela's father in the supermarket parking lot. I grabbed the steering wheel just in time.

Of course, the incident also made me wonder what Felix would have done in that situation. Or Erin-Joi. I'm pretty sure Erin-Joi would have run him over and tossed the body in the trunk.

I roll out of bed and head down the hall to the bathroom. I miss Erin-Joi. And Felix, the talking car. And Ethan.

Most of all, I miss Ethan.

I perform my morning ablutions (brush teeth, wash face) and join mom in the kitchen.

"Sweetheart!" My mother looks up from her laptop with a supremely guilty look on her face.

I slump into a chair. "How bad is it?"

"It's getting a little better."

"That bad, huh?"

When mom gets up to pour me a mug of coffee, I swing the computer screen around.

#Porn star tips for Amy.

#How not to lose your fiancé.

#If you were Amy, you'd...

So much for this blowing over quickly. I'm not sure Angela is even instigating things at this point. Every time it looks as though it might die out, it respawns anew.

I Facetimed with Ethan last night. Which only made me miss him harder. Most of the call was me talking him down off the ledge. He wants to buy up a competitor to Danny's fitness studio and crush him out of business. He wants to endow a football chair at Avondale's arch rival, hire a pro football coach, and ensure that Avondale never wins another state championship. He wants to run down Angela's entire family in a parking lot.

Mom sets the coffee and a plate of pancakes and bacon in front of me. I dig in, suddenly aware of just how ravenous my appetite is. "Thanks, Mom."

She closes the laptop and slides it away. "So what are your plans for the day?"

This is Mom-code for "you can't just spend all day every day in bed." Which I know. I have to start facing the music, even if I'm not the one who started the music.

"I need to go to Danny's and drop off the shoes. And the car. Can you pick me up after?"

Erin-Joi came through for me and shipped a pair of size nine black Christian Louboutin fuck-me pumps. My bank account feels screwed, but my karma should be in alignment again soon.

I am not looking forward to seeing Danny. It has to be done, though. I'm taking the higher road by replacing the shoes.

"I'll do that after I swing by the school. Charlie wants me to come in." I hold up crossed fingers. "Maybe Malcolm Jones got a better offer in another school district."

At eleven o'clock, I am showered, dressed, and knocking on Charlie Gardner's office door. In another five weeks, I'll be back here, preparing for the new school year.

"Come on in," I hear Charlie say. I push open the door. Charlie is seated behind his desk. It's weird to see him not wearing the suit he sports every day during the school year. Today he's wearing a Get Fit with Danny tee shirt.

I try to tell myself that someday this will just be a funny story I tell my grandchildren. *And then I went in to see my boss and he was wearing the same tee shirt the porn star wore pole dancing!*

"How's your summer been, Charlie?" I take a seat in one of the visitor's chairs.

"Good. Good. You look tan."

"I was in the Bahamas for a bit."

"Sounds fun."

"You ever been?"

"Nope. Can't say I have."

We stare at each other for a good minute. I don't want to jump the gun and inquire after Malcolm. *So ... Malcolm. What happened? Eaten by sharks? Abducted by aliens? Poached by a prep school?* Charlie's greatest fear is that the tony boarding school fifteen miles from Avondale will steal away his best teachers.

Sometimes it does.

"So. Amy," he says finally, like I haven't been sitting here for five minutes. "The Board of Education is not exactly thrilled with the events of late."

I watch as his eyes settle on his "Administrator of the Year" paperweight, then on the stapler, on the trendy blue mirrored sunglasses that look entirely out of place on a principal's desk—on everything but me. And now I know where this conversation is going.

"You do know that wasn't me," I point out. Anyone who both knows me in person and is not blind could see that I'm not the body in that video.

"It's a matter of perception, Amy. It doesn't reflect well on the Avondale School District."

"Is it a perception problem for Coach Walker, whose girlfriend is actually the person *in* the video?" This is, of course, a rhetorical question. I already know the answer.

He's silent.

"I'll take that as a no. The Board of Education also wants another state football championship, is that it?"

"I need you to resign, Amy. For the good of the school. Think of the students."

"And if I don't?"

"The board will make me fire you. I'd rather you resign peacefully."

This is so not how I saw today going. Although I've been pretty bad at predicting my days lately. So probably I should have anticipated this. I take a deep breath.

"Fine. I quit."

"I'll escort you to the classroom to get your things."

"I'm not going to steal the water fountains if you let me go unescorted."

I'm numb as I collect my things from the room where I've taught for the past eleven years. I put everything in the box Charlie helpfully provides and then walk beside him to the front entrance. I stop to allow him to open the door for me, since my hands are full with the box. But he doesn't.

Instead, he just says, "Good luck with things, Amy."

As he walks back to his office, I arrange my middle finger into the appropriate position against the cardboard box. (I'm hardly the first person to flip Charlie Gardner the bird. Not even the first teacher.) Then I bump my hip against the door and push it open with my body. When I reach the car, I drop the box and let out a primal scream like I'm a senior on the last day of school.

Or my last day of school.

Twenty minutes later, I pull the BMW up to Danny's house. The house I was supposed to move into this summer. It's a nice house. Nowhere near as big as Ethan's, of course, but I had painted myself a lovely museum-quality picture of what my life was going to be like inside it.

The short version: blissfully happy.

The long version: blissfully happy, having hot sex with the hottest guy in Avondale, going off birth control every two years to procreate, hosting big family dinners at Thanksgiving and

Christmas and Easter, throwing birthday parties for the kids, catching lightning bugs at night.

Part of me always knew it was too good to be true.

I get out of the car, taking the shoe box with me. I didn't wrap it or anything. That would have required going to the store to buy paper and I'm trying not to show my face around town anymore than I have to.

Ethan assured me that The G.O.D. Squad has a plan but, whatever it is, it's not bearing fruit yet. I feel awful for the girls. It'll be hard for them to get funding at the August Fund-off, having failed at my real life case.

I ring the doorbell and wait patiently for someone to answer. I can't say whether I'd rather it be Danny or Angela. I'm not looking forward to a conversation with either.

It's Danny who comes to the door. He's wearing a stained sweatshirt with absolutely no branding of any sort. He's unshaven and barefoot. His toenails need trimming.

"You look like hell," I blurt out.

"Thanks. Err—right. I know."

He looks surprised to see me. But in a weird way, he sounds a little relieved, too.

"Do you want to talk inside?" He opens the door wider.

I'd rather not go inside. For one thing, I can hear the distinct sound of someone puking their guts out in the background. On the other hand, if this conversation deteriorates into a knock-down, drag-out fight I'd rather that not happen outside where all the neighbors can see.

So I step inside. The puking has turned into dull moaning.

"Is everything okay?"

"Yeah, uh, morning sickness."

It's then that I notice the wedding band on his finger. My heart seizes up for a second. I don't want him back—heavens no—but it hurts a little that he immediately married Angela. I figured she was just a fling.

"Who is it?" Angela's strained voice comes from upstairs.

"Uh, just Girl Scout cookies!" Danny calls back.

"Get me a box of thin mints. Make that two."

Danny flinches. I can't help him there. I do not have two boxes of cookies on me. He looks miserable. Not that it makes me feel one bit sorry for him. He made his bed and yada yada yada. I thrust the shoebox at him.

"Here. I bought a replacement pair of shoes for the ones I threw in the toilet. I'm sorry about that. I shouldn't have done it."

He takes the box. "Thanks. She was pretty pissed."

"Apparently. I was asked to resign from the school."

His eyes widen. "You're kidding."

"I assure you that I am not. Charlie gave me the option of resigning or being fired."

"That's not fair, Amy."

"No, it's not. Kinda late for you to worry about that, though."

"I didn't have anything to do with this." He glances upstairs. "I swear to god, Amy. My parents are furious. I made her stop posting, but it seems to have taken on a life of its own."

"Seems that way." I hand over the BMW key. "Here. You can have the car back."

"No." He pushes the key back toward me. "Keep it. It was a gift."

I shove the key into his unbranded sweatshirt. "I don't want it. Every time I drive it, it makes me think of you. And no offense, but I don't want to think about you ever again. Congratulations on the baby."

"Thanks." He doesn't exactly look like an overjoyed parent-to-be.

I don't care. I turn to go. I take two steps and turn back.

"Can I ask you something?"

"I guess."

"Why did you want a relationship with me? It never made sense to anyone in town. It didn't make sense to me either, but I ignored those voices in my head."

He sighs. "My parents wanted me to marry a nice girl. As a condition of their investing more money in the business."

"And I was the only unmarried girl in town whom you hadn't already slept with?"

His sheepish look is my answer.

"You know, you could have gone with a mail order bride."

"Danny! Bring up those thin mints!"

"Yeah, that would have been a better idea."

CHAPTER 37

Ethan

I slam on the brakes of the tin can I've just driven from the airport like a bat outta hell. It was the only rental car they had left. Sadly, Felix is not a flying car. Brad's company is working on a prototype for a flying car, but it's not sky-worthy yet.

When I get out of the tin can and close the door, the whole thing shudders. "Sorry." I pat the hood and look down at the right front wheel. How on earth did I jump the curb in this thing? I could never have pulled up to Everly's house in a car like this. But Amy's house? She's just going to laugh at it.

I ring the doorbell and Mrs. Casales answers.

"Oh Ethan. You just missed her. She's out at Smithy's Rock."

"The Rock?" My heart stops. There are only three kinds of people who go to Smithy's Rock. Underaged drinkers, hang gliders, and jumpers. Amy is not underaged or a hang glider.

"How long ago did she leave?"

"An hour or so?"

Oh damn. I sprint back to the car. "Buddy, I am sorry to do this to you." I floor it and peel away from Amy's house. She's at Smithy's Rock? No good can come of that. "Come on, car. You can go faster than this." The Rock is a good three miles outside town—if Amy left an hour ago, she's already there.

Tin Can sounds like a lawnmower as I urge it across town. I should be worried that it's going to fall apart around me and I'll be left driving just the chassis—with the weird bulge in my shorts visible to everyone.

I can't worry about that now.

I pull into the small parking lot at the Rock and slam on the brakes again, this time sending a shower of gravel through the trees and over the edge of the cliff. I narrowly miss slamming into Mrs. Casales's car. I don't bother shutting Tin Can's door. Instead, I race up the short path that leads to the main clearing and ...

Amy is sitting there on the ground, her legs criss-cross applesauce like a Buddha. If Buddha had been an attractive young woman whom I'm wildly in love with.

Which I don't believe he was.

I let out a giant sigh of relief. "Amy!"

She turns her head toward me. Well, her head and the giant hoagie she's eating. She chews fast and swallows.

"Eeth? What are you doing here?"

I glance at the edge of the mountain's outcropping, where it drops off to several hundred feet of nothing but air. She starts laughing. Not quite the reaction I was expecting.

"You thought I was going to jump?"

I sit down next to her. I'm out of breath and her lips are going to taste like salami, peppers, and extra virgin olive oil, but I don't care. I kiss those salami-scented lips.

"Who else comes here?" I answer after a full five minutes of kissing. "You're not an underaged drinker and you don't hang glide."

"I like to come here when I need to think. Here." She holds out the other half of her sandwich, which I take because there was no food on my flight.

"I hope you're thinking about us," I say between bites.

"Us. And other things. I lost my job today. And my former fiancé is already married to his pregnant girlfriend. And 'porn star tips for Amy' is trending."

I nudge her shoulder with mine. "I might be interested in some of those." She gives me a baleful look. "But that wasn't trending when I got off the plane."

"Well, good. I'm sure it's been replaced with something equally charming."

"Actually, it has." I set down the sub and pull my phone from the pocket of my shorts. "The G.O.D. Squad is getting traction." I show her the screen."

"Hashtag what I learned from Amy?" she reads.

I scroll down so she can read the posts.

Who Oscar Wilde was.

That history never repeats itself, but it does often rhyme.

"Pretty sure that was Mark Twain and not me."

She giggles softly, which might be a good sign. I'm holding my breath.

What a codpiece is.

"I should have paid more attention in English class," I say.

The difference between effect and affect.

"What? Who posted that?" She squints harder at the phone. "Oh. Sagittarius Smith."

"You had a student named Sagittarius?"

"A couple years ago. Her given name was Star. She thought it wasn't specific enough."

"We're not naming any of our kids Sagittarius. Or Elana."

"Why not Elana? I like that name."

"It terrifies me." I'm feeling hopeful, if she's not shutting down discussion of kids' names. *Our* kids' names.

She hands the phone back to me. I glance at the screen and the time. Speaking of Elana, she said she couldn't guarantee an exact time. Although I can also picture her on the phone with Jack D., *demanding* an exact time. He'll give her one, too, if he knows what's good for him.

"So what are you going to do now that you don't have a job here?"

"I don't know. Look for another one. But what am I going to say when they ask why I left my previous job? I was forced to resign because someone posted a video of me on the internet that wasn't actually me?"

"Work for me."

"The parents of your students won't be any happier with this situation than the Avondale Board of Education is."

"I already emailed all the parents. They're fine with it. They understand what happened. And even if they weren't, I'm not a school. They're free to take their kids elsewhere."

"I don't know, Eeth. What would I do at Chaos?"

"Whatever you want. I could use some help attracting more girls to the Lab. And heaven knows the kids all need help writing their business plans."

"My mom would miss me."

"I'll fly you home to visit whenever you want. Or fly her to New Athens. Move her to New Athens, even. Buy her a house." I glance back in the direction of the parking lot. "Buy you a car. I'm guessing Danny took back the BMW?"

"No, I gave it back. I don't want to be reminded of him every time I drive somewhere. Plus, Angela would probably end up keying it."

My phone buzzes with a text. It's Elana. I tap open Twitter and show it to Amy again. *#Ethan loves Amy because ...* I navigate to the Chaos Labs account. (Yes, The G.O.D. Squad wrested control from me.)

She always shared her cookies.

She doesn't hog the covers.

She laughs at my jokes. Even the ones that aren't funny.

That's most of them.

"Okay, I didn't write that last one."

"Who did? This is your account, right?"

"My account under temporary new management. Elana and the girls are posting pre-planned tweets. And some not-so-pre-planned, apparently."

She has a big heart.

She kisses really, really well.

She lifts an eyebrow as my phone buzzes again. That's my cue from Elana. Like clockwork, the video post appears.

CHAPTER 38

Amy

In the video, Ethan is kneeling in his backyard, wearing a Chaos Labs tee shirt and jeans. The image bounces a bit, as though the person holding it is laughing. I'm guessing it's Erin-Joi.

"I know we say that we've known each other forever," Video Ethan says. "But that's not really true. We've only known each other up until today. Forever is a journey still ahead of us."

After what happened with Everly and *that* proposal, I can't believe he's doing this online. For anyone to see. I lean my shoulder into his as we listen to the rest of what Video Ethan has to say.

"Will you take that journey with me? I love you, Amy Casales. Please marry me."

Video Ethan picks up something from the grass next to his knee. A small black box. He tries to flip open the lid one-handedly, but ends up flipping the entire box into the air. He juggles it for a moment before it falls onto the grass. He picks it up again.

"Fumbled the ring there." He pulls open the lid. "But I promise never to fumble your heart." The camera zooms in. It's not the ring I wore in the Bahamas, the one Erin-Joi picked out. This one is a little less ostentatious. But the diamonds still sparkle in the sunshine of Ethan's backyard.

When I woke up this morning, this is not where I saw the day going. (I think I've said that once already.) But now that we're here, it feels *right*. We love each other. And if we *still* love each other after all these years, we must be meant to be.

The video goes black and Ethan is pulling something out of his pocket. A small black box. He expertly flips open the lid with one hand.

"I've been practicing."

The ring is even more gorgeous in person.

"Will you marry me, Amy?"

My eyes sting with tears. Happy tears. Tears of emotional whiplash as this day throws yet one more unexpected thing at me. Finally, it's a good thing.

"Yes. I will marry you."

Ethan slips the ring onto my finger and then he is kissing me. My tailbone is waltzing around in delirious delight until it collapses into a dizzy heap. We come up for air when his phone starts buzzing frantically.

#She said yes!

EPILOGUE

Ethan & Amy

So Amy did come to the bachelor auction with me.

It was for a good cause.

Yes, it was.

But I had to bow out of the bidding fairly early on. You were too expensive for the likes of me.

Fortunately, Everly had to bail out early as well.

You looked like you were going to faint there towards the end.

Yeah well, I was picturing myself on a date with The G.O.D. Squad. At homecoming or something.

They crowd-sourced the money.

Some people have more money than brains.

I'm not touching that one.

They also managed to pull in a reporter from CNN.

And People Magazine.

True. Can't forget them.

And Theodore Fernsby the Third.

I really need to schedule a debrief with them to learn how *that* came about.

You really need to give them funding in the August Fund-off.

Now that they've discovered the joys of crowd-sourcing, they may not need it.

I think they want the win as much as the money.

Well, since they donated the date to you, I'll consider it.

We're not at homecoming.

No, we most certainly are not.

Dear Reader,

Thanks for reading *Anything for Her!* If you're new to my books, you might be wondering what to read next...

If you like heartwarming small town romance that's not super-steamy, the St. Caroline Series is for you! You can even start the series for FREE with **Hearts on Fire**.

On the other hand, if you like super-steamy romance, I promise that **Muse** will set your e-reader on fire.

And if you've read all of my books already ... I love you! (heart emoji heart emoji heart emoji!) Are you signed up for my email list? I don't email all that often, so no worries about being inundated with email. (I know how it is!) But subscribing to my emails gets you access to excerpts of upcoming books, fun giveaways, and notice of limited-time book discounts.

Alternatively, you can follow me on BookBub and stay abreast of new releases and Featured Deals that way.

Last but not least, if you enjoyed *Anything for Her*, please leave a review and tell others!

XOXO...
     Julia

ABOUT THE AUTHOR

Julia Gabriel writes contemporary romance that is smart, sexy, and emotionally-intense (grab the tissues). She lives in New England where she is a full-time mom to a teenager, as well as a sometime writing professor and obsessive quilter (is there any other kind?). If all goes well, she'll be a Parisienne in her next life.

Her books have been selected as "Top Picks" by RT Book Reviews, and critics at RT Book Reviews, Kirkus, and others have called her work "nuanced," "heart-wrenching and emotional," "well-crafted contemporary romance," and "deeply moving storytelling."

Say "hello" on social media ...

BB bookbub.com/authors/julia-gabriel
a amazon.com/Julia-Gabriel
f facebook.com/authorjuliagabriel.com
O instagram.com/juliagabriel.author

Sign up for Julia's Coffee Break email for the chance to win Coffee Care Packages, get bonus scenes, learn about new releases and sales, and more!

Sign up at www.authorjuliagabriel.com.

St. Caroline Series

Hearts on Fire

Two of Hearts

This Reminds Me of Us

Summer Again (standalone)

Phlox Beauty Series

Next to You

Back to Us

Drawing Lessons Duet

Drawing Lessons

Chiaroscuro: Light & Dark

Muse: A dark romance

Made in the USA
Coppell, TX
09 February 2024